CW00516486

THE PROBABILITY
OF SUCCESS

THE PROBABILITY OF SUCCESS

THE CHINA AFFAIRS

BOOK 3

BRAD GOOD

The characters and events in this book are fiction. Any similarities to real persons, living or dead, is coincidental and not intended by the author.

Copyright © 2022 by Bradley Good.
All rights reserved.

ISBN: 979-8-9865821-1-5

The scanning, uploading, and distribution of this book without permission is a theft of the author's intellectual property. If you would like permission to use material from the book (other than for review purposes), please visit www.bradleygood.com to make an inquiry.

Published by Jack Gold Publishing, Austin, Texas

The publisher is not responsible for websites (or their content) that are not owned by the publisher.

CHAPTER 1

Sometimes, Jack Gold found he still marveled at the fact of everyday technology—things that would have sounded like science fiction only a few generations prior—that people all over the world took for granted now, like the fact that so many now walked around with a tiny computer in their pockets, the world's wealth of knowledge just a few finger swipes away.

Jack poured some coffee out of the French press as he waited for his father to answer his FaceTime call. Jojo's dog, Mini, a border collie mix, followed Jack back to the living room and lay at his feet. Jack's father's face suddenly appeared on the laptop screen.

"Jack," his dad said. "Hi. I knew it was you—you're the only who calls me with FaceTime."

"Hi Dad," Jack said. His father, who lived year-round in Cabo after retiring from a successful ob-gyn practice, looked tanned and relaxed. "And you know I call you on FaceTime so I can better tell if you're bullshitting me or not." Jack's dad smiled. "How is living in Cabo year-round anyway?"

"Can't complain. I can go fishing anytime I want. Weather's always beautiful. After seeing patients for thirty-five years, I think I've earned it."

"No one's going to argue with that," Jack said. Of course his father would feel he had to "earn" any leisure time he now had—he'd ingrained that exact sentiment into Jack from an early age.

"How are you?" his father asked. "How's Jojo?"

As if on cue, Jojo came into the room, smothering a yawn, her hair still a little messed up from sleeping. "Hello, Dr. Gold," she said in English, with a slight French accent, as she pulled a chair closer to Jack. "I'm still not fully awake yet."

Jack's father smiled. "Hi, Jojo. You're looking great, fully awake or not. You've gained a little weight—it suits you."

Leave it to his dad to instantly notice such a little thing from seven thousand miles away. Jack put his arm around his wife's shoulders. "Dad, we do have some news we'd like to share with you. Jojo is three months pregnant. So . . . it would appear you are going to be a grandfather."

"You don't say." The smile that had been on his father's face was replaced with a look of surprise, which quickly morphed into another smile, this one congratulatory in nature, but also, Jack felt, a little forced. "Congratulations to both of you. You'll be excellent parents."

Jojo seemed to take him at his word, but Jack knew his father was less than thrilled about his impending grandfather-hood when he immediately pivoted the conversation to another topic.

"So, Jack, what have you been up to? Did you find a job? Are you making any money?"

The answer to the last two questions was no, which made Jack uncomfortable to admit, despite the fact that he did not need a job. He had risked his life on more than one occasion in his bid to help the citizens of China have more say over their own lives, and he'd been paid handsomely. But for all his previous efforts, he was realizing how difficult sustained human change really was. With the help of his good friend Ari, he had addressed the nation of China, from the country's very own Control Center. The previous administration was removed and Jack's own father-in-law was named the president. Yet despite having more freedom now, the average Chinese citizen did little to exercise those freedoms, and this surprised Jack.

"I'm taking some time to chill out," Jack told his father. "Things will come together, and I've got more than enough money. The bounty for those two guys was about fifty million. We're doing okay right now."

His father raised his eyebrows and nodded. "Yes, I'd say you are. Though a man your age should still find a way to meaningfully contribute, I never understood these people that take an early retirement in their fifties, some of them even in their forties. You've got a lot of useful years left, Jack, don't let them go to waste just because your bank account's flush."

Jack sighed. "I won't, Dad."

"Think you'll have the chance to visit before the birth?"

Jack glanced at Jojo. She gave him a smile and then turned her attention to the laptop screen. "We would certainly like that," she said. "We'll have a better idea on things within the next few weeks; we still haven't seen a doctor so it's a little early to plan long-distance travel."

"We're here all the time so you can come whenever's convenient. Jack, I want to take you marlin fishing, this season should be great. Remember that huge one you caught when you were eight?"

"How could I forget?" Jack asked. That had been one of his life experiences he'd never forget, despite that it had happened decades ago, when Cabo was still just a fishing village and not a thriving tourist destination. His father had been the one to hook the marlin, but he'd handed Jack the fishing rod. "It's yours!" he'd told him.

Finally, he would get to catch a huge marlin like his father had done so many times before. Even now as an adult Jack could recall how that exact excitement felt, rushing through him as he gripped the rod and tried to reel in the fish. But that excitement started to wither as the fish's resistance increased and his hands began to ache. He'd reel the fish in a little only to have it pull the opposite direction a moment later. It was a never-ending cycle, the truest example of *one step forward, two steps back.*

After thirty minutes, his hands were rubbed raw and bleeding. But the fish's resolve was wavering, its strength ebbing. Jack was keenly aware of his father's gaze on him.

"Come on, Jack," his dad said to him. "You got this. Never quit. Reel him in. Keep the rod high so the line doesn't break!"

Even now, years later, the conversations, the feel of his blistered hands, the weight of his father's gaze, his expectations—it was as easy to recall as if it had happened yesterday.

"I'd love to catch another big one," Jack said.

"Well, it's not going to happen unless you come out here."

"We're going to try to make it happen, Dad," Jack said. "Things have really settled down for us, so I'm sure I'll be seeing you sooner rather than later."

"Okay, good. Keep me posted. Jojo, congratulations. I'm excited for you both."

They said their goodbyes and Jack disconnected the call. Jojo stretched and yawned. "You know, I think I'm going to go back to bed for a little while."

Jack took a sip of his coffee. He wanted to follow Jojo back to bed, but he felt mildly unsettled. Was it that he sensed his father was not really that excited about the baby? Or that his father disapproved of the fact he wasn't working, despite the multimillions he had in his bank?

"Get some more rest," Jack said. "I'll try to keep it down out here."

"I'm glad I overheard you and got to say hi to your dad. He seemed excited to hear the news!"

Jack did not dispute this, though he disagreed with Jojo on that point. She squeezed his shoulders. "You're tense."

"I must've been a little nervous to tell my dad the news," he said. "But yeah, he took it pretty well."

Jojo went back into their bedroom. Jack found himself thinking about his dad, both the dad of his childhood and his dad now, retired. The dad of his childhood worked all the time, at the hospital, helping others, saving people's lives. Often, it would be in the middle of the night or at some other inopportune time, like a birthday party or a holiday. His dad now was retired and lived in Cabo where he spent his days fishing, reading, relaxing on the beach. Jack had the financial wherewithal to do the same, but he'd not put his time in, the way his father had. Never mind that he'd gone to a great college, an excellent graduate school, spoke fluent Chinese, and had helped both China and America. Jack had tried—and mostly succeeded—to excel in everything he did. He always finished a job because that was how he'd been programmed. That was the example he'd seen growing up and that was the sentiment that was hardwired into him. Living a life of leisure had to be earned through long hard work, and Jack knew that in his father's eyes, he hadn't earned it yet.

Could his dad ever change? Would he ever stop having such expecta-tions? But really, did the fabric of a man or woman ever really change? It was nearly impossible, Jack knew; he shouldn't expect his father to change any more than he could expect himself to change. He had always tried to accept his father for who he was: a hard worker, someone others could count on, a man who kept his cards close and did not ever see the value in showing his affection, at least to his children. Jack could not ever recall his father giving him a hug or speak of his feelings beyond the superficial small talk people engaged in when first beginning a conversation.

Maybe my dad's actually Chinese, Jack thought, smiling. Showing affection or talking about love were not things most Chinese people felt comfortable doing. Fortunately, Jojo did not fall into this category.

Turning his attention back to the computer screen, Jack saw an advertisement for cruises going to Cabo. His mind drifted for a moment;

a visit to Cabo might be just what he and Jojo needed before the baby was born. But before his daydream went any further, Jack looked more closely at the computer. The ad for Cabo hadn't been there prior to his FaceTime call; that seemed a little too coincidental. He frowned at the image of the white cruise ship in the turquoise blue water—it was as though his computer had been listening.

He shut the laptop. There were still a few hours before his eleven o'clock meeting with his father-in-law, the president of China, Wang Yang. He wasn't entirely sure what the meeting was about, but when the president of China requests to meet with you, you don't turn him down.

"I haven't been able to fall back asleep." Jojo's voice beckoned him from the bedroom. Jack stood up, stretched, and went to her, removing his clothes as he crawled back into bed.

"How about we just go back to bed for the rest of the day," he said as she wrapped her arms around him.

"I thought that's what Sundays were supposed to be for," she said. "But you're the one who's going to be leaving soon. Why are you meeting with my dad on a Sunday, anyway?"

"Well, I didn't feel like I was really in the position to specify the day or time."

"It's okay. I have a few things to do around the house today, anyway."

"Oh yeah?"

"Yeah, I have to set up those shelves that just got delivered and I want to replace the front doorknob and lock; I got a much nicer one. And that sliding glass door in the back, it's good quality but it wasn't installed correctly. It needs a few small adjustments and then it should work just fine."

Jack smiled. "That's quite a list. You know, if it were me, I'd just call someone to do it. And hey, you forgot something on that list."

"Did I?"

"My massage."

She pushed back from him enough so he could see the playful smile on her face. "Your massage? Let me get your phone so you can call someone to do it."

They both laughed as Jojo pushed the covers back and sat up. "Roll over," she said.

"You don't really need to massage me right now. I should be massaging you—not only are you pregnant, you've got a full day of house restoration projects ahead of you."

"That's why you'll be giving me my massage later, once all my projects are complete."

"Ah," Jack said, turning onto his stomach as Jojo straddled his back. He let his eyes close as his wife's fingers, made strong from her years of sculpting, pressed the knotted muscles along his shoulder blades, either side of spine. "Now that's a plan."

CHAPTER 2

Though he'd now visited Zhongnanhai many times, Jack still could not help but be in awe of the place, the headquarters of the Communist party and other senior officials; it was the epicenter of power in China.

After entering through the back entrance of Zhongnanhai, Davis, the special agent from the United States Bureau of Diplomatic Security, navigated the SUV to the "Leadership Compound," which was housed in a traditional Chinese building with an ornate, green-tiled roof. Despite its traditional looking exterior, Jack knew inside, everything was ultra-modern.

He stepped out of the car and told Davis that he'd see him in a little while. Though Davis's nature was always a bit standoffish, Jack considered him a friend—they had certainly been through plenty together.

Liang waiting for him at the entrance. Liang was head of the security regiment at Zhongnanhai and someone Jack knew was a trusted friend of Wang's. Liang was tall, nearly Jack's height, and in excellent shape, particularly compared to the average Chinese citizen.

"Jack," Liang said. He had a warm smile on his face as Jack approached. "Hi. Welcome back."

"Good to see you, Liang," Jack said as they shook hands.

"Tell me, Jack, what brings you here today? Or are you just here to visit your father-in-law?" He looked amused, Jack thought, at the fact that Wang was also Jack's father-in-law.

"This isn't just a social calling, I'm afraid," Jack said. "I've got a meeting with Wang. Other than that, I can't tell you much, because that's all I know."

"After all you've done, Jack, I figured you'd be taking some well-deserved time off. I know I would."

Jack smiled. "That's what Jojo would like."

"And how is Jojo?"

"She's great." For a moment, Jack was overcome with the urge to share the news of Jojo's pregnancy with Liang. His father was the only one they'd told so far, and it seemed a natural segue in the current conversation he was having. Liang was not a friend, though he'd always been friendly to Jack and he was a trusted confidant of Wang. Jack swallowed the words though and instead pulled his two phones out of his pocket, which he handed to Liang. He knew what was expected of him when he came to Zhongnanhai.

Liang escorted Jack to the conference room where Wang was waiting. "Have a good meeting," Liang said before he left, giving Jack another smile.

"Jack, thanks for coming by today," Wang said. "I read that book by Milton Friedman you had recommended. I thought it might be interesting to talk about it with regard to China," Wang said. "The trade deal with the US is helping us grow, but there are just too many people in China. If the lives of Chinese citizens are going to improve, we need the economy to grow much faster than six percent."

Jack looked at Wang Yang, the leader of China but also his father-in-law and a good friend. "China's large population is not the problem," he told him. Though Wang was from Suzhou and spoke Suzhou dialect, they spoke Mandarin, as it was spoken by nearly everyone in China, despite the fact there were over two hundred dialects spoken within the country.

"You don't think so? China has 1.4 billion people. That's far greater than any other country."

"What's more important to look at is population density—people per square kilometer of land area. China might have the largest population, but there are many other countries that have higher densities than China, such as Japan, Germany, the United Kingdom. So the question to me is: Why hasn't China's economy grown faster? Why aren't salaries higher? Everyone thought the One Belt One Road initiative would change things, but it was an ill-conceived idea from the start."

Wang nodded, but the frustration on his face was evident. The initiative was meant to connect China to sixty-eight countries, using the Silk Road from East Asia as a starting point and ending in Europe, in the hopes that, along with the building of ports, it would drive trade and commerce, helping all connected countries thrive. What many did not understand, though it seemed rather obvious to Jack, was that many of the countries, such as Malaysia, Thailand, and Indonesia, were slow-growing, low-tech economies.

"I know," Wang said. "The One Belt One Road initiative has been a bust. We've already spent $6 trillion with no return in sight."

Jack nodded. "Having a way to deliver inferior products to a larger market more quickly is going to do little in terms of helping countries thrive. It seems that it's been only the Chinese construction companies that have made any money from this, instead of the participating countries that had already contributed funds."

"The innovation that we hoped would come after investing such a huge amount in the high-tech sector did not materialize. And Jack, equally concerning is the fact that there are more great Chinese doctors, businessmen, and teachers in America than there are in China. How can China succeed if its greatest talent goes elsewhere? We want to launch a new China during the Olympics next year. A re-branding, if you will. Now this seems it won't happen unless we make some rapid progress. Tell me what you're thinking." Wang looked at Jack imploringly.

Jack appreciated the fact that his father-in-law was the sort of leader who could admit when something wasn't working and was open to guidance and suggestions. Jack wouldn't always have the right answers, but when he did, he knew Wang would always be receptive to at least listening to what he had to say.

"Imagine," Jack said, "if all that infrastructure money had gone into massively ramping up China's education systems. What would have happened if all the money spent on those new aircraft carriers and missiles had gone to science and education instead?"

Wang frowned. "I'm imagining what you have said and yes, clearly, the six trillion would have been put to much better use had we invested in education. Unfortunately, we can't turn back the clock and get that money back."

"Of course not. And I don't bring that up to dwell on the past or make anyone feel bad. Have you considered how things are managed?"

"I'm not sure what you mean."

Jack shifted in his chair, exhaling. "Plans for the country are still largely developed top-down. That could be changed and it would help things significantly." This was something he'd thought about before and he was pleased that he was going to have the opportunity to talk to Wang about it.

"I'm listening," Wang said. "Continue."

"Each of China's twenty-one provinces could be run more like a separate country, though China would maintain central control. You could have one province end up like Germany, one like Japan, another like Singapore, etcetera. Deng Xiaoping started something like this in Guangdong Province, which, as we know, was successful. This could certainly be done elsewhere."

In a way, China and the United States were similar: each country was made up of states or provinces that had within them many cities, and within that, smaller cities and towns. Just as there were multiple cities within the County of Los Angeles, Shanghai had a massive number of smaller cities and towns, making it the most populous city in the world. The difference was that, unlike states in the US, the provinces in China had limited independence.

Wang reached into the inner pocket of his suit and pulled out a pack of cigarettes. "You mean twenty-three provinces, don't you?" he asked after he lit the cigarette.

Jack smiled. Wang returned the smile. Jack had intentionally left out Taiwan and Hong Kong, though he knew they should be included as provinces of China.

"So," Wang said. "How would it be done?"

"The head of each province, or municipality, could put up a plan for *what* they plan to accomplish, *how* they'll do it, and *what* will be the impact to tax revenue over a two- to three-year period. They would first have to drill down to the key city level and make such plans. They'd need to look afresh at their area and become creative as to where opportunity for growth is and how to capture it. It would require some out of the box thinking for sure. Get each head to present their findings and ideas and after they've made their presentations, the key would be to track the right things, like tax revenue, crime, jobs added, social welfare. From there, you could compare the reports from each province. The same sort of reporting could also be done for each city within a province. These reports could be used by you to easily and quickly find where actual performance is falling short of the plan. Conversely, you'll also be able to see which plans succeeded, and you can then share that information with the other provinces."

Wang sat in silence for a few moments, smoking, an intrigued but also skeptical expression on his face. "All sorts of problems would arise.

I don't want another well-intentioned idea that we sink trillions into and have nothing to show for at the end of it."

Jack nodded because Wang was correct. Some of the province leaders simply wouldn't be able to develop and implement a plan. Some would resist any change from that status quo. It would likely require a significant reshuffling of leadership within the provinces. Problems would arise, yes, but it was nothing insurmountable.

"That's true," Jack said, "but governors should be encouraged to actively shift resources within their provinces, and you'd only allocate resources to those plans that you believe in. A key feature of this is that the Central Government can assist them in implementing their plan, where and when it is warranted. Some individuals will thrive and can be given more responsibility. Provinces will evolve. The plans will need to be presented to you to evaluate and then eventually, approve. These presentations will really give you the opportunity to learn a great deal about the provinces and their leaders. They will need to focus on what they are good at and what makes sense; there will be competition for resources and talented people, and both these things need to be able to freely move around and go to the most deserving province. One province may end up specializing in sports, another in music, another in modern pharmaceutical manufacturing. Either way, the provinces could present their plans to you and others for input. Also, I'd imagine that knowing their plans would be very helpful when deciding what national infrastructure projects are necessary."

"You never think small," Wang said. "I've talked to over a hundred people and no one has focused in this area. You're essentially introducing a bottom-up strategic planning process, and this is something that China has never really tried. And I must say, Jack, you've given this more thought than I ever expected, but I'm so glad you did. Can I trouble you to write your thoughts down and send them to me over via WeChat? I'll think about what you've said in the meantime. This bottom-up approach could potentially help to ignite creativity, innovation, and produce real results, which, up until now, has been elusive."

Jack could tell from Wang's tone and the expression on his face that he took his responsibility as president seriously and was trying to do what was best for all the people in his country. It wouldn't be easy but it certainly wasn't impossible. After successfully addressing the entire nation from the Control Center, Jack knew that almost anything could be accomplished.

"Yes, I'll send something over," Jack said, wishing that his writing in Chinese were better so that he didn't have to write in English, which meant Wang would need to have someone translate it into Chinese.

"Thank you, Jack. And—one more thing. President Sutton does not need to know about this chat, please."

Looking into changing how China operated would be of huge interest to the US, though the idea of sharing this conversation had never occurred to Jack. "Of course," he said.

When their meeting concluded, Jack bid Wang goodbye and made his way through the now-familiar hallways to the front entrance. He recalled the first time he entered Zhongnanhai, which seemed like ages ago now; back then, never did he think it would be a place that he regularly came to.

Approaching the exit, he replayed his conversation with Wang. China's slow growth was frustrating. He knew the real reason, but he had kept it to himself just now, not wanting to offend his father-in-law. But the truth was: there was no diversity of people in China, and that impacted everything. People could not readily hear different perspectives. People mostly took direction from authority, which hindered innovation. People seemed content with the status quo. Even after his address to them at the Control Center, the citizens of China had not evolved socially, intellectually, or politically.

Though the economy had opened up, there were still many limiting regulations for any true progress to be made. People needed and wanted to make money. Beyond just surviving, they wanted to thrive—but this meant Wang's position and that of the Communist Party could be at stake. The Party had always managed to preserve its position, but at what cost? The cost of its citizens prosperity.

Before Jack exited the building, his two phones were returned—his black phone, which was his connection to Cooper and the CIA, and his own personal iPhone. As he stepped outside, he saw Liang again.

"Good meeting?" he asked.

"I think so. Every time I come here I learn something new."

Liang blinked dramatically. "Huó dào lǎo, xué dào lǎo!"

Jack smiled at the Chinese proverb: *One is never too old to learn.*

Jack responded with the less known second sentence to the idiom, "Hái yǒu sān fēn xué bú dào." *There is always three things that you have not learned.*

"Jack, you know Chinese better than most Chinese." They both laughed and Jack bid Liang goodbye as he headed over to the black SUV that Davis was waiting by.

Jack got in and they left; as they drove away from Zhongnanhai, Jack recalled that day, over a year ago now, right after he had delivered a broadcast from the Control Center Building to the entire nation of China . . . He'd made his way over to the China World Hotel and Davis walked right up to him. *I'm from the US Embassy. For your safety, please come with me. There's a flight out of China you need to be on.*

"You know," Jack said. "It's been over a year since you came up to me at the China World Hotel and here we are, still in Beijing. Have you had many opportunities to check out any other places?"

"Just Beijing and Shanghai." Davis shrugged. "I've been meaning to visit some other places but the time just hasn't been right yet." He turned his head slightly to give Jack a wry half-smile. It was ensuring Jack and Jojo's safety that kept him so busy.

"Well, you might have the chance soon," Jack said.

Davis perked up. "Can you share any details?"

"Not yet," Jack said. "But soon."

CHAPTER 3

The boutique hotel Jack and Jojo lived in had been a wedding present from Wang Yang. It had been converted into what Jack saw as both a comfortable but practical home, with an abundance of space for Jojo's sculpting and whatever other creative endeavors she wanted to pursue.

Jack entered on the ground floor, which was expansive and had a decidedly industrial feel, with its raw concrete floors, though this was balanced by several Persian rugs and overstuffed sofas that were artfully arranged throughout the space.

There was no sign of anyone; Jack took his shoes off and made his way through the large space, passing by the floor to ceiling shelving where she had just placed her sculptures. Jack reached the back door and stepped out. Jojo was sitting in front of an easel holding a stretched white canvas; the dog was wrangling a chew toy nearby. She had a paint-brush in hand with a pensive expression on her face. At the sound of the door closing behind him, she looked up, smiling.

"Hey."

Jack smiled and went over to her, his gaze missing the canvas completely as he bent to kiss her. They had been married over nine months, and their marital life came so easily that Jack still couldn't believe he'd initially had his reservations about the whole thing.

"What are you working on?" he asked.

She looked at the canvas, though he still kept his face turned away. "I couldn't remember the last time I'd picked up a paint brush. And I realized I kind of missed it. So I bought some supplies on Taobao the other night, and they got delivered today."

Jack kissed her again. "Can I see what you're painting?"

"Of course. Though with the caveat that I'm just getting back into the swing of things. I really can't remember the last time I painted."

Jack turned his head. Jojo was immensely talented at anything she tried, which of course he knew sounded biased, seeing as he was her husband, but it was also a fact. It was a watermelon and two bright yellow flowers. Jack frowned; it was like a picture he was certain he'd seen before—and that was how realistic it looked, like a photograph.

He looked past the canvas to their garden, where there was a watermelon and two bright yellow flowers. He let his gaze go to the canvas and then the garden again before alighting back on Jojo.

"Looks to me like you're more than back in the swing of things. I can't even tell the difference between the two. That's incredible."

Jojo smiled but her brow creased a little as she looked at the canvas. "I'm still a little rusty," she said. "I'd originally wanted to be a painter, but it seemed like so did everyone else. And—I admit—I chose sculpting because I didn't want to be like everyone else."

"Now that would be impossible."

She set her paintbrush down and stood. "And you somehow always know the right thing to say. How'd it go with my dad?"

"He's got a lot on his mind. Understandably."

"What did he want to talk about?"

"Remember that book by Milton Friedman that I'd mentioned in my speech? He wanted to chat about that for a little bit."

"I heard that book has been downloaded over a hundred and twenty-five million times. Apparently, that's some sort of world record."

"Wow," Jack said. "I didn't know that. But I'm glad to hear the book recommendation was so well-received. Never mind all that, though," he said. He touched Jojo's stomach, which was still flat, giving no indication of their impending parenthood.

Jojo put her hand over his and then looked at him, gave him a playful smile. "Shàng chuáng ma?" The literal translation: *Would you like to get on the bed?*

Jack returned her smile and took her hand, leading her back inside. "Lái shàng chuáng." This was not an invitation he would ever turn down.

* * *

A few hours later, Jack was in his home office in front of his laptop and Jojo had returned to her painting. He opened a new file and titled it

Provincial Strategic Planning. Within the document, he created different headings:

- Objective
- Methodology
- Key Steps
- Risks & Mitigation
- Timeline
- Estimated Budget
- Monitoring
- Expected Benefits
- Results

This would be the framework for each province's presentation. Ideally, all Province Secretaries and Governors would meet with the Standing Committee beforehand to explain the importance of the project and what would occur. Presentations would be limited to fifteen minutes with questions afterward. Absolutely no reading of presentations—a favorite approach of nearly all government officials. Jack included this in the document.

The last thing he suggested was that it might be useful to gain the assistance of a major management consulting firm to help in the process and compilation of information. The firm would need to visit each province and work with the officials there to brainstorm fresh ideas.

Jack reviewed the document and then sent it via WeChat to Wang Lang, along with a voice message in Chinese: *President Wang, I hope this summary document is what you were looking for.*

Once the file was sent, Jack leaned back in his chair. Wang would appreciate receiving the information so promptly, and, Jack hoped, he'd like what he read. Jack knew that what he was suggesting would be met with fierce resistance from some. He'd done a similar project for a large financial institution, and he was confident that the same approach could be applied to the world's most populous nation. But it would require secretaries and governors to look at their responsibilities from an entirely new angle. It would not be easy, as people invariably feared change; they wanted safety and security.

Positive and lasting change—the sort that Jack had hoped would flourish after he addressed the nation at the Control Center—was generally not the purview of the powerful and influential. And it would be these government officials who would be required to critically assess their provinces and make recommendations that would help the lives of the average citizen instead of enriching themselves further.

There would be significant resistance. Jack knew Wang knew this, and surely that would be a consideration when he reviewed the file Jack had sent over. Wang did not know it yet, but there was a grandchild of his very own who would soon be here. Jack had no idea if he and Jojo and their unborn baby would remain in China forever, but there were babies being born every day and children who deserved to have a life that included the freedom to make their own choices and not be told by the government what they are and are not permitted to do. Everything Jack knew about Wang pointed to a man who would not be swayed to maintain the status quo for fear of upsetting those in power. Wang would want to make the changes necessary to ensure a better future for the everyday citizen.

And Jack did, too.

CHAPTER 4

The next morning, Jack stood at the kitchen counter, pouring yesterday's coffee into his mug. Jojo was already out back, working on her painting. Jack loved the way she allowed things to completely absorb her; she looked like a painting herself, right now, bathed in the mid-morning light. She wore a men's white button-down dress shirt, tied at the bottom, which would protect her clothes from the paint. Jack took his old coffee and sat in front of his computer to check out the day's headlines in America.

The DOW, NASDAQ, AND S&P had all hit historic highs. President Sutton had secured trade agreements with all the other Asian countries. Unemployment was at a historic low.

All good things, yet Jack could not help but feel the world was changing without him. This was a new feeling, and one he was not entirely comfortable with. The fact of it was: He was witnessing all this change yet not causing it. Which he realized might sound odd and he wondered if he'd become accustomed to the high stakes, high tension—and often dangerous—situations he'd found himself in over a year ago. His life prior to that time, before that "chance" meeting with Ari, had not been a bastion of fast-paced action and danger. And once everything started to return to normal after his address at the Control Center, Jack had assumed things would, more or less, go back to how they'd been. He was a husband now, so that was a new role, and also, there was a baby on the way.

The feeling that he should be doing more did not want to relent, though. He took a sip of his stale coffee. He was married to an incredible woman. They were about to start a family. He had more money than he would ever need. Shouldn't that be enough? Why this stirring of restlessness? It wasn't something he wanted to talk to Jojo about; he'd always felt they could speak about anything yet he knew the way something like that could be construed, and anyway, his restless feeling had nothing to do with *her.*

His iPhone chimed—a WeChat alert. It was a voice message from Wang: *Thanks for your write-up. Are you free today at 2pm to discuss further at Zhongnanhai?*

He'd been about to take another sip of coffee but stopped. He put the mug down. Something was up. There was a reason when things moved fast like this.

Jack sent a return message, affirming that he'd be there. He returned his attention to his laptop and went to Google news, which, unlike a few months ago, he could access in China only with a VPN. After he had addressed the nation at the Control Center, all news was freely accessible online. He typed "China" but nothing of new of significance came up.

He closed the laptop. He'd find out soon enough.

Downstairs, he found Jojo working on a new painting. "I just got a voice message from your dad. He wants me to go see him this afternoon."

She glanced at him. "Does he? I was thinking we might go for a walk in a little bit. I might be thrilled to be painting again, but my lower back isn't thrilled about sitting in this chair for so long."

"I'm sure we'll have time for that," Jack said. "This is your dad, after all, it's not like I can say no to the president of China. I'll be back soon."

Jojo smiled as Jack leaned down to kiss her cheek. "I know you will. We'll go for a walk then."

*   *   *

Jack sat in the black SUV as Davis drove them to Zhongnanhai. Like yesterday, Jack was dressed in a formal dark blue suit and a yellow tie.

"Seems like you're bouncing in and out of Zhongnanhai quite a bit," Davis said. He knew better than to ask what this meeting was about. "I can't remember the last time someone from the US Embassy visited there."

"I've never visited the US Embassy," Jack said. He had wondered why the US needed seven hundred people at the Beijing Embassy. He'd even be willing to take it a step further and close all the US Embassies and Consulates throughout China; the benefits of such a thing were numerous. It would save money. Visas could be issued online, and documents could be sent to the US via FedEx. It would never happen, Jack knew, because America was wasteful and things with inertia were also hard to stop.

"No kidding?" Davis said. "I find that surprising."

"Wang and President Sutton seem to have a pretty good relationship, so they probably speak directly," Jack said.

"That's true. Faster that way, too."

"Right." Jack looked out the window at the blurred buildings as they drove by. He still couldn't shake the feeling that something was going on, something beyond what he and Wang had talked about yesterday. Yet despite this feeling, he didn't have the slightest idea what it might be. He thrived on challenges, on analyzing situations, solving problems. But he felt he wasn't doing anything even close to that right now.

"Davis," Jack said. "Have you heard of anything going on in China that's unusual? Or anything that stands out?"

Davis met his gaze momentarily in the rearview mirror. Jack had never asked him such a question before. "No," he said. "I haven't, and I receive briefings every day."

"Could I get a copy of those?"

"Shouldn't be a problem. I get them as emails on my phone, so I'll talk to Cooper and arrange it."

"Thank you," Jack said. They pulled into Zhongnanhai, where things seemed the same as usual. It was a different young man and young woman there to welcome him, and he went through the regular routine of turning off his black phone and leaving both his phones at the entrance. This time, though, instead of going into the room they'd met in yesterday, Jack was led to a new area of Zhongnanhai that he had never visited before.

This section was even more modern and elegant than the areas Jack was familiar with. He walked past paintings and sculptures and other priceless artwork. Zhongnanhai was adjacent to the Forbidden City, where twenty-four emperors had previously lived.

Jack thanked the man and the woman who escorted him to the meeting. Wang was waiting for him in a room at the end of the hallway.

"Jack, thanks for coming by," he said. "I shared your write-up with a few others; I hope you don't mind. And, well . . . they wanted to meet with you. I hope that's okay?"

He had assumed this would be another discussion with Wang, much like yesterday, though he did not let the surprise register on his face. Besides, he didn't mind speaking with others, especially if they were interested in learning more about what a bottom-up approach could do for the country.

"Of course it is, President Wang," Jack said, addressing him in such a manner so he would know Jack would respect him as president while in this meeting even though he was also his father-in-law.

Wang smiled. "Thanks, Jack. Come on." He escorted Jack into an adjacent, larger room where six men already sat around a conference table. The men stood as Wang entered and then remained standing to introduce themselves and shake Jack's hand. They were all smiling and seemed genuinely pleased to see Jack; he realized they were members of the Standing Committee of the Communist Party of China. Some of them he knew Wang had replaced, such as Li Keqiang. Wang had simply taken a page from Mao Zedong, the founder and chairman of China's communist party until his death in 1976, who had done the same thing and unilaterally replaced a number of the members.

Jack took his seat as the others did, his feelings of being outside of everything suddenly inverted; now he felt uncertain about the fact he was here, that these men wanted to talk with him. What had he gotten himself into?

Wang, from his seat at the head of the table, looked around before his eyes settled on Jack. "Jack. Thank you for coming by on such short notice. We liked the Provincial Strategic Planning paper you put together." He nodded and the six other men followed suit.

"That's excellent," Jack said. "I'm happy to hear you think it will be useful."

"Yes. Well, it will be useful only if what you have drafted can be utilized properly. Which is why we would like you to do it."

Though it was flattering, Jack was not the right person for the job. "I appreciate the vote of confidence," he said, "but it is really the head of the provinces who should conduct the strategy planning process. People will need to be replaced and resources will be shifted and allocated. That person must have the authority to do so and stick around afterward to implement it. Though I will say, the prospect of such a challenge is quite intriguing."

Wang smiled and looked around the table. Jack had seen such a smile before and knew it meant that the rationale that had just been offered was already considered as his likely response.

"Jack," Wang said. "We will all see each presentation. We will make sure that what you say is done. The reason that we want *you* is because you are uniquely suited to help these people focus and address their questions. We need an outsider who we respect and trust."

"You want me to go to each province?"

"Yes," Wang said. "You will be traveling to each of China's *twenty-three* provinces. Actually, we think it makes best sense to cover all thirty-three Administrative Divisions for greater coverage. Also, you estimated it would take six months. Well, it needs to be done in three."

For several moments, Jack was speechless. He looked around the table at the men, all of them older than Jack by several decades, in their gray and dark blue suits. Was this some sort of joke they were all in on? He replayed what Wang had just said and did some mental math: he'd need to visit three divisions each week to be done within three months. A huge undertaking.

"Three months," he said. "That works out to be an average of three divisions each week, if you're looking to have this done within three months. And speaking of three months, have you gotten my wife's permission for me to be unavailable for that length of time?"

"She's aware of why you are here today," Wang said. "I called her while you were on your way over. And I spoke with President Sutton earlier and he is okay with you working on the project. China needs to get this initiative going and for it to be known there is an aggressive undertaking occurring."

Clearly, there was more going on than they were willing to divulge right now, but they also needed his help. And, Jack noticed, Wang had affirmed that permission had been granted by Sutton, but not Jojo, just that she knew about it. Jack imagined he'd have to do a little creative reasoning to get her to agree. Three months was a while to be away.

"I'll need three very smart people to assist me," Jack said. "And no one from Beijing or Shanghai." His reasoning was general but true: people from Beijing might have relationships with leadership and those from Shanghai were simply too arrogant and would be too difficult to work with in the limited time that he had. "And again—they need to be intelligent."

"Say no more," Wang said. "Consider it done. And thank you for helping." He reached into the inner pocket of his suit and extracted a small red booklet that he slid across the table to Jack.

Jack looked down. The cover read: *Diplomatic Passport of People's Republic of China.* He glanced at Wang before opening the booklet, revealing a photo of himself and his information.

"Sutton said he has no problem with you simultaneously holding this passport," Wang said as Jack closed the cover, stunned to see his picture attached to a Chinese Diplomatic Passport. He was the only non-Chinese person in the world to have one, as far as he knew. But he also wasn't entirely sure what he would use it for.

"This will help confirm your identity during your visits to each municipality which will help with security," Wang added. "And you had recommended we hire a consulting firm to do this. Well, we checked and the cost was around $3.5 million. We'd like to pay you three million for the assignment."

"That's fine," Jack said. "I accept it. For the record, all such money will be going to charity in China. I would not want there to be any appearance of nepotism, given our relationship. However, if the Chinese government provided a small token of appreciation in the form of Maotai, it would be appreciated."

Wang grinned. Maotai was the national drink of China, a strong, aromatic alcoholic beverage that Jack had grown quite fond of. "Then it's settled," Wang said. "Next Wednesday all the municipality secretaries and governors will visit Zhongnanhai. Thank you again for coming in, Jack."

"Certainly." Jack knew that, though it was hard to get anything done in China, once things got going, they went very fast. Still, he couldn't help but be impressed by the speed with which they were moving.

He thought about how productive the five-minute meeting had been as Davis drove him back home. Wang's confidence that Jack would accept was undeniable; now that he was replaying the meeting, his recollection seemed to be that the six other men had exuded a similar confidence.

They might be certain about getting me to agree, Jack thought, *but I doubt they'd have the same confidence about convincing Jojo.*

On the one hand, of course she would understand, wouldn't she? Not only was it the right thing to do for China, Jojo's father was the president.

It was a family matter. Yet at the same time, Jojo hadn't seemed entirely thrilled about his two-meetings-in-a-row at Zhongnanhai, and if she felt like that when he was only gone briefly, such a short distance from home, what were the chances he'd really get her on board with him traveling all over the country for the next three months?

CHAPTER 5

He found Jojo on the couch with her iPad when he returned home. He sat down next to her.

"How was the meeting?" she asked.

"Interesting. I heard your father called when I was on my way over?"

She kept her focus on the tablet for a moment longer and then set it down. "Yes," she said, looking at him, her expression neutral. "He called me right after you left. He was a little vague, but said that he needs your help. That the whole country, once again, needs your help. Oh, and that it's going to involve you visiting every province and it will take a few months."

Jack winced. "Yeah. Like three months. Which is a lot, I know."

"You know, when my dad told me, my initial reaction was *no*. How could it not be? You've already put your life at risk trying to help this country become a better place for *all* of its citizens—you addressed the nation from the Control Center! No one ever thought something like that would happen. So of course there's a part of me that wants to be selfish and say that you need to stay here; I *am* pregnant, after all. But, the other part of me knows how lucky I am to have had so few side effects and that surely I'll manage just fine while you're doing this very important work. I know my dad—if he says it's important, it is. He wouldn't be asking this of you—and of me—if it weren't. I will say, I don't like you being away, and I'd rather you didn't do it. But I understand, and I know that it's not all about me and what I want. And how can I not help but admire how you are so willing to go to such lengths to try to change things for the better, for people you will never even meet?" She smiled, though Jack sensed there was some sadness there, too.

"I was thinking that maybe you'd be able to come with me on a few of the trips? The meetings themselves won't take too long, or at least the part that I have to be involved with. We could even start with Dali. You've mentioned wanting to go there and I hear it's a beautiful city."

"That doesn't sound like a bad idea at all," Jojo said. "I'd love that, actually." Her smile widened and the previous sadness Jack had sensed evaporated. "Afterward, I could spend some time in Suzhou and visit some relatives and old friends I haven't seen in a while. It's been a while since I was last home."

Jack relaxed back into the couch cushion, relieved that Jojo not only understood that he needed to participate in this project but she was actually excited herself about it.

"And I give you my word," he said, "that I will always be there for you. I will not get so caught up in this that you ever feel like you have been abandoned. I'm not that sort of person."

"I know you're not. And that's just one of the many things I love about you."

Jack leaned forward and gave her a kiss. "You—and our child—are the most important things in my life. I know you know this, but it's worth saying again. And I appreciate that you understand the importance of this. Your father is really committed to seeing things change. I want to do what I can to see him be successful."

Jack picked up his iPhone and opened WeChat to send Wang a voice message. "*Jojo and I will visit Dali after the meeting on Wednesday, so I'll begin there. Kindly send over the three assistants to our home when they are ready. Thank you.*"

After that message was sent, he texted Cooper from his black phone with their plans to stay in Dali. Cooper would liaise with China to arrange transport and the three-night stay for the two of them, starting right after his meeting in Zhongnanhai next Wednesday.

Jack put his phone down and wrapped his arms around Jojo. "Work is such an inconvenience," he said, breathing in the pleasing botanical scent from the shampoo she used.

"You don't look like you're working too hard."

"Some very important instructions were just issued having to do with our upcoming stay in Dali."

Jojo raised her eyebrows. "All that just happened?"

"Just this moment."

"While you were sitting here next to me on the couch?"

"Affirmative."

She couldn't contain her laughter any longer. "You make it look so easy."

A melodic ringing filled the air, though it seemed to be emanating from inside. Jack and Jojo looked at each other.

"Oh," Jack said after a moment. "It's the doorbell." He stood. "I guess everyone who's ever visited us here has knocked? I don't think I've heard that before."

Jojo laughed. "Me neither. I wonder who it is."

Jack went to find out. He opened the front door to find two young men in dark blue suits and a young woman in a conservative orange dress standing on the step.

"Hello, Mr. Gold," the woman said in flawless English. "We understand you are expecting us. We are from President Wang's office."

Jack tried not to hide his surprise at the speed in which they showed up. "That's great," he said, stepping back. "Come on in."

They followed him inside and removed their shoes. Jojo had gotten up and came to stand next to Jack.

"Jojo, I'd like to introduce you to my three new colleagues," Jack said, but then he paused because he realized he didn't know their names. "This is my wife, Jojo. And I'm Jack."

The woman smiled. "Yes, we know," she said. "My name is Susan." She shook Jack's hand and then Jojo's; the two men—Jason and David—did the same.

"It's great to meet you," Jojo said.

"We're just going to talk for a few minutes, if that's okay with you," Jack said.

"Of course it is. I'll bring out some tea."

Jojo went to the kitchen and Jack motioned to the three to have a seat at the table near the windows that faced the garden. "I've been looking forward to meeting you and working on this exciting project together," Jack said, looking at each of his new colleagues. They nodded earnestly, each taking out a notepad and a pen. Jack was glad to see this, instead of a smart phone or a tablet.

"Have you seen the draft project description?"

The three of them nodded and in unison said, "Yes."

"Great," Jack said. "Let me describe our goal and then what we need to do. Our objective is to help China's municipalities to become more successful at growing tax revenue. To do this, they need to start thinking more creatively. Things cannot continue on as 'business as usual' if there is any hope for real, lasting change." He paused. Jason and David were scribbling notes, their heads bent over their notepads. Susan had her pen in hand but was listening intently, clearly absorbing everything Jack was saying.

"As we visit each provincial secretary and governor, we'll emphasize this point—the outside the box thinking—and encourage their creativity. This will be likely be an uncomfortable exercise for some of them at first; they're not used to this sort of approach. But it's what needs to happen if this project is going to succeed. You'll see. In the meantime, we need to prepare for the meetings so that we have our own ideas to share with them."

Jack glanced over his shoulder as Jojo arrived with a tray containing a tea pot and four teacups. She poured Jack's tea first, then filled the other three cups before passing them out. Jack realized that this was something she'd done countless times for her father and his guests; in China, what she had done was the quintessential duty of any wife or daughter, and Jack felt a deep appreciation for the gesture.

"I'll let you get back to work," Jojo said, giving Jack a wink, before she took the tray.

Jack looked back to his colleagues as they sipped their tea. "We need a five-page briefing paper on each municipality prepared before we visit. One of those items must be the city's P&L, their Income Statement."

"The cities and provinces don't have that," Jason said.

"Well, we need to know where their revenue and key expenses come from, by year, for the past five years. We don't need everything broken down, just the main items and totals. I'm sure that information can be obtained."

"That shouldn't be a problem," Susan said, and now she did write something in her notepad.

"We also need a description of the municipality's financials. This should be less than half a page long. Then I need a description of the city itself: demographic information, what makes it special or unique—or not. I'd like you to put together a simple SWOT analysis of their Strengths, Weaknesses, Opportunities, and Threats. There needs to be an insightful biography of each secretary and governor. And finally—one page that contains the most relevant maps of the area."

Jack picked up his tea while Susan, David, and Jason wrote down what he just said. He held the cup in his hands and inhaled, taking in the fragrance before he took a sip, much in the same way someone would do with a good glass of red wine. Then he took a sip, and when he put his cup down, the others had finished writing and were taking sips from their own cups.

He was pleased with the way things were going so far. His new colleagues were young, yes, but they were focused and intelligent. And he relished being able to come up with ideas and processes to implement in this new bottom-up approach.

"Our first province is going to be Yunnan," Jack said. "So why don't you put together the first briefing paper on Yunnan, and then let me take a look at it. That will be our first real meeting. Jojo and I will be going to the city of Dali for a few days beforehand; then she's going to fly to Suzhou to visit with some family and friends. Hopefully you three can divide the reports for the municipalities and review each other's work before getting them to me, at least a day before each of our meetings. Upon arrival, we should try to arrange a brief car tour to any areas you think might be of significance."

He took out his iPhone and opened WeChat to his QR Code. "Here, let's form a group," he said.

Susan, David, and Jason followed Jack's lead and took out their own phones and scanned his code. Just like that—they'd made a group. It was that easy.

"So the other thing I'd like you to begin working on," Jack said, "is compiling a list of the cities we should visit, and when we should visit them. Just tell me where we need to be when, including weekends. How does that sound?"

"That sounds fine," Susan said. Jason and David nodded. "I'll also create a Cloud Group and send out links so that documents can be uploaded and accessed there."

"Excellent," Jack said. "And all the documents should be written in English because my Chinese sucks." They all laughed; he had been speaking Chinese fluently with them this whole time. But reading and writing Chinese was a different matter altogether. "And the last thing for today," Jack said, "because I think we've definitely covered a lot of ground, is that everything we are doing is confidential. Secret. President

Wang is the only person, aside from myself, that you may discuss what we are doing. Otherwise, you must get approval from one of us beforehand, prior to talking about anything in regard to this project. Is that okay with everyone?"

Again, the three of them nodded in earnest. They looked as eager about this as Jack felt inside—perhaps his address at the Control Center had only been the first step in ushering in a new future for China. He felt good about the direction they were moving.

When the meeting was over, they said goodbye to Jojo and Jack walked his new colleagues back to the front door, where they put on their shoes and told him they would begin right away with the tasks he had mentioned. They had only been gone a few moments when Jack's phone beeped; he looked at the screen and accepted their invitations to connect via WeChat.

Jack went and sat back down on the couch next to Jojo, in close to the exact positions they'd been in before the doorbell rang. She put her iPad down. "I've never seen you run a meeting before. I liked what I saw. To the point with no wasted time, but fair and willing to hear other opinions. No wonder my dad feels he needs you on board for this to be a success."

"You're welcome to come to all of my meetings and help out, if you'd like."

She gave him a smile and slowly shook her head. "As tempting as that is, you really don't need my help. And I can see just how much your new colleagues respect you." She nudged him with her elbow. "I think Susan thinks you're handsome."

Jack let out a loud laugh. "That's a good one."

"Well, why wouldn't she? You are. Incredibly so."

"Coming from my wife, I take that as the compliment it is. Though I respectfully disagree with her assessment that my newest colleague has a crush on me."

"Crushes take time," Jojo said. She laughed. "I'm just kidding. At one point, though, when I was bringing over the tea, you were saying something and they were all looking at you with such rapt attention it was like they *all* had crushes on you. It was cute. But honestly, I'd like to spend some of this time focusing on my painting. I really can't believe I let so much time go by without picking up a brush. And now I'm sort of feeling like I want to really dedicate some time to it now, before the baby arrives and I never have a moment to myself again."

"You will definitely still have time for yourself after the baby's here," Jack said. "I promise. But I understand. And I love to see you painting; I can tell it's something you're not only excellent at, but you also thoroughly enjoy."

"You know, that's exactly how I feel after listening to your meeting today. You're in your element, Jack, and I'm glad you get to do it. I'm sorry for my hesitancy about all of this."

"Come here." He pulled her into a hug.

"Are we still planning on visiting Jiankou tomorrow?" Jiankou was a section of the Great Wall, known for its precarious path on a steep and winding mountain ledge.

"Would you rather not?" Jack asked.

"No, I want to. I've spent so many hours in front of my easel now that a vigorous walk like that will do me some good."

"I'll make sandwiches to take with us."

"You make the best sandwiches," Jojo said, grinning.

CHAPTER 6

The section of the Great Wall they were going to hike was called Jiankou and it traversed green mountaintops and gave anyone willing to make the trek a stunning vista view. And unlike other places along the Great Wall, there were no snack shops or souvenir stands, there were no gondolas to make the ascent easier. Jack liked this, and he knew Jojo would appreciate it also.

Davis drove them; leading the way in an identical black SUV was their security detail from the US Embassy; behind them was another SUV with their Chinese security. There were no known threats—at least that Jack was aware of—but he felt reassured at their presence.

They drove for about ninety minutes, during which time Jack and Jojo dozed; it was still very early; the sun had not even started to rise, though the sky to the east had begun to lighten. Davis pulled up to a semi-official looking roadblock. He put down his window and Jack heard someone outside say, "That'll be forty RMB for each of you."

Jack was seated behind Davis; he put his own window down. "That cost is 20 RMB," he said in Mandarin.

If the man he just addressed was surprised to hear Jack's fluency, he did not show it on his darkly tanned face. "It's 40 RMB per person."

But Jack had checked, just last night, about the "unofficial" cost of entry. It was 20 RMB. There was no one formally collecting fees and issuing entry tickets; this man likely shared whatever money collected with various officials of the city, which was a normal way of doing things. The man clearly thought he could charge more since they were foreigners.

Jack reached into his pocket and withdrew his Chinese Diplomatic Passport. He handed it to the man, whose face now could not help but register his shock.

"Oh. Oh! I'm sorry." He hastily handed the passport back. "Please proceed."

"Thank you. But first—here." Jack handed the man 60 RMB.

"What'd you show him?" Davis asked as he started to drive again.

"Wang gave me a Chinese diplomatic passport. It seemed like a good time to test it out." Jack slipped the passport back into his pocket.

"Does the US State Department know about that?" Davis asked, catching Jack's eye in the rearview mirror.

"Wang said he cleared things with Sutton."

Jojo began to stir as Davis pulled into the nearly empty dirt parking lot. She yawned. "We're here?"

"We're here."

"I think I slept the whole way." She smothered another yawn. "Tell me again why we're here at such an ungodly hour?"

Jack had jogged on the Great Wall before, though he'd never been to Jiankou. "Well, Jiankou's supposed to be beautiful. And just look." He gestured to the parking lot. "We've practically got the whole place to ourselves at this hour. We don't have to deal with any crowds, and plus, we'll get to watch the sunrise. Come on. Let's do it!"

Jojo laughed. "My husband sounds like a Nike commercial."

They got out and readied themselves, inserting their earbuds, getting their playlist queued up. Davis and Willie, one of the Chinese military guards, would accompany them while the rest remained below to observe anyone who arrived and follow them if warranted.

Davis stood next to Willie, in a pair of Adidas sports pants and a black shirt and a fanny pack. "You guys ready?" Jack asked.

"I'm ready," Davis said. "But we should wait a few minutes until it gets lighter. Jiankou is very steep and is not fully restored. It can be dangerous to hike, even during the day."

The sun would be rising soon, and the light right now was diffuse, gray, still a little murky. "You're right," Jack said. "The Sky Stairs would be difficult to navigate in the dark."

"The Sky Stairs?" Jojo asked.

"It's a very steep and narrow stretch, and it can be difficult to get a foothold, especially if you can't see well. But the view from there is amazing." As he drifted off to sleep last night, Jack had considered whether he should bring Jojo here now; she was, after all, pregnant, but it was still so early in the pregnancy that her center of gravity was still the same that it had always been. It certainly wasn't something he'd feel comfortable doing once she reached her second and third trimesters.

He touched her lower back. He knew her well enough to know that asking if she'd rather not because of her "delicate state" would not go over well. If Jojo didn't want to do it, she would have told him. Her forthrightness was one of the things he appreciated most about her.

They waited in the parking lot, taking sips of water and doing some light stretching, for several minutes as the day began to brighten more. When they started to walk, they headed through a long path toward the entrance.

"Wow," Jojo said, looking around. "Those rocks are beautiful." Her eyes were wide as she took in the natural scenery. "I should have brought my painting supplies."

After finally passing through the main entrance, they turned to the left to begin their climb. The sun had appeared over the horizon as they took careful steps.

Davis was in front, and he braced himself against the wall on his right to help navigate the steep stairs. Jojo went next and Jack kept both a close eye on her as well as his own footing. The wall dropped down and then went back up, almost vertical.

They'd stop and rest after a steep vertical ascent before continuing onward. They stopped at a watch tower to take in the sunrise; Davis and Willie waited outside. Jack took Jojo's hand, their faces bathed in the early morning light. Though their security detail was just nearby, Jack felt as though he and Jojo were alone here on the Great Wall, watching the natural beauty of the changing light transform the landscape before them. He gave Jojo's hand a squeeze.

"It's as beautiful as you said," she told him. He loved the awestruck look on her face as she looked out.

"I have a feeling there's an incredible painting of this exact scene in our near future," he said.

"I'm taking a mental picture as we speak. This was totally worth getting up so early for, Jack." She turned to him and tilted her head back. He leaned down and kissed her. "You always bring me to the best places," she said, smiling.

They were about fifteen minutes from the Sky Stairs. When they arrived, Jack looked at Jojo. The stairs were incredibly narrow and they went up at an angle of seventy to eighty degrees.

"So, we're just going to take this nice and steady," he said. "And I'm here to assist if you need it."

"That's sweet of you. But I bet I'll be able to manage."

"I know you will." Jack glanced over his shoulder. "You good, Willie?" he asked.

Willie grinned and nodded, looked like he was having a fine time. They began to climb the Sky Stairs.

Halfway up, Jack paused to take in the view. His leg muscles burned with the pleasing pain of moderate exertion; the air was still crisp and he could see fog gathering below him.

What a sight, he thought.

No sooner had the thought crossed his mind when he caught a sudden movement from the corner of his eye. It looked like a metallic object, floating in the sky. Was it coming toward them? He couldn't tell from this distance. But it got larger and larger, which meant it was getting closer. It was a drone.

And it was coming toward them.

"Drone incoming!" Jack yelled. "Nine o'clock!"

Everyone froze except Jack, who sprinted ahead to Jojo and shielded her with his body.

"Get down!" Davis shouted. He unzipped the fanny pack and pulled a taser gun out. "Get as small as you can!"

But they couldn't move. The steps were too narrow and the wall too steep. They were a vulnerable, stationary target and there was no way they could flee without putting their lives at significant risk were they to misstep and fall.

Adrenaline poured through Jack. Jojo was safe for the moment, but he needed to get them out of here. Whoever was controlling the drone had pulled it back; for a moment it seemed as if it had vanished altogether.

"Where'd it go," he said softly. Davis navigated his way to them, positioning himself so he was now in front of both Jack and Jojo.

The drone reappeared, now at their eye level, headed straight toward them.

When the drone was about twenty feet away and still coming, Davis pulled the trigger on the taser gun. Immediately, he reloaded and fired another two probes into the drone.

Jack heard, rather than saw, the drone hit the ground. They stood there for a moment, no one saying anything. Two of the taser wires had become intertwined with the drone's semi-vertical propellers.

Davis pulled his radio from the fanny pack. "One drone down," he said, "confirmed targeting Gold and Wang. Search area for more and its controller."

Jack and Jojo remained right where they were until Davis got the all clear.

"Okay," he said. "Everything looks okay. Let's head back down."

Jojo said nothing as Jack helped her up and they began their careful descent back down the Sky Stairs.

At the bottom of the stairs, Davis inspected the drone. "It's consumer, not military," he said, holding it carefully. "But the sides and rotary blades have been sharpened, see? It could have caused some significant—but not deadly—damage."

Jack frowned as he looked at the sharpened blades. "China requires that all drones be registered. So it shouldn't be difficult to figure out who this belongs to and then hunt them down as soon as possible."

Davis took his radio back out and relayed the drone's serial number.

Jack looked at Jojo. "You okay?" he asked.

"That's certainly not anything I thought would happen this morning," she said. "You guys sure know how to show a girl a good time. I thought you were trying to take advantage of me back there, when you got on top of me like that."

Jack winked. "Shàng chuáng ma?" He was relieved that Jojo wasn't upset, and that no one had been injured. He looked at Davis. "Thanks for jumping in front of us like that."

"That's my job," Davis said. "Fortunately, it was just a little toy. I hope we can find its owner; I'd like to give it back."

By the time they made it back to the parking lot, Jack felt physically and mentally drained. What had started off with so much tranquility and enjoyment had been completely upended. No one was hurt, but his anger that it had happened in the first place did not want to be quelled.

They got back into the SUV while Davis spoke with Willie. "After that near life and death experience, I think I'm ready for a sandwich," Jojo said.

The driver's side door opened and Davis got in. "We're going to sit tight for a few minutes," he said. "There's going to be a twenty-five-mile roadblock and everyone will be searched for drones and their IDs checked against drone purchases. If we don't get a hit soon, then they'll close the circle to search inside the perimeter for the operator. The military is on their way to lead the effort. All incoming traffic, except for residents, will be diverted for the time being."

"That's good," Jack said. He reached into his backpack. "While we wait, can I interest you in a sandwich?"

"I won't say no to that," Davis said. Jack passed him a foil-wrapped baguette.

"Pastrami with cheese and onions," he said. He handed an identical sandwich to Jojo, and then began unwrapping one for himself.

The food provided a necessary distraction, and when they were done eating, it was okay to go.

They drove back in the same procession they'd arrived: Jack and Jojo's SUV sandwiched between the American security in the front, the Chinese security in the back. Yet even with this measure of security, something had almost happened. The drone attack had been planned before they arrived; there was no way anyone would know that unless their home had been bugged.

Jack had goosebumps on his arms and an unsettled feeling in his stomach. It seemed unthinkable yet at the same time, it was entirely possible that their place had indeed been bugged. There was no other way anyone would know their whereabouts this morning.

He leaned forward and shared these thoughts with Davis, who nodded and then picked up his phone. Jack wasn't sure who he was speaking to, but he could hear the person reply when Davis told them their house would need to be swept.

"We'll coordinate with China," the voice said.

"No," Jack said, in a low voice. Davis nodded.

"Let's take care of this ourselves, please. We don't know what's going on or who might be involved."

The person must have agreed, because Davis hung up the phone a moment later, right after saying, "Thank you."

"Someone bugged our house?" Jojo asked.

"It would seem that way."

She shuddered. "I hate to even think that. That someone was listening to us and we didn't even know it."

"I know," Jack said. "And I'm sorry if it's true. But I can't think of another way that someone would know exactly where we were going to be, and when, if our house wasn't bugged. I guess the silver lining is that now we know and we'll take all the necessary precautions to ensure this doesn't happen again."

Jojo pressed her lips into a thin line, her brow furrowed. She did not look pleased and Jack didn't blame her.

"My dad said that everything would be fine if you worked on this project," she said. "But we just tried to take an early morning walk and were attacked by a drone."

"I know. I'm surprised too."

Jojo didn't say anything else, and Jack didn't want to press her right now. She was upset, and that understandable.

They drove in silence for a while, the quiet broken when Davis's phone rang. He took the call, which was brief, and then hung up.

"There was a bug in your house," he said, looking first at Jack, then Jojo, in the rearview mirror. "It was high-tech and from China."

Jack sensed Jojo's tension rachet up a few notches. He turned to her. "Please send your dad a message that we need to see him urgently. I'm thinking maybe we should just drive there directly from here."

Jojo took her phone out and sent the message, which Wang replied to almost immediately. "He said to drive to Zhongnanhai," she said. "He'll be waiting for us."

* * *

At Zhongnanhai, Jojo led the way to the entrance, where Wang was waiting to receive them. After she gave her dad a hug, she turned and gestured to Davis. "Dad, I'd like you to meet Davis. He just saved our lives, he put himself right between us and a drone with sharpened propellors. He literally stood in front of us."

"Davis." Wang had a look of solemn gratitude on his face as he shook Davis's hand. "I cannot thank you enough. Let's go inside so I can hear everything that happened."

They followed Wang down two hallways into a relaxing private room with good lighting and comfortable sofas. Jack hadn't even sat down yet when Wang asked them to explain what happened.

Both Jack and Jojo translated Davis's English for Wang, whose expression became more and more stricken with each detail. By the time Davis was finished, Wang was slumped back in the sofa, his gaze on the ceiling.

He let out a long sigh and reached into his jacket side pocket and took out his cigarettes. He extracted one and then wordlessly handed the pack to Jack.

"Dad," Jojo said, and her voice sounded small. "How could our house be bugged? You told me when you called me about getting Jack involved with this project that there would be nothing to worry about. That we would be safe. We had your *protection*, that was how you put it." Her tone was not so much accusatory as it was let down. Which, Jack thought, was actually worse. The expression on Wang's face made it clear he felt the same way, too.

"Xiǎo Chūn Juǎn'er," Wang said, and despite everything that had happened this morning, Jack felt a surge of delight at hearing the nickname Wang had just called his daughter: *Little Spring Roll.* He'd never heard the moniker before.

Wang leaned over and picked up the phone on the side table next to him. "Get Lieutenant General Wang Shaojun for me please. Yes, I'll hold." Wang looked at Davis. "Is the bug still in the house?"

Jack translated for Davis. "Yes," Davis said. "The bug is there, downstairs."

Wang might not have understood the rest of what Davis said, but he certainly understood the *yes.* "Have the Central Security Bureau take over the security detail and find out what happened immediately," he said. "I'll keep Jojo and Jack here for the next hour or so. That should give you enough time to go through the house and review the observation video tapes."

Jack felt reassured just hearing Wang's end of the conversation. The Central Security Bureau was professional and knew what it was doing. Liang was not only head of the security regiment at Zhongnanhai, he was also a member of the Central Security Bureau and Jack knew how much trust Wang had in him.

Wang hung up and looked at Jojo, and then Jack. "General Wang Shaojun is the head of the Central Security Bureau, which is responsible for the security of senior Chinese government and party leaders. I know I'm probably telling you things you already know, but I do so to reassure you that you *do* have my protection and we are going to do everything we can to ensure the two of you are safe. General Wang Shaojun will get to the bottom of this, rest assured."

"Thank you, Dad," Jojo said. Jack realized that Wang had said *the two of you*—he didn't yet know that Jojo was pregnant. Jack glanced at her, but he knew now was not the time to break the good news.

*   *   *

They arrived back at their home later that day to find three military security guards posted out front. They held submachine guns and each man had a handgun strapped to his chest.

Davis grinned at the sight of it. "Now we're talkin'," he said as the gate to the hotel opened.

"Will you stop for one second?" Jack asked. He put the window down as one of the officers came around his side. Jack recognized him immediately.

"Liang," he said. "Good to see you again. I'm relieved you're here, it makes me feel better already. And, Liang, I'd like you to meet Jojo Wang, and the man driving, who was the hero today, Davis."

"Jack, it's a terrible thing that happened, but we're glad you're okay," Liang said. He looked past Jack into the car at Jojo. "It's so nice to meet President's Wang's daughter, finally," he said.

Jojo smiled. "We might only just be meeting now, but, like Jack, I feel better knowing you're around!" She looked at Jack. "He's said good things about you."

"We will do whatever is necessary to ensure the leaders of this country are safe," Liang said. "Please know we take this very seriously." He stepped to his left, so he was at Davis's window. The two men shook hands, their mutual respect for each other clearly on display.

Liang stepped back so he was in front of Jack's window. "Everything looks fine inside. We've taken out the listening device. You should feel safe at home now."

"Thank you so much," Jojo said. "It really means a lot to us."

Liang gave her a reassuring smile. "It's what we're here for," he said. "I hope you enjoy the rest of your day."

They waved goodbye and Davis drove through the gate, into the compound. Jack craned his neck to look at the three men standing watch outside. It had been a close call today but now they had armed security right out front; not only that, but Jack knew one of the guards, and knew that Liang was someone Wang held in high regard.

"Back home, safe and sound," Davis said. "With a few minor detours along the way."

Jack opened the door to get out. "It was quite the day," he said. "We'll have to do it again soon."

CHAPTER 7

The following Wednesday, Davis dropped Jack off at the Great Hall of the People. "I'll meet you right here when the meeting's over," he told Jack.

"Thanks," Jack said. He took a deep breath. "Why, I almost feel like you're dropping me off at my first day of school. I'll see you after, Davis."

As Jack walked toward the massive building's entrance, he tried to clear any residual thoughts about the drone incident from his mind. He needed to focus today and be on top of his game. Supposedly the drone operator had been captured, but Jack hadn't been given any further details, such as any additional leads or who was ultimately behind the attack.

Jack turned his focus to the Great Hall, an enormous space capable of holding ten thousand guests. Usually, it was used for legislative and ceremonial activities by the People's Republic of China. Today, Jack suspected they'd use one of the smaller auxiliary halls.

He realized as he began walking up the stairs that nearly everyone was looking at him. He was used to being the only non-Chinese person in any given situation and the looks didn't bother him. A man about his age fell in step next to him.

"Hello, Jack," he said. "My name is Zhang Li."

"Hi there," Jack said. He knew Zhang Li; he was one of the newer Standing Committee members recently appointed by Wang.

"We're excited to hear what is going to be presented today. And I wanted to personally thank you for what you did at the Control Center. It's quite remarkable. There are many of us who are committed to seeing through the work that you started."

"I appreciate it," Jack said.

At the entrance, he presented his pass that had been sent over by Wang's office and then he was directed to the room for the event. He checked his pass for the seat number, which was in the first row. They were in one of the smaller conference halls within the Great Hall; the room was still opulent though it was meant to hold a smaller crowd, maybe about a thousand. Jack estimated there were maybe one hundred people there, taking up the front rows. They were nearly all men, and all dressed in similar dark suits. As he made his way down, he scanned the room, taking in its grandeur—the white walls with gold accents, the vaulted ceiling and the enormous domed light that reminded Jack of a lotus blossom.

There were two manned CCTV cameras on either side of the room; was this going to be broadcast? Jack hadn't considered that. He found his seat and sat down, looked to the stage where Wang and the other Standing Committee members were seated at a red table, in quiet discussion with each other. Behind them were ten Chinese flags, a hammer and sickle in the middle. Everything felt very regal, grand. A hush fell over the room as Wang leaned forward and pressed the button on his microphone.

"Ladies and gentlemen," he said, "welcome to this Provincial and Municipality Strategy Planning Session. The previous five-year plan emphasized a number of important issues, on which great progress has been made. These include bridging the welfare gaps between country-side and cities by distributing and managing resources more efficiently. Urbanization will continue to centralize essentials services, such as education and healthcare. China also sought to open up with deeper participation in supranational power structures, and more international cooperation."

Jack listened attentively to everything Wang said. Unlike other Chinese leaders, Wang spoke without notes or reading from a prepared speech. "As China moves to develop its next five-year plan" Wang continued, "these and other core values will not change." He paused to let the words sink in. "But there is something that will change. Historically, plans have come top-down. We are going to try a different approach. Your more active participation is now required to carry this nation to its next level of development and further enhance the lives of all Chinese citizens." Wang looked to the other Standing Committee members, who all nodded their agreement. "In short, you will need to do create the plan for your province and municipality and present it to us. You will be limited to a fifteen-minute presentation—which you cannot read from. You'll be given the specifics of what each presentation must cover, and we'll allocate resources to those with the best plans. Performance will be tracked closely thereafter. We hope you can be creative in figuring out the best ways to be more successful, so as to better contribute to the country."

There was some murmuring from the people around him, though Jack didn't think Wang could have phrased it any more clearly. Wang looked at him and caught his eye and Jack gave him a quick nod of approval.

"We understand that this will be new for you," Wang said. "It is new for us, too. So, the Standing Committee has engaged Jack Gold to visit each province and meet with you. He will provide instruction and guidance as needed. Jack, why don't you come up here." Wang gestured for him to join them on stage.

For a moment, Jack didn't move. He had not expected to speak today, especially in such a formal setting with all the provincial leaders of the country. But Wang, and now it seemed, everyone else in the room as well, was looking right at him. Jack stood.

"Come on up here, Jack," Wang said. "I believe everyone knows Jack Gold."

Jack made his way from his seat to the stairs leading up to the stage. Someone brought a standing microphone that had been tucked away at the back of the stage to the front. Wang stood in front of it and motioned Jack over.

"Jack," Wang said, speaking into the microphone. "Did I leave anything out? Is there anything you'd like to add?"

Jack looked at the microphone but hesitated. He had not planned on addressing everyone, and though Wang was clearly giving him the invitation to, Jack felt it would be more effective for the room to hear only from Wang right now. He took a step closer to him and spoke quietly into his ear.

Wang listened intently, nodding, a smile coming to his face after Jack stopped speaking. "That's a great suggestion," he said to Jack, before turning to speak into the microphone. "What Jack has just suggested: If a governor disagrees with the plans of a province secretary, he or she *must* present their plans to us also." Wang shot a look at Jack. "I like that you used the word *must*."

Jack stood there and said nothing; he hadn't at all used the word "must" but had instead said "should." Clearly, Wang thought the stronger word should be used.

After Jack returned to his seat, Wang continued speaking for another half an hour before the meeting concluded. When it was over, those closest to Jack swarmed him, eager to introduce themselves and their province; they were already trying to seek his favor. This was not surprising; he had just received the endorsement of China's president and the all-powerful Standing Committee.

* * *

"How was your first day at school?" Davis asked when Jack met him outside.

"It was okay," Jack said. He climbed into the SUV. "I was there for show and tell."

Davis smiled. "Now that sounds like a great first day."

They drove back, passing by Tiananmen Square, where the student protests occurred in 1989. But long before the students protests, the British and French, during the second opium war in the 1860s, pitched their camp in Tiananmen Square, right near the gate. It was almost burned down along with the Forbidden City.

Back at home, Jojo was drawing on her iPad with her Apple Pencil. She looked up as Jack walked over.

"How'd it go?" she asked.

"As expected. I was the only foreigner. Everyone was looking at me like I was an alien. But your dad was up on stage with the other Standing Committee members, and guess what? He called me up there too and mentioned I'd be helping with the project. Now I'm everyone's best friend."

Jojo laughed and rolled her eyes. "Funny how that works, isn't it? Some of those provincial secretaries and governors are very wealthy and influential."

"I can tell."

"Did my dad say anything to you about the drone attack?"

"No. But we didn't really have time to speak privately."

"Well, he called me a few minutes ago, so maybe he just wants to tell us at the same time. They learned some more information, so he's going to stop by in a little bit and tell us what he knows."

Jack looked pointedly at Jojo's stomach. "Should we tell him?"

She frowned. "I think it's still too early. I'm not even showing. I know we told your dad already but . . . I think we should wait a little longer. I'd like to."

"Then we will." Jack peered over at the iPad. "What's that you're working on?"

"Oh, nothing much. Just some flowers." She turned the tablet toward him so he could see. It was a bunch of daisies and pansies, the colors bright and vivid.

"They're beautiful," Jack said.

"Oh, I got a present for you."

"You did?"

"I stopped by the Apple store and got this pencil, but I also picked up the newest iPad Pro for you. I figured you could put it to good use while you're working on this project. Plus, it came with a pretty cool keyboard."

"Wow, babe, thanks," Jack said, genuinely pleased with this unexpected gift. She was right; it would be perfect for this new project.

She had left the iPad on the table, so Jack went and retrieved it, feeling like a kid on Christmas. Even though he had more money than he ever thought he would, he did not spend freely and buying things for himself and Jojo was not something he often did. More so than the cost of the iPad, though, was the thought that Jojo had put into getting it for him.

It only took a few minutes for him to get the new iPad up and running; once he connected to his iCloud account all his documents were immediately accessible, thanks to the fact that their home was equipped with ultra-high-speed internet. The average internet speed in China was less than 5 Mbps. In America, it was well above 50 Mbps. This, in Jack's mind, said a lot about the relative development stages of the two countries.

When Wang knocked on the door, Jack and Jojo were sitting side by side on the couch, working on their iPads. They both got up and followed Mini to the door. The dog sat, wagging his tail, as if he knew who was on the other side. Wang came in, said hello, patted Mini. He took his shoes off and then turned to face the dog.

"Sit," he said, and Mini immediately sat, tail still thumping. Wang took a dog biscuit from his pocket and gave it to the dog. "Good boy."

"So, how do you think it went earlier?" Wang asked as they walked over to the sofa.

"I have to admit," Jack said, "it was impressive. More importantly, I thought what *you* said was perfect for setting the stage for my upcoming meetings."

"Provincial secretaries and governors always resist change," Wang said, crossing one leg over the other. "And they will resist you, at least until they discover it's futile. Then, they'll acquiesce. Think of it like a surly child who doesn't want to take a nap. They'll resist mightily until they realize there is no other choice."

Jojo came over from the kitchen with some tea, which she placed on the table between the two sofas. Jack watched as she elegantly poured the tea, first for her father, then for Jack. Because he was her father, Wang got his tea first.

He picked up his cup as Jojo was pouring some for Jack, and he first inhaled it deeply and then took a sip. He set the cup back down on the table and waited until Jojo had sat down next to Jack to speak.

"I wanted to update both of you on what happened regarding the drone. We caught the person who was controlling the drone, as well as the person who placed the listening device here. The intent was indeed to seriously injure you. The blades on the drone were laced with a chemical called tetrodotoxin."

"What is that?" Jack asked.

"It's the venom from a puffer fish. A small dose would shut down your nervous system and paralyze your muscles. If you had actually been cut, it would have been absorbed directly into your bloodstream and you would have most likely died."

"Oh my gosh," Jojo said, her mouth open. "Dad, that thing got *really* close to us!"

Jack's insides twisted. He didn't want to replay the events from that morning, but the truth was, the drone had almost succeeded in its attack.

"How many people knew about my involvement on this project?" Jack asked. "Prior to today, I mean."

"From our interrogations, we found out that the purpose was to seriously injure or impair you, to keep you from working with the provinces," Wang said. "The provincial secretaries and governments knew of your upcoming involvement from an announcement we previously sent out to them. Unfortunately, it doesn't seem likely that we'll be able to find out who shared the information."

"Can you find out where the venom's from?" Jack asked. "Is it trace-able that way?"

Wang shook his head. "There are people looking into it, but I wouldn't hold out much hope for that, as puffer fish venom is fairly common and easy to get. I'm very sorry to both of you. We simply did not see this type of attack coming, but rest assured, this sort of thing will not happen again. You will both have security, just like mine, until this thing is over. Of course there was going to be resistance to further opening China. Certain wealthy people do not want competition. Moreover, some just do not want any change at all. These are the same people who are fiercely opposed to recognizing and formalizing an independent Taiwan. They are trying to influence people and the press. You two got in the middle of all of this, I'm afraid."

"What you say makes sense," Jack said. "Are you getting any closer to diminishing their impact?"

"Yes, we are," Wang said. "Actually, we're using computers and getting better at it all the time."

"You're using AI to predict what they'll do?"

"Huh?" Jojo said. She looked at Jack. "What are you talking about?"

Wang frowned. "Nothing you need to know about," he said. "And nothing Jack needs to talk about."

Jack raised his eyebrows. Of course China would have evolved at least some level of expertise in the area of artificial intelligence. As for Taiwan, he knew that some were pushing China's claim to Taiwan and restricting its membership to all international organizations.

"I'm confident you two are out of danger now," Wang said, in a softer tone. "They'll likely disrupt things through other avenues, and I assure you we are getting closer to a plan to deal with them once and for all. I don't want you to be surprised if some unusual events happen in the future. But that's all I can say."

Jojo got up to pour some more tea. She said nothing but Jack could see the tension around her mouth, her eyes. She refilled her father's cup, then Jack's. She did not pour any for herself, but sat back down and looked at her father. For a moment, she said nothing, though it seemed that she was about to, or wanted to, and Jack wondered if she was going to pull the plug on all of it, tell Wang that they were expecting a child, that he couldn't expect Jack to continue work on something that would jeopardize their lives. But how could he back out now? If he did that, the likelihood of any of this succeeding was almost nullified. Certainly another person besides Jack could travel to each province and work with the secretaries and governors to implement a bottom-up approach; but if he stepped down now, after Wang had just introduced him as the man to lead the project . . . It would never stand a chance of being taken seriously.

Jojo brushed a few loose strands of hair back from her face and cleared her throat. Jack consciously made the effort to relax his shoulders and stop jamming his tongue against the roof of his mouth. "I'm going to join Jack in Dali tomorrow, for a few days," she said. "He can go straight to his meeting in Kunming. Afterward, I'm off to Suzhou for a while to see some friends and family. Actually . . . could Mini stay with you? I'm sure he'd enjoy Dali but I'm not going to bring him to Suzhou and I don't know what Jack's schedule is going to be like when he's there."

"It'll probably be fine," Jack said, relieved to hear that Jojo was going to join him.

"I'd be happy to take this guy with me," Wang said. "And you'll have a wonderful time in Suzhou. I should really get over to visit soon, too." Wang looked at his watch and then stood. "I've got to get going, but why don't I take Mini with me now, since I'm here. And please, believe me when I say you two are safe now. I don't want you to worry."

"I'll try not to, Dad," Jojo said.

After Wang had left, with Mini and a bag of his food and toys, Jojo went up to the office, without saying anything. Jack went back to the couch and took his black phone out of his pocket. He typed a quick message to Cooper: *Did you hear that?* Jack did not know the specifics of everything his black phone was capable of, but he knew that it was likely Cooper was able to listen in from his post back in Washington DC.

Cooper's response was almost instantaneous. *Yes,* his reply read. *We did. But there is nothing else I can say right now.*

Jack frowned but slipped his phone back in his pocket without responding. Even though it annoyed him that information was clearly being withheld but he also understood that there might be a reason for it. No, that there *was* a reason for it; Jack had full faith in Wang that he would not keep him in the dark about important matters, especially as it related to the success of this new project. And their own personal safety.

He went to the kitchen and got two beers. No point in remaining on the sofa fixating on what he didn't know. He headed upstairs. Jojo sat at her desk, which faced one of the room's two windows; Jack's desk faced the other.

"I brought you a beer," he said.

She swiveled in her chair, an unhappy expression still on her face. "Thanks," she said, holding her hand out for it.

"Everything okay?" he asked, taking a seat in his own chair.

Jojo took a sip and then held the bottle on her lap. "Is everything okay? I wouldn't necessarily say so, would you? I mean, I know we escaped Jiankou unscathed, but that whole situation could have ended quite differently. Jack, do you really think this is the right thing to do? You haven't even visited any of the provinces yet, things aren't even really underway and people are already trying to take you out. I just . . . I didn't think it was going to be like this."

"I hear you," Jack said. "I do. And you know I would do anything to keep you safe."

Jojo raised an eyebrow. "Anything? Like stop working on this project?"

Jack took a deep breath, knowing that he needed to walk a fine line. He didn't want Jojo to feel as if he were ignoring her very legitimate concerns. But he wasn't ready to give up yet.

"Listen," he said. "I know what just happened with the drone was scary. It scared me. But we were lucky to have the security that we did, and now they've tracked down the people involved."

"*Some* of the people."

"Yes, some of the people. But you know what I think? I think they played their hand too early, and did so in a pretty amateurish way. Your father has given us the same level of security that he has. We will be more protected now than we've ever been, and because of that, I feel okay about moving forward. They *want* us to go away, Jojo. They don't want to see this bottom-up approach succeed, because it spells the end for the influence the wealthy wield. And then nothing would change." He shook his head. "Nothing would change."

"I know you're doing this because it would help others. But you don't have the assurance that your participation will result in lasting change. What if you do everything you can and it still doesn't work? What if something else happens? What if one of us gets injured?"

Jack took a sip of his beer and tried not to feel as if he had put himself in an impossible situation. How was someone supposed to make a choice when there were clear reasons on each side for either continuing or stopping?

"You know I don't want that to happen. And I believe your father, and I believe that we'll be safe with the heightened security. We're leaving for Dali tomorrow, and I know you've been looking forward to that. I have, too. And after, you'll get to go see some of your family and friends you haven't seen in a while, and I think that'll be good."

A smile flickered across her face at the mention of friends and family. "Okay," she finally said. "I *have* been looking forward to that."

"And you still should. I'm looking forward to going there with you."

Jojo said nothing for a moment but then lifted her beer, tilted it slightly toward him. "To Dali, then," she said. Jack raised his own beer.

"To Dali," he said.

CHAPTER 8

Despite Jack's earlier assurances to Jojo, late that night he found himself unable to sleep, troubled by something Wang had said.

It had nothing to do with the puffer fish venom or whoever was behind operating the drone; it was Wang's vague comment about AI. And the fact that he didn't want divulge anything further about it.

Next to him, Jojo slumbered peacefully, her breathing slow and even. Jack did not want to wake her up with his tossing and turning, and he couldn't bear the thought of lying here awake all night while his thoughts ricocheted around. He quietly slipped out of bed and went into the office, closing the door behind him.

He got his new iPad and opened FaceTime. There was only one person he could think of who might be able to shed some light on what was going on, and that was Jeff Hern, a classmate of Jack's at Berkeley, and now a professor at Stanford, specializing in Artificial Intelligence.

Only after Jeff's face appeared on the screen did Jack realize he'd gotten out of bed without putting clothes on. He adjusted the iPad so the camera angle only showed his face.

"Jack," Jeff said. "To what do I owe this pleasure? Wonderful to see you. But it's two in the morning in Beijing; shouldn't you be sleeping?"

"Good to see you, too, Jeff," Jack said. "How's Stanford treating you?"

"Can't complain. Just got a second big grant for my new company that deals with Big Data. Never mind me, though, I've been tracking you all over the news this past year. How's China and the exotic life?"

Jack suppressed a smile. "I wouldn't call it the exotic life. I'd love to be in Palo Alto, actually. But I'm married and currently working on a project for the Chinese government."

"Ah," Jeff said. "So. What's on your mind?"

"AI is on my mind," Jack said. "Hence the call. I couldn't think of anyone better to help with a question about the subject. What can you tell me to get me up to speed?"

Jeff cupped his chin, frowned. "Well . . . it's not as simple as that. Why don't you start with telling me what's piqued your interest?"

"Sure," Jack said. He let out a breath. "It's piqued my interest because I think it will soon impact China, and, likely, my family."

"So, real AI has the ability to predict future events, outcomes, and even actions of individuals. It's ultimately about outcomes. Do you remember back at Berkeley when I told you the coming of AI was limited by processing speed and memory?"

"Uh . . ." Jack laughed. "No, I don't recall that. Though in my defense that was over fifteen years ago."

"Well, those barriers no longer exist. So much of our lives are now digital, which means there is more to easily integrate into a computational matrix that leads to very accurate prediction outcomes."

"How might that be used by a government?"

"Well, they would use AI to understand the social environment and then seek or input scenarios that maximize the chances of success for a particular outcome."

This made sense, though Jack knew Jeff was certainly dumbing everything down for him. "Do you think the US is using AI in that way?"

"Absolutely," Jeff said without hesitation. "You can see Sutton saying something one day that seems crazy, but then, days, weeks, or months later, when other events occur, it seems insightful and in fact it helped out. The key is that when trying to maximize the chances of success, there are specific things you should and should not do and say. Then, the chances of the outcome occurring as you'd like are much greater."

"But what's the danger of it?" Jack asked, sensing that Jeff wasn't telling him everything.

"With the advent of digital devices and the use of applications like texting, search engines, Facebook, Instagram, what Joe Rogan's guest is saying on the podcast—it's very easy for a computer to run algorithms to understand the emotions of individuals. The computer knows what will make them happy and how to do it. You can give a computer an outcome and the computer will tell you how to get there."

Jack raised his eyebrows. "Shit."

"Kind of puts a damper on the whole notion of 'freedom of choice.' Just think for a moment about the applications of such a capability. It could be used for business or for war. Elon Musk is right when he said AI is an existential threat to humanity and it should be regulated. Computer self-learning is truly scary and that's an essential component to real artificial *human* intelligence. Consciousness is an outcome and requirement of true AI. The ramifications of that alone should be deeply contemplated."

Jack knew the operative word in that last sentence was *should*. Yes, it *should*, but had governments who were utilizing this technology actually doing that?

He rubbed a hand across his eyes, finally feeling the fatigue of the sleepless night catching up to him. "I appreciate the quick tutorial, Jeff," he said. "Thank you."

"Have I put you to sleep? One last thing, though, Jack. The word AI is being thrown around out there. But the vast majority don't know what true AI is—and what it is not. Having motion sensors adjust traffic lights is not AI. Amazon's Alexa and Apple's Siri are not even close to human intelligence. Anyway, I'll send you a few papers that will provide more insight. That should help you get up the learning curve."

Jack thanked his old friend again before they said goodbye. After his iPad screen went dark, he sat in the office for several moments, his mind racing.

What does Wang want? What does China need?

Faster economic growth was one thing, for sure. Also, Wang wanted to settle the Taiwan issue and free them, in the face of harsh opposition from influential critics. And Wang would want a new constitution, instituting elections and freedoms.

Jack thought back to the meeting with Wang and the Standing Committee. The impression he'd gotten then was that they all had great confidence, and it was because they'd gotten Jack to play his role.

He got up and went back to the bedroom and into bed. He thought about Ai Weiwei, the artist and human rights advocate who once said: "One little fire can cause a huge fire and that can happen anytime."

Jack stared at the ceiling, trying to make sense of everything that had happened recently, everything he'd been a part of and all the information he learned. Regardless of AI's role in this, he was going to take part in another significant change in China, a change that would hopefully last, that would benefit the lives of a billion people. Knowing what to expect was one thing, but Jack was determined to enjoy the journey as well.

CHAPTER 9

The next afternoon they took a three-and-a-half-hour flight to Dali. Davis accompanied them on the flight and then drove them to the two-story house where they'd be staying, about thirty-five miles away.

Erhai Lake dominated the view, with high mountains on all sides. Small farms dotted the area, creating a peaceful and bucolic environment. They were about sixty-five hundred feet above sea level, which meant there was no air pollution. As Jack gazed up, it seemed that he was close enough to pluck a cloud straight from the azure sky.

Their new home was refurbished but traditional, with an open, modern kitchen and a large living/dining area with many windows and an unobstructed view of the city, the farms, the lake, and beyond that, the mountains. Upstairs was their bedroom, a room with clean lines and elegantly appointed furniture. Their bedroom had an equally grand view, as did the adjoining bathroom.

"That bed looks comfortable," Jack said. He glanced at Jojo, who had gone over to the window to take in the view. "Shàngchuáng ma?"

She came over and took his hand. "Why yes I would."

* * *

Later that day, Davis drove them to Erhai Lake, which, though they could see it from their new home, was too far to walk to. The streets were lined with restaurants and shops and crowds of Chinese tourists bustled around them, though Jack noticed he was the only white person. As they approached the lake, they turned right onto a new concrete path that traveled parallel to the lake. On one side was the lake, on the other were traditional homes, nearly all of which looked the same, in varying sizes, with the same tile roofs and white walls and larger than normal windows.

They held hands as they walked, breathing in the clear fresh air and enjoying the tranquility of the area. Jack looked at the expanse of water; it looked clear and inviting though no one was swimming in the lake and he couldn't see any boats. A little further along, they came to a pier where three teenagers were hanging out. They looked at Jack and Jojo as they approached.

"Hi," Jack said, addressing them in Mandarin. "Do you go swimming in the lake?"

"No," one of them said, and all three shook their heads in unison.

"Why not?"

"It's dangerous."

The waves were little more than ripples, gently lapping at the shore. "Why is it dangerous?" Jack asked.

The three kids looked at each other. For a moment, no one said anything. "It's because of the weeds," one of them finally offered.

Jack thanked them and he and Jojo continued on their way. It wasn't because of the weeds, he knew; it was because they didn't know how to swim.

After they walked the lake for a little while, they began to head back by way of a road a little further inland. Their security roamed both in front of and behind them, which reassured Jack and allowed him to feel like he could really just relax right now and enjoy this time with Jojo.

They passed by new homes still under construction but also ancient walls that were crumbling and had yet to be restored. There were a handful of small farms with plots full of various vegetables. Scooters zipped by them periodically.

They came to a wall emblazoned with four large Chinese characters written on it. Jack studied the characters for a moment but had no clue what they said. He looked to Jojo.

"Those four characters represent and explain the name of the family. This was evidently common for this area, but not so much now," she said.

"I wonder why," Jack said.

"It's something unique to the Bai people of this area. So those characters represent not just the family name, but also their heritage and family tradition."

"I see," Jack said. He was not familiar with the Bai people, but he knew they were one of the fifty-five ethnic minorities that were officially recognized by the government. "So much of this architecture feels like art as well. It really does seem like it tells a story."

Jojo smiled a little bashfully. "I might have done a little reading up on this place earlier. So I also know that we need to go to Old Town Dali for dinner. And, when we get the chance, there's a hidden hiking trail near the university."

"I like the sound of that," Jack said, thinking all the way back to the first date and Jojo went on, a picnic at a university park. So much had happened since that day, and despite some of it being very challenging and even dangerous, he was relieved and grateful that he had Jojo with him through all of this, by his side.

*   *   *

They had dinner in Dali's Old Town, seated outside on low chairs around a circular hotplate that looked like it was made of yellow marble. For dinner, they ordered lamb, pork, mushrooms, and spinach, all thinly-sliced and served with a plate of romaine lettuce leaves. Diners helped themselves to whatever sauces they wanted at the sauce bar, and Jack loaded up on the garlic and chili. The meat was dipped into the sauce and then wrapped in lettuce leaves and eaten taco-style. Jack savored the first bite, which was a savory and spicy explosion of flavors.

"My god, that's good," he said, sighing as he chewed. He looked around at the other tables around them; most were full of other people who appeared to be enjoying their meals as much as Jack was enjoying his.

"I love eating outside," Jojo said as she assembled another lettuce leaf for herself.

Jack flagged down a waiter and ordered some Dali Beer. He poured a glass for Jojo, then himself, and they toasted, but Jojo paused, lowering her drink.

"Do you really think it's okay if I drink beer while I'm pregnant?"

When Jojo first told him she was pregnant, Jack had gone out and got himself a copy of What to Expect When You're Expecting, and though he hadn't read every chapter, he'd thumbed through most of it. "So in that pregnancy book I was reading," he said, "it says you can do pretty much anything in moderation. Except eat raw fish, apparently, but try telling that to pregnant Japanese women."

He picked up the bottle of beer and tried to read the label. "The alcohol content is only 2.4 percent, which is very low."

Jojo grinned. "That's what I wanted to hear," she said. She took a sip. "Ah, now that's good."

After their meal, they continued their walk, this time turning onto People's Street, an ancient road that was now bustling with tourists, locals, street vendors, and shops. And he still hadn't seen another white person; it almost seemed that Dali was a hidden place white people couldn't find, despite the fact that the infamous Shangri-La was only a few hours' drive away.

Jojo reached out and took Jack's hand. "I love it here," she said. "This really is a traveler's city." She nodded to one of the old-looking shops as they walked past. "All of this here has been developed to cater to the travelers, even though it looks old and traditional. All the buildings are new, but they made them look like they've been around forever."

"This is like having my own personal tour guide," Jack said.

"That was just one other thing I remember from my reading."

Jack inhaled deeply. The clean, clear air was not something most were used to in China. He would love to live, at least part of the year anyway, in such a beautiful, tranquil place. He was pleased that Jojo seemed to be enjoying herself as much as he was. "I'm looking forward to our hike tomorrow," he said.

"I am too. As long as we don't have to worry about drones."

"Well, since we've got your father's level of security now, I would say that's something we have little to concern ourselves over."

"I can only imagine how beautiful it's going to be. Everything we've seen here so far is just so gorgeous." Jack could tell being in a place of such resplendent beauty really inspired Jojo's artistic eye. It was probably very inspirational for an artist or creative type to live in an area such as this.

"Also, tomorrow—what would you think if I invited my three assistants over for dinner tomorrow? David, Jason, and Susan. I'd like to meet with them briefly before the meeting and also, it would be nice to get to know them a little better."

"That's a great idea," Jojo said. "What should we have? I can pick up some things tomorrow."

"Or we could do takeout, you don't have to cook."

"No, I don't mind at all. The kitchen in this place looks great, so it should definitely get put to good use. With all the traveling you four are about to embark on, you shouldn't say no to a home-cooked meal, anyway. It's going to be takeout and hotel room service for you for the foreseeable future."

"Well, when you put it that way . . ." Jack took his phone out and sent a message to the group, inviting them to their place tomorrow, first for a brief meeting and then an informal dinner with Jojo. Their replies came in almost immediately, and Jack thought he could sense the enthusiasm in their typed words.

CHAPTER 10

The next morning, Jack and Jojo met Davis out front. Standing with him was a tall woman Jack didn't recognize. Davis introduced her as Rio, from Hangzhou. She was one of the new Chinese agents that would be working security with Davis. Like Davis, she wore a fanny pack and had her running shoes on.

"I heard what happened at Jiankou," she said. "Nothing like that is going to happen today."

Jack found her words reassuring, perhaps because she was tall and muscular and looked as if she could singlehandedly take on any danger that might come their way.

They headed toward Dali University, which was built into the side of a mountain. The front entrance was heavily guarded by security and certainly did not look very welcoming.

"Is the university closed to outsiders?" Jack asked. Had that been the case at Jiao Tong University, they would not have been able to have their first picnic date there.

"I'm not sure," Jojo said. "That's not something I came across in my reading. Maybe they don't want lots of tourists walking around."

They kept walking along a wall that surrounded the university. When they came to the end of the wall, Jojo pointed to a gravel path on their right, just as she had read about. They followed the path, again with the university's wall to their right, the sound of a rushing stream was audible to their left but any view of it was obscured by the overgrown brush.

Jack glanced over his shoulder and saw Davis and Rio a little ways behind them, attentive to their surroundings but also seeming to enjoy each other's company, as they chatted about something that Jack couldn't quite make out. It's almost like a double date, he thought as he focused his gaze in front of him again. Davis had never mentioned a wife or a girlfriend before.

The path narrowed and became steep as they approached a stone bridge. The bridge had different levels, so they went to one of the lower levels so they could get a better view of the river. They were the only people on the bridge.

"I think we've found another great place for a picnic," Jack said. He and Jojo stood side by side, looking down the flowing water.

Jojo smiled. "I remember our first picnic. That was so romantic. And you looked so handsome!" She gave his arm a squeeze. "You still are."

They stayed on the bridge admiring the view a little longer and then continued on. After about twenty minutes of walking, they came to a portion of the wall in which a red steel door had been installed. Jack glanced at Jojo.

"Let's give it a try," he said.

The door, to his surprise, was not locked, and it led into the university. At this location, Jack couldn't see any buildings, but instead his gaze took in the expansive lawns and the tops of trees as he looked down the mountain. They stayed on the main path, which Jack guessed would lead them to the main entrance at the bottom. Down a hill to his left, he could see rows and rows of small tea trees. The scenery was beautiful, but as they walked further into the university, Jack realized something: the place felt nearly empty. Where were the groups of students—walking to class, hanging out on the green, throwing a frisbee? Every bench he saw was unoccupied.

"Why is this place so empty?" Jack asked.

"It's lunchtime," Jojo said. "Everyone's probably in the mess hall."

Though Jack had lived in China for years, he still sometimes forgot that most Chinese people still ate lunch right at noon.

"Even still," he said. "We just walked up an amazing trail—empty. We found our way into this university—empty. It just seems like such a waste. These spaces should really be utilized, but they're not."

"I'm not sure why it's not open to the public," Jojo said. "Someone must be claiming this place as their own territory."

Jack shook his head. "Yeah, things seem a little . . . off."

Even if it was lunchtime, there was no good explanation as to why the place appeared so deserted, other than it wasn't being used to its full potential. When they arrived at the main entrance they had first passed when they started their walk, they exited, and the guards paid them no notice.

Their next stop was not planned, but as they went by a small shop called Simple Stone, Jack found the aroma so tantalizing that they went in to order. The woman behind the counter greeted them in perfect English. Jack ordered three lattes and a double espresso, plus four of the freshly-baked croissants, two chocolate and two plain. The woman told them she'd bring their drinks and food to their table when it was ready.

They sat outside; Jack and Davis on one side of the table, Rio and Jojo on the other. The sun was shining and the sky was a deep azure blue. Rio, from what Jack could overhear from her conversation with Jojo, also had an interest in art, though she had never formally studied it. Jack looked at Davis.

"Is this the life or what?"

Davis grinned. "My first foray outside of Beijing or Shanghai has been good so far. This is a nice place. And even nicer—to finally get a real cup of coffee."

As if on cue, their orders came out, the woman had the plate of croissants and, to Jack's surprise, a Caucasian man behind her was carrying the tray of coffees.

After everything had been set on the table, Jack introduced himself. "I'm Jack," he said. "Is this your place?"

"It is," the man said. "I'm Lachlan. We opened up about five months ago."

All the other outside tables were occupied, and as they spoke, another group of people went inside. "You've done really well," Jack said. "You've grown fast. Where are you from?"

"Australia. But the pastries are from France."

"Mmm, I can tell!" Jojo said in English, which she spoke with a French accent. "They're superb."

The croissants were indeed superb, and Jack savored his, along with his espresso. He chatted with Lachlan and found out a little more about his history. He was an avid climber who had visited China and ended up meeting his wife, who he decided to open a little café with.

"And it worked out better than either of us expected," Lachlan said. "We bake everything downstairs in a kitchen that's barely big enough for two, but we make it work."

"That's great," Jack said. He knew how much the Chinese liked it when a foreigner opened a business that allowed them to purchase something that was good and they might not otherwise get, such as the croissants they were indulging in now.

"Life has been good for us," Lachlan said. "I better get back to the kitchen; nice to meet you guys and thanks for stopping in."

Jack turned his attention back to the table, though he was pleased to have met Lachlan, to get this great cup of coffee and fabulous croissant. Lachlan and his wife had a successful business and a good life for themselves. It was something he thought that all Chinese citizens should be able to achieve.

CHAPTER 11

That afternoon, while Jojo was at the market, Jack got on his iPad and opened WeChat. He found the document his assistants had sent over on Yunnan Province and he started to review it. The province had two main cities, Kunming and Dali. He started with Dali and looked at the Description, then the SWOT analysis and the financials that showed five years of performance. He was intentionally looking at the cities as businesses. There wasn't enough information here to do a full evaluation, but after carefully reading through what he did have, he felt he had enough information to ask some penetrating questions and get them started on the right track.

Not that the province secretaries and governors would look at things the same way. Well, maybe some of them would be open, but Jack knew he was going to meet with significant resistance from many of these officials. They wanted to implement their part of the country's five-year-plan; if they succeeded in that, then there was no way they could get in trouble with Beijing and they'd keep their jobs. That's the course they would want to stay, and Jack was going to have to convince them to do things differently. If the other provinces were similar to the one he was looking at right now, then this upcoming change would be both bold and drastic.

* * *

When the doorbell rang, Jack answered it and found Susan, David, and Jason standing on the other side of the door. He greeted them and stepped back so they could come in.

"Please make yourself at home," he said, as they slipped their shoes off. "Jojo will be back downstairs in a minute, she's looking forward to having a meal all together. Can I get you guys something to drink? Beer? White wine? Soda? A glass of warm water?"

Susan eyed David and Jason before looking back at Jack. Jason and David looked to Susan. No one said anything.

"I'll be having a glass of white wine," Jack said. "Jojo probably will, too. We are going to chat briefly about our upcoming meeting, but I want everyone to relax and enjoy themselves tonight."

His three assistants nodded. "I'll have some warm water," Susan finally said. David and Jason exchanged another long look.

"We'll have a beer," they both said as they walked into the house.

"Great," Jack said. Susan, who was nearest to him, cleared her throat.

"Actually," she said, "I'll have a glass of wine."

Jack suppressed his smile as he went to the kitchen to get the drinks. He handed David and Jason each a bottle of Asahai beer, along with a glass. He poured three glasses of white wine and gave one to Susan.

"Come see the view," he said. "It's quite nice."

He motioned for them to follow him over to the window, where there was the view of the lake, accompanied by an expansive, darkening blue sky, the mountains in the distance.

"Wow," Susan said. She set her glass of wine down on the coffee table so she could take a few pictures with her phone. "This view is incredible."

"It's really something, isn't it?" Jack turned at the sound of Jojo's voice. "Nice to see the three of you again," she said. "I'm so glad you're able to join us for dinner tonight."

They took seats on the couch and sipped their drinks. "Where are you originally from, Susan?" Jojo asked.

"I'm from a city in Shandong called Jining. I come from a family of farmers. I went to Beijing University, and the rest is history." She smiled. "Oh! And I wanted to tell you . . . that story you had written, about how you and Jack met—it's one of the most romantic things I've ever heard." Jack again suppressed a smile, though Jojo did not, as she reached over and took his hand.

"Oh yes," she said. "We certainly took a long path to get here. Though it was worth it. And now we all find ourselves here."

Like Susan, David and Jason were also from smaller towns. There was a name for people from smaller places around China who moved to Beijing or Shanghai—Wàidìrén, or "outsiders." In order to have gotten to the positions they were in now, all three had to be incredibly honest and hard-working. There was no other way.

"Well, I'm so glad you've joined us for dinner. Which I'm going to go start, so they'll be something to eat when you guys have finished your meeting." She looked at Jack. "Does that timing work?"

"It's perfect," he said, standing. His three assistants followed suit. "Let's go sit at the table and have a brief chat about tomorrow."

They brought their drinks as they re-settled around the table. "I reviewed the documents," Jack said. "Thank you, they look great. Can we make sure to bring a copy for the party secretary and the governor. I want to give them a copy. If we made a mistake, they can let us know."

Susan jotted something down in her notepad. "That's a good idea."

"A copy of these briefs will be given to the Standing Committee, so we need to make sure all are correct. Also, during the meeting tomorrow, if we find out any new relevant information, let's please put it where it should go, for example, under the SWOT analysis. The documents were very thorough but there will certainly be things that we'll be finding out as we go along." Jack paused and took a sip of his wine. "Have we figured out how to organize our other visits?"

"Yes," David said. "We divided China into six regions: northeast, northwest, etcetera . . . We figured this is easy to understand and the provinces near each other might overlap in characteristics and needs."

"That sounds excellent. Let's use that designation. Also, I want to share something with you." Jack reached for his iPad and used his Apple Pencil to draw a matrix. "I'd like this to be prepared for each city, and roll the cities up into one for the province. We'll need to have one for city profit. Past years profit will be on the top, then you can have months for the current year, then list the *planned profit*, followed by the *gap*, on the top at the end. We'll need similar sheets for expenses—that are broken down, if possible—and revenue. Does that make sense?"

Jason raised a hand. "I'm not sure I understand what you mean by *gap*."

"Sure," Jack said. "Good question. So, let's say if, in July, a province's revenue is planned for ten million, but the actual achieved is eight, then the gap will be two million. Show it as a negative two million. In this way, everyone will be able to see very clearly how they are performing."

He slid the iPad to Susan, who took a photo of the screen with her own phone, and then David and Jason did the same.

"The goal is that the cities will roll up into provinces, and provinces will roll up into the nation. If done correctly, this will be a powerful tool for Beijing to use to manage plans. Ideally, we'll automate it and they'll get a hard copy monthly."

Susan was unable to keep the smile from her face. "Brilliant," she said. "No one will be able to escape. They'll have to achieve their plan—otherwise, everyone will know. So even if the planning exercise itself isn't a success, the monitoring part will be."

They talked for a little longer until Jojo came out and asked Susan if she would help her bring the dishes out.

Susan immediately pushed back from the table and hurried to the kitchen. She and Jojo reappeared a moment later with the food. She had made eggplant with pork, spinach, spicy chicken and onion cake, which Jack knew was a version of comfort food and would likely remind them of home.

It was nice to have dinner guests, and Jack was pleased to see that his assistants seemed to be enjoying both the food and themselves. They had relaxed noticeably since they first arrived, thanks in part to the alcohol, but also, Jack hoped, because they felt they were having a good time.

He took another bite, noticing that David had stopped eating and was looking around the table at each of them.

"Everything okay?" Jack asked.

David looked at him, smiled a little bashfully. "I just . . . I'm having a really good time tonight. This food is incredible." He nodded at Jojo. "Thank you. And . . . I was just thinking that it seems inconceivable, at least to me, that we're going to visit all of these provinces and meet all these people. I know we will, but . . . I never thought I'd be part of something like this. It's a really big deal."

His voice had a note of awe in it, or maybe it was plain disbelief at the magnitude of their task.

"We'll all learn a great deal about China," Jack said. "And I bet we'll encounter some things along the way that we didn't expect, but you know what? I have full confidence in you, in us, as a team, and I know we'll be able to handle it. Whatever comes our way."

David nodded slowly, as if taking the time to first taste, then digest fully what Jack had just said. "I haven't gone into much detail at all, but some of my family is very interested in this project. They are eager to see how it turns out."

"I have high hopes for its success," Jack said. "Your family should, too. This will be a great thing for the nation, and I'm sure they're proud that you get to be a part of it." He gave David what he hoped was an encouraging nod; he could understand why being part of such a thing might seem hard to believe, but he also knew that, as the days turned into weeks, and they racked up the miles traveling across the entire country, things would get rather grueling.

After the meal, they moved over to the living area and sat on the sofas. The moon had risen and reflected off the water's surface in undulating ripples.

"It's beautiful," Susan said. "It must be so lovely living here." She had taken the seat next to Jack on the sofa, her face slightly flushed, her eyes bright. "I used to daydream about living in a home like this, when I was little," she said, almost more to herself. "The architecture wasn't the same, but I always wanted a body of water to look out on, mountains as the backdrop. I can't think of anything nicer than that."

"It is a very nice view," Jason said gamely, looking around. Jack hid his smile. Maybe Susan had had more to drink than he realized; she was relaxing back into the sofa, one leg crossed over the other, her gaze toward the window with the view that she had used to daydream about.

They ended the evening early, since they had the meeting tomorrow. Jojo said goodbye to their dinner guests and Jack walked them downstairs and said goodnight.

"Thank you again for everything," Susan said. "I had a really good time tonight."

"We did too," Jack said. "It's nice to have people over for dinner. You all sleep well tonight, and I'll see you tomorrow."

Back upstairs, Jojo had a wry smile on her face as she wiped down the dining table.

"What?" Jack asked.

"Your assistants are very sweet," Jojo said. "They're like little puppies, just waiting for your order. Especially Susan. She might even have a little crush on you."

Jack laughed. "Come on," he said. He went over and put his arms around Jojo. "Now you're being funny. And you know you have nothing to worry about anyway."

Jojo smiled and touched the tip of his nose with her forefinger. "Who says I'm worried? I think it's cute."

Jack leaned down and gave her a kiss. "Well, I think you're cute." He took her hand, pulled her toward the bedroom. "I'll finish that later," he said. "I can think of a few other things we should be doing right now."

CHAPTER 12

The next morning, they travelled together to the Kunming government office. It was a massive, ten-story building with many windows. One of the first things Jack saw was the huge flag of China. From his days in Chicago, he recalled that the five stars on the flag symbolized the great union of revolutionary people under the leadership of the Communist Party. Perhaps it was a unifying symbol during the days of Mao Zedong, but it certainly did not fit modern China.

A man in a dark suit greeted them and led them to a large room taken up mostly by a U-shaped table that looked like it could comfortably seat seventy people. Jack took a seat as others began to filter into the room; the governor and the party secretary were last in, and sat directly opposite Jack, about twenty-five feet away. They looked at him but did not say anything or make any move to come over and introduce themselves.

"Welcome to Yunnan, Mr. Jack Gold." Jack turned at the sound of the voice; a man to his right was speaking into a microphone. "We would like to take this opportunity to share with you the background and history of this great province."

Jack glanced at Susan, David, and Jason. Susan sat to his right; Jason and David were to his left. "Follow me. Susan, please translate."

He stood up and Susan, Jason, and David, followed. He stepped inside the U-shape and over to the party secretary. He held his hand out. "Hi. I'm Jack Gold. Nice to meet you." Susan dutifully translated. Jason pulled his phone out and took a few photos. "This room is set up more for a United Nations meeting," Jack continued. "It is not conducive to a working meeting. And, we're here to help *you* develop *your* plan, not receive an overview of your province. Our guidance will be essential to your success."

Jack could have easily said everything he just did in Mandarin, but he purposefully spoke English, as he knew most Chinese citizens felt those from America were more senior and smarter—which didn't make sense to him, but it was a reality.

"Please find a suitable working meeting room, where no more than eight people can attend. Then we can continue. We will wait outside until you are properly prepared. We only have sixty minutes to meet with you. Your time is limited, and you have already wasted much of it." Susan continued to translate. Out of the corner of his eye, Jack saw Jason hold his phone up and take a picture of the scene.

Jack turned and walked away without saying anything else or waiting for the party secretary to respond. It was perfectly clear what was happening—they were snubbing him and trying to sabotage the meeting. They would have used the entire time talking about the province but not talking about the actual plan. Fortunately, Jack knew how to deal with these types of people: tell them as politely as you can that they're idiots and they'll lose out. This was not his first barbeque in China.

Jack heard hurried footsteps behind him as he walked out of the room. He turned and saw the governor, his hand extended.

"Jack," he said. "I'm Governor Bo. My apologies for all that inside. We have a suitable room already set up." Jack shook his hand. "Let's start anew," the governor said.

Jack smiled, sensing that he could work with this man. They followed Governor Bo into a smaller room, with a conference table that could seat ten. When the party secretary entered and took his seat at the head of the table, Jack walked over. He held his hand out again, which the party secretary just looked at in confusion.

"I thought we could start again," Jack said, his hand still extended. The party secretary begrudgingly stood and shook it, though Jack could tell from the man's stiff body language that he was not pleased.

"Party Secretary, Governor—the Standing Committee sent us here to help you with your plan," Jack said. "More to the point, as President Wang specifically asked, *what* will you do, *how* will you do it, and *what* will be the results?" Jack paused and let his words sink in. "Why don't we start with Dali."

The silence stretched. Jack looked around the room as he took his seat. Still, no one spoke. "You must have some idea on how to decrease expenses," Jack said. "Or how to increase revenues. What is there within Dali that can be changed or used?"

There was some shuffling of papers, some shifting in chairs, some sharing of uncomfortable glances, but no one offered a single suggestion.

"May I ask a question?" Jack said, purposefully trying to keep his voice nonconfrontational. "Why are the interest expenses so high in Dali?"

A look of shock crossed the party secretary's face, as if he could not believe someone would dare pose such a question to begin with. Though he still had no answer to offer.

"No one has even a single suggestion?" Jack asked. He saw Jason, from the corner of his eye, get up and begin taking photos with his phone.

"You are a foreigner." The party secretary's voice was tight with anger. "You're not Chinese. How could you know anything of China? Why don't you just go away." He shot Jack a look of disgust.

Jack exhaled, could feel the tension in the room grow. But he was unphased; this sort of outburst was not entirely unexpected. "I've done business all over China," Jack said. "All over the world. Much more than you, for sure." He removed his diplomatic passport from his suit's inner pocket. "And, I might not *be* from China, but, evidently, I am a Chinese diplomat." He slipped the passport back into his pocket, the disgust on the secretary's face turning into disbelief. "Secretary," Jack said, "your non-participation is counterproductive. You are dismissed from this exercise. Govenor Bo, we will see you in Dali tomorrow to discuss some ideas we have and any that you might want to share. You will present to the Standing Committee, instead of the secretary."

The shock in the room was palpable as Jack stood. "Susan," he said, "please set up a time with the governor, at his convenience. We can meet at my house."

And with that, the meeting was over.

*   *   *

They re-convened the next morning at ten at Jack's. Governor Bo arrived shortly after Susan, David, and Jason.

He was a younger man, slightly overweight, with a round face and an easygoing disposition. Jack could tell he was the sort of person others felt comfortable around.

"My apologies for yesterday," Governor Bo said. "We look forward to another chance and appreciate your time."

"Of course," Jack said. "And no need to apologize. Yesterday is behind us. We're looking forward to setting the foundation to make some good progress. Thank you for making the trip down here."

Before he took a seat, Governor Bo looked around, his gaze stopping at the windows with the view of the lake. "What a wonderful view," he said. "You were smart in selecting this place."

"The reflection of the moon in the water is especially beautiful against the backdrop of the mountains," Jack said. "It's one of my favorite views."

Governor Bo gave Jack an appreciative smile as he took his seat at the table. "I was hoping to start the meeting by answering the question as to why we have such high interest expenses."

"That'd be great," Jack said. "I'm curious."

"Well, on a well-positioned piece of government-owned land, we built two rather large commercial buildings. The buildings have been running at seventy percent occupancy, so we've been unable to refinance or pay back the loan."

"Your rental revenue is less than your interest expense?"

"Exactly." Governor Bo nodded vigorously. "And some of the space is occupied by government administration, which doesn't pay rent. All of this drains the province's resources."

Jack looked at his assistants, who had their notepads open in front of them. "All costs should be properly assigned nationally; if a government department occupies a government building, they should pay market rent. This must apply in all other areas, too—not just real estate." He shifted his focus back to the governor. "Why don't you just sell the buildings?"

"It's not so simple. Some feel the market will change, and they don't want the risk of having to move the government department elsewhere."

"You mean there is space elsewhere for the department?"

"Yes."

"How much would the savings be from selling?"

"We'd be able to pay back the loan and we'd be left with about twenty million in extra funds. That would be our net profit."

Jack nodded. "That doesn't sound so bad, then. Why don't you get some quotes from real estate brokers. Tell the committee why you want to sell, and then benefit of selling. That's an easy one."

Governor Bo reached out and took one of the water bottles Jack had put in the middle of the table. The governor twisted the cap off the bottle and took a sip. "Well . . ." he said. "Well, to be honest, the secretary is quite attached to the two buildings."

"I see. But if the Standing Committee knew about the current financial situation, they would urge you to sell, right?"

"You're probably exactly right."

"Then make the tough decision. You are not better than industry experts in timing the market. And, tell the committee you want to have the government offices pay market rates."

"Okay," Governor Bo said, though he still sounded unsure.

"We had an idea and we wanted to share it with you," Jack said. He reached for his iPad. "May I show you a few pictures of some lakes in America?"

Governor Bo visibly brightened. "Sure!"

Jack opened the photo album he'd saved several screenshots in. "Please, everyone," he said, "come around and see."

Susan, David, and Jason came behind them as Jack scrolled through the pictures. "This is Lake Arrowhead, in California," Jack said. "It's a small lake, only one square mile of water." The picture showed the pristine water, a sailboat, two speedboats, a backdrop of mountains and sky. The next picture showed another body of water, with some fishing boats and jet skis. "Big Bear Lake is smaller," Jack said, "and it gets snow during the winter." He went to the next picture. "This is Lake Mead. It's a very active lake with wakeboarders and jet skiers." The last lake he had to show was Tappan Lake, in Ohio. "I was once at this lake and a neighbor won a wakeboarding scholarship to Florida University. I don't care what anyone says—wakeboarding is a serious sport."

Jack closed the iPad and waited for everyone to return to their seats. "We think the Erhai is substantially underutilized," he told the governor. "There are so many possibilities with a body of water like that—but here, what we see, is how substantially underutilized it is. Think of how it could be transformed, though, for water sports, sailing, fishing, swimming . . . Like with other lakes, all over the world, this will drive up real estate prices and *meaningfully* increase tourism and domestic consumption, and also have a sizable impact on tax income. There is ninety-seven square miles of lake. It's huge. The seventh largest in China."

But despite the enthusiasm in Jack's voice, the governor looked crestfallen. "Jack," he said slowly, "that's a great idea but I know what the party secretary will say. *Erhai is a jewel of China. Its clean water must be preserved and the fish are the pride and livelihood of the indigenous people.* That's what he would say. Realistically, if we opened the lake to swimming, lots of people would start bathing in it. There'd be a serious pollution concern."

"Those are valid concerns, but there are remedies," Jack said with a smile. "You can fine people for illegally bathing. And, you can explain how extra boat gas taxes will go to *increasing* water quality; prices for fishing licenses will be as high as they need to be to ensure the lake is not overfished. More importantly, though, you can tell him that zero percent of the province population knows how to swim. That's a national embarrassment. How can China compete in the Olympics with that sort of attitude? Swimming, sailing, water polo—all Olympic sports!"

Jack paused. He didn't want to discourage the young governor or make him feel like the project was going to fail before it even got underway. "You have to understand why I'm here," Jack said. "China must evolve. This is the reason the Standing Committee sent me here—to help change attitudes. All you have to do is present recommendations and how you'll do it, and what will be the impact on revenue over a few years. President Wang selected me to do this, so if you run into any problems, I can contact the president directly." Jack reached for his iPhone and pulled up his WeChat QR code. He slid the phone over to Governor Bo, so he could scan the code.

"I do have another question," Jack said. "What's going on with Dali University?"

The governor frowned. "What do you mean?"

"How is it performing? How many students are attending? Is it making money? It covers four hundred and ten acres and has almost one thousand teachers. It should be serving twenty-five to thirty-thousand students."

The governor looked down at the table before meeting Jack's gaze. "It's actually not doing well at all," he said. "A few notable research papers have been published, but that's about it. And . . . student admission is low. You're right about that."

"What is it?"

"About fifteen thousand."

"So something needs to be done about that."

"It's one of Secretary Ho's favorite projects. I can't do anything."

"Let's just take Secretary Ho out of the equation for a moment. Tell me what you would do if you had total control and the secretary was not an issue."

Such a question had never been posed to the governor before, Jack could tell. But Jack could also see in Bo's face that he *did* have ideas, probably good ones, that had likely been thwarted because they did not align with what Secretary Ho preferred.

"The problem," Governor Bo said, "is that the university is loaded with professors who got there through their connections. It's not run as a business."

This was nothing new, but it irritated Jack to hear it. "Every Chinese person who could —but does not—receive an education, is a sad loss for the nation." He let these words sink in. Susan nodded as she wrote something on her notepad. "I see three options. One: replace the university president. Two: send in a team to re-organize and re-position the university. Or, three: Privatize the university. Sell it, and the land."

Governor Bo had a wide-eyed, bewildered expression on his face. Yes, Jack's three suggestions would result in great upheaval from the current status quo. But that was the point. That the university was only serving half the number of students it could and the greater emphasis sounded like it was on providing well-connected professors with cushy positions . . . It was a travesty.

"My own initial preference is that you privatize it," Jack said. "Whoever buys it can clean it up. Either way, whatever you decide, you should view things as if a big hotel rented that beautiful land for a period of thirty years. Their annual rent would be what that university should be paying in rent to the people of Dali. Put together a P&L and share it with the Standing Committee. You cannot permit wastefulness. If every province is so casual about such things, the nation will suffer horribly. I will be at the presentation, and I'll ask you pointed questions. You'll have fifteen minutes to concisely make your recommendations. I'm sure there are many more things that you'll come up with to mention in your presentation. Prioritize. Keep me posted. If you need help, I'm available. We have a draft copy of our internal report about the entire province. Here it is." Susan slid a copy of the report to the governor.

"Please let one of us know if there are any inaccuracies or omissions," Jack said. "It will be shared with the Committee." He purposefully looked at his watch, signaling the meeting was over.

Governor Bo stood. "Thank you for your time," he said. "It was great meeting with you. You've given me a lot to think about."

Jack walked Governor Bo to the door. Before he stepped out, he extended his arm and shook Jack's hand. "You are well-informed and very helpful," he said. "I wasn't expecting that. Thank you."

"Remember what I said," Jack told him. "Don't let what the party secretary prefers to factor in to your presentation or muddy your ideas. And be in touch if you need to."

Jack bid the governor goodbye and went back inside. His assistants were packing up their own belongings and getting ready to take off.

"Thank you, everyone, for a good meeting," Jack said.

"You are fearless," Susan said, looking at him. "Thank you."

"For what?" Jack asked, smiling, genuinely unsure why she thought he was fearless, or why she was thanking him.

"You really care about China," Susan said, a little bashfully. "And its people. That's very obvious. I mean, I suppose it was when you addressed the nation from the Control Center. But it wasn't just a one-time thing for you, like you do that and you're gone." She tilted her head a little. "Because you're still here, and it seems quite obvious to me, to us–" she gestured to David and Jason, "that your ideas and guidance could really help everyone in this country live a happier life with more personal liberty and opportunity." Susan's cheeks were flushed, and she stopped speaking and looked down at the ground. "I'm sorry," she said. "I shouldn't keep going on like that. This . . . this is just unlike any opportunity that we–I–have had before, and I'm thankful for it. Even if it's a small part, I'm glad for the chance to do something to try to make things better for others."

"I appreciate the feedback," Jack said. "Thank you. We all work very well together; I couldn't have asked for three better assistants."

He walked the three of them out, David and Jason echoing sentiments of what Susan had just said. When they left, Jojo came down and asked Jack if he was done working.

"For now," he said.

"How many more of these meetings do you have?"

"We've got to do one for every municipality in China. So, thirty-four. Which means we're now down to thirty-three."

"Thirty-three. That's a lot. But it's really the only way to get this done, I can see that. I know why my dad wanted *you* to do this. How'd it go, today's meeting?"

"Pretty well, actually."

"I wasn't eavesdropping, but I did hear the tail end of that conversation. Your assistants are really quite enamored with you."

"I don't think they've ever had an opportunity like this before. It's exciting for them."

"Well, there's no one better for them to learn from. Now, on to more serious matters: I'm starving. And I want a pizza."

"Then we will get you a pizza." He put his arms around her. "Now, I must tell you, I did a little reading on Dali too, and I happen to know the best pizza place here, but . . . it's not that great from what I read."

Jojo turned and smiled up at him. "Maybe you can give them some suggestions on how to improve that, too."

CHAPTER 13

For the trip to Suzhou, they all flew together: Jack, Jojo, Davis, Rio, Susan, Jason, and David. It was a large group, but Jack felt traveling all together would be more efficient, plus, it strengthened their group bond. Jack was pleased with how well this particular group coalesced; and it wasn't just him and his assistants, or Jojo and Rio—everyone, Jack noticed, seemed to enjoy each other's company, and genuinely respected.

Jack sat with his assistants. He could hear snippets of Jojo and Rio's lively conversation at the back of the plane. "This is a five-hour flight," he said. "I like all of us flying together, so let's make sure that happens for subsequent trips; I'd like us all to say in the same hotel, too. In fact, I was thinking that we might be able to speed things up. As long as your municipality reports are in good shape, I think we can do up to five or six cities a week. If necessary, we can do meetings on Saturday or Sunday. So, we'll basically be living with in hotels and on this plane." He looked at Susan, then Jason, then David. "That okay with everyone?"

"Yes," Susan said. Jack had not expected a different response from them, yet he also knew that it would be a grueling schedule that would take at least eight weeks. Their enthusiasm was strong now, but he knew they'd feel differently in a few weeks.

"I'm glad to hear it," Jack said. "But, it will be a challenge after some time. You need to exercise daily, eat well, make sure you take time for yourself. We'll all be staying in the same hotel, but you'll each have your own room. Order room service and use the hotel's laundry service to get your clothes cleaned. If you have any problems or need something, you must tell me." He went around and looked at the each of them in the eye. "Okay?"

The three of them smiled and nodded, looking pleased but almost as if the news were too good to be true. It wasn't, though Jack knew that's what they were used to: Chinese managers were notorious for having two standards, one for themselves and one for their staff. The boss would stay in a nice hotel and eat extravagant meals. Staff would typically stay elsewhere, in inferior locations, most often sharing a room. Whether or not that was the situation his assistants were expecting, it wouldn't be the one they were going to get.

"Thanks for looking after us," Susan said. "You've certainly been the best boss that I've ever had." She handed Jack some papers. "By the way, here is a printout of the Suzhou brief, which we also uploaded to the group."

"Excellent," Jack said, taking the papers from her. "Thank you." He was not new to Suzhou. The city had been founded over 2,500 years ago and was a charming place, and with its numerous canals, it was sometimes referred to as the Venice of the East. The city's growth was primarily related to its satellite cities, where many manufacturing and high-tech companies made their home. Suzhou was doing well, better than Dali, but there was always room for improvement. Convincing the party secretary and governor of Suzhou of this might be a challenge; success often led to complacency, at least, that was what Jack had seen.

When the plane was about half an hour from landing, Jack walked to the back of the private plane they were in to speak with Jojo.

"We'll be landing soon," he said. He took her hand. "I know you'll have a good time. But I'm going to miss you. I don't like being away from you for extended periods like this."

"Then let's go home." Jojo managed to keep a straight face for a few seconds, but then she couldn't help it, she smiled, started laughing. "Jack, I'll miss you too, of course, but I'm looking forward to it. Well, the visiting with family and friends, not the missing you part, but maybe that'll be kind of nice, too? That's how I'm looking at it, anyway. There's nothing wrong with missing someone, and, in fact, it can be quite nice when you know you're going to see them again. So that's how I'm looking at this."

Jack returned her smile, felt relieved. "What about *Shàng Chuáng*?" he asked.

She squeezed his hand. "The bed will have to wait."

* * *

They arrived at the W Suzhou, after Jack had said goodbye to Jojo, and Rio, who would be accompanying her on her travels. Jack went up to his corner room, with a nice view of the lake, and plugged in his computer, his iPad, and his two phones. He reviewed the report the team had prepared and then supplemented his review with an internet search. Like many cities, Suzhou, over the years, had sought to urbanize. People were brought into the city from farms. In this way, education, healthcare, and other services could be more effectively and efficiently provided, as things were more central. Those living in urban areas could theoretically get higher paying jobs and, as a result, spend more money. The goal was to drive domestic consumption up as a way to fuel economic growth. That was the idea, which sounded easy enough, but Jack knew what a challenge it could be to get there. Suzhou was a tier-two city in China, and it was neglected in some respects.

The challenge was that when problems occurred, the local governments hid them and tried to look the other way instead of facing them head-on. Beijing was far away, so no one knew. This was an ineffective way of dealing with *anything*, never mind the running of a city, but Jack knew this was going to be one of the most difficult things to change. He thumbed through the report again that Susan had given him. Dividing China into six regions was insightful. If there was a head of each region, there would be greater oversight to ensure plans were implemented and other issues addressed. If it were up to Jack, he would have mystery shoppers, but instead, they would roam the country, ensuring laws were adhered to and plans properly executed.

CHAPTER 14

After successfully completing their meeting in Suzhou, they took a high-speed train to Shanghai. The journey was sixty miles and took them twenty-five minutes. From there, they had another ten miles to their destination at the Ritz-Carlton Portman Hotel, which took fifty minutes in a car. To go from one mode of transportation directly to another just made the stark difference between train and automobile travel all the more obvious. Trains were fast and efficient; navigating auto traffic was the worst. Even if you weren't the one driving.

Despite all this, Jack couldn't feel like he was returning home. He had lived in Shanghai for a number of years; it was where he and Jojo met. In a way, it seemed like a lifetime ago.

Jack gazed out the window as they drove through the Former French Concession, on Wukang Road. The settlement was beautiful with its old French architecture, which was built starting in the mid-1800s and lasted until the Japanese occupation in 1943. Until that time, it had been the most fashionable place to live in Shanghai and was home to people from nearly every major country. Since then, almost all the foreigners had left. The homes were still occupied, by families and groups of families, but very few of them seemed to have an interest in maintaining the upkeep of their homes.

Davis inched the SUV along, and they made their way onto Nanjing Road, where you could find stores such as Tiffany's, Rolex, and Gucci. Up ahead, their hotel. Jack always stayed at the Portman when he was in town, with its convenience to restaurants, the market, and other parts of town. There was even a Shake Shack ten minutes away.

After everyone was settled in, his three assistants met Jack around the table in his suite. They were on the forty-fifth floor and the windows overlooked the Shanghai Exhibition Center.

"I'm not sure how tomorrow's meeting is going to go," Susan said. They each had a copy of the five-page briefing in front of them.

"What do you mean?" Jack asked.

"Well . . . I just don't think it's going to be that easy for us to add value. They have a big group of people responsible for all their planning and they always work closely with Beijing." She glanced down at the document in front of her and thumbed through the pages. "I'm just not sure how receptive they're going to be to us."

Jack could hear the apprehension in her voice and he wanted to assuage her concerns; even if they *weren't* receptive to them, it didn't matter. Those that stood in the way or were disruptive or trying to block progress would be removed.

"Let's first talk about who we are meeting tomorrow," Jack said.

"Well, as you know, Shanghai has been the home of some of China's most esteemed leaders, including Wang Yang and Zhu Rongji. Shanghai has a mayor who performs the same duties as a governor; his name is Yang Xiong. He's fifty-three and is from Zhejang, where he went to school for engineering and later got a PhD in accounting. He has an eleven-year-old daughter. Interestingly, he has yet to be voted into the 205 Central Committee members."

Jack frowned. "Do we know *why* they haven't voted him onto the Committee? It seems rather unusual, since he's the mayor of such an esteemed city."

"We don't," Susan said. "They meet every five years, so it may just be a matter of time."

"Who is the secretary?"

"Li Qiang. He was born and raised in Chengdu. At university, he majored in agriculture mechanization and he holds a BA from Pepperdine University, in Malibu, California. He has two boys—eleven and fifteen. He has been on the Party Standing Committee since 2005. Both speak good English."

Susan did not read straight from her notes, Jack noticed, but only glanced at them every now and then. "Do they have a plan?" Jack asked.

"Yes. I got access to an internal document. They plan on investing heavily in 5G, AI, cloud computing, industrial internet, R&D areas, and in other more traditional areas like high-speed rail. They'll be investing on their own and supporting the private sector."

None of what she said surprised Jack. "Sounds like they want to be known as a global leader in these areas. I guess we'll hear more about this tomorrow." He looked out the window toward the exhibition center. There were four guards at the entrance, checking what few cars entered. It was a huge piece of land with a spider-like structure occupying a small portion of the footprint in the center. The top of the structure was adorned with a star, three hundred sixty feet above the ground. Jack knew China and Russia had designed and built the exhibition center sixty years ago, hence the Russian neoclassical design. Jack always wondered why they kept the property, since there were many other bigger and better exhibition centers in Shanghai. It seemed like a waste of prime real estate. Better for the residents of the city would be to turn the place into a park, like a smaller version of Central Park.

"I have an idea," Jack said. "I'd like to get whatever information is available on the exhibition center, whatever you can find." He pointed across the street. "Ideally, let's find out key data like earnings, costs, and utilization. Let's find that out and pass it to me before our meeting."

Susan nodded. "I'll look into it."

"What suggestions will we make tomorrow?" Jason asked.

"We-ell . . ." Jack paused. He had some preliminary ideas but he wanted to see how the meeting was going to go before bringing anything up. "This is Shanghai, and anything can happen. Let's find out what we can about the exhibition center, and we'll go from there."

His three assistants smiled. None of them were from Shanghai, but they all knew what a unique place the city was—though this was not meant in a complimentary way. The Shanghainese tended to think they were better than others, for no substantial reason. It was even harder to get a job if you were from elsewhere since they heavily favored their own. It was known that the Shanghainese looked down on people from other parts of China, and it was likely that such attitude would be on full display tomorrow at the meeting.

*   *   *

"I'm sorry I didn't get this to you sooner," Susan said. She handed Jack two typed pages. They were in the car over to the meeting with the Shanghai government officials. "This is the information on the exhibition center that you asked for." Jack began skimming the document. "Only ten percent of the land is used for the center and utilization of the center is at about thirty-five percent on a yearly basis. A state-owned enterprise owns it and loses about three million dollars a year."

Jack nodded. "Thanks, Susan. That's what I expected. They could sell the property for over one billion easily and earn more on interest—or, they could open it as a park to the public. Either way, it's just a waste of resources right now."

Their car pulled right up in front of the seventeen-story building where they'd have the meeting. There was a single flag of China on a shiny stainless-steel flagpole in front of the building. They checked in at the front desk and were given nametags on lanyards to wear, then they put their briefcases and bags through the x-ray machine while they walked through a metal detector. Only after they were each checked with a hand-held scanner were they allowed through. The building's interior was modern and spotless, with its stainless-steel columns and abundance of windows. Jack tried to compare it to other buildings he'd been in, in places like New York and Hong Kong, but honestly, none of them could compare to this.

The elevator was ultra-modern and it almost felt like they were teleported to the top floor. They were escorted to a conference room with frosted glass walls and an unobstructed view of the entire eastern portion of Shanghai. Through the bright haze they could see where the Bund was, a protected historical district in the central part of the city. There was a sea of commercial buildings of all heights, sizes and shapes. He deliberately went over to the windows, not just to get a better view but because he knew Susan, Jason, and David would follow him. Then, when Secretary Li and Mayor Yang entered, they would feel compelled to let Jack and his assistants sit on that side of the table; Jack wanted the light from the windows in their eyes, not his.

The two men entered the room a few minutes later, both wearing spotless dark blue suits, a Chinese flag pin affixed to their left lapel. Jack moved from the window around the table, extending his hand to the man closest to him, who did the same. Jason stood and photographed the interaction.

"Hi, Jack," he said in English. "I'm Secretary Li. Welcome to Shanghai."

"Thank you, Secretary Li," Jack said, shaking his hand. "Nice to meet you."

He shook the mayor's hand next. "Jack, I'm Mayor Yang. Welcome." Mayor Yang was shorter than the secretary, and he wore silver-rimmed glasses and his short black hair was sticking up in some places, as if refusing to obey the orders of any previously applied hair gel. "Please feel free to help yourself to a drink before we get started."

Jack grabbed a Diet Coke from the array of beverages that were set up on a side table. Everything was very western, almost as if they were not in China at all. Susan, Jason, and David all took bottles of water and they sat down with Jack, their backs to the windows. Two more people came in—the young man sat next to Secretary Li and a woman, probably in her forties, sat next to Mayor Yang. Both had a pen and a pad of paper, like Jack's assistants.

Jack cracked his can of soda open. "How can we help you today?" Secretary Li asked, a benevolent smile on his face.

Jack took a sip of his soda and set the can down. "We came to help you, actually," he said.

The secretary's smile did not waver. "Help us?"

"Yes. With the plan that you will be presenting."

"We've been working with Beijing on a rather significant plan," Secretary Li said, glancing at the mayor. "They'll be gaining approval for it separately, when it's finalized."

Jack didn't say anything for a moment. He took another sip of his soda. "I think the president and the Standing Committee were pretty clear that you'd present the plan for approval," he said.

Secretary Li gave Jack a sympathetic look. "Jack," he said, "Shanghai is different. Plans get done in a more collaborative way when we work with Beijing. I'm sure you understand how an international city like Shanghai necessitates a different approach."

From the corner of his eye, he could see the tense expression on Susan's face. He had expected this from the top officials in a city whose people thought they deserved special treatment. It was something Jack had observed time and again in Shanghai, but not in Beijing. It seemed to do with the Shanghainese feeling *they* were responsible for the city's illustrious past, even though it had nothing to do with them—it was really due to the French, English, and Americans who had made the city their home.

"Let me clarify whether this is the case or not," Jack said. He wasn't going to argue with them. He took out his phone and opened WeChat, then passed the phone to Susan. "Please ask President Wang if Shanghai Secretary and Mayor must present their plans, just like other municipalities."

Susan typed the message and pressed send. Then, they all sat and waited, the stillness and tension in the air palpable. Secretary Li and Mayor Yang were doing their best to keep their expressions neutral, but it was clear neither had expected Jack to just get in touch with Wang like that.

Less than a minute later, Wang's reply came through: *Definitely!*

Jack turned his phone and slid it across the table so the others side could see it. He suspected they knew the WeChat icon for the president and would know that the message was authentic.

"I'm glad that's been cleared up," Jack said. "We don't have much time, so would you now please tell us any plans you might have? Again, we are here to help."

The smile was long gone from Secretary Li's face. His brow was furrowed and a muscle in his jaw quivered. "Certainly," he said in a tight voice. "Mayor Yang, let's please share our plans with Jack and his team. Since they're here to help."

"Sure," Mayor Yang said, and he offered a smile which did not seem angry, which Jack found surprising but was also hopeful about—maybe they would be able to make some progress here. "Over the next three years, Shanghai will invest over thirty-eighty billion dollars to develop 5G networks, cloud computing industrial internet, AI, and R&D institutions, making Shanghai the global leader in high-tech and innovative industries of the future. In some of the areas, China will allow foreign co-investment and will work with world-class strategic partners. All of this will help ensure that China's economy soon matches that of the United States."

And that was it. Jack waited a few moments to see if there would be anything else, but there wasn't. Secretary Li and Mayor Yang looked at Jack. He looked back at them. Finally, Secretary Li leaned forward, his forearms on the table. "We have a nine-hundred-page document with Beijing that deals with everything. We're not going through nine hundred pages right now so you can offer your 'help.' We don't need it."

David was looking nervously from Jack to the two Shanghai officials. Jason fidgeted with his notepad. Jack could feel the thickening tension. Susan sat perfectly still, her pen down, her hands in her lap.

Jack took a deep breath and exhaled slowly. "President Wang was very specific in his requirements for all provincial heads when it came to presenting plans. Do you recall what those requirements are?"

"Those do not apply to Shanghai," Secretary Li said. "We are a special case, for obvious reasons."

"Such as . . .?"

The secretary shot him a look of thinly veiled disgust. "We are the financial capital of China."

Jack nodded. "Okay," he said. So the secretary had just seen a text message from the president of China and still he resisted. "Secretary, you deny reality. The president just communicated very clearly that each province is to present its plan. You saw it on my phone, with your own two eyes. Would you like to see it again? Should I switch to Chinese and explain things to you in Mandarin? Or should we just end this meeting now? There's no reason for us to be here if you are going to continue to deny what it is you need to do. Like I said, we are here to help, but we cannot do that if you are unwilling to uphold your end of the arrangement. And in this case, the arrangement is that each province will create a plan to present to the Standing Committee." Jack reached for his briefcase and started to stand.

"Wait!" Mayor Yang waved his hands in the air. "Please. Don't leave. Let's stay here and talk further. We understand that we have to present. This just caught us off-guard and it's taking a moment to sink in, is all." He gave Jack an imploring, earnest look. He really did want them to stay, Jack could see. He sat back down.

"This isn't Jack's decision," Mayor Yang said to the secretary. "He's here to help, and we should take him up on is offer."

Secretary Li nodded begrudgingly.

Jack knew how people got attached to what they created; people would put a lot of work into something and then when things changed and they needed to start over, their resistance would almost always be because of a strong emotional reaction. It was natural, but it did not mean it was the correct way to do things.

"What should we do?" Mayor Yang asked, looking directly at Jack.

After all that, Jack felt his own inner resistance now toward offering the help that they were there to offer. Rather—he did not feel inclined to rush to answer the question or provide them with any immediate assistance. The Secretary was arrogant and obtuse. In this moment, it would be easy enough to allow those feelings to eclipse what he knew to be right—the whole reason they were here in the first place—and that was to help the mayor and the secretary in any way they could, while they were here. Jack let out a breath, aware that the silence had continued to stretch, that Susan had turned slightly in her chair and was looking at him.

"You have to go back to what Wang carefully said to you at Zhongnanhai," Jack said, exhibiting far more patience than he actually felt. "He said that your plan and presentation must be limited to fifteen minutes and 'will need to describe *what* you want, *how* you will do it, and *what* precisely you will achieve.'"

"Fifteen minutes?" Secretary Li waved his hand dismissively. "Our plan is too long for a fifteen-minute presentation."

"It's not too *long*," Jack said. "It's *too complex* and *doesn't make sense.* That's the problem."

"What do you mean, it doesn't make sense?" Mayor Yang asked, worry etched on his face.

"You want Shanghai to be the global leader in technology, and for China to surpass America in GDP, right? That's your goal?"

The mayor and the secretary both nodded earnestly.

"No one will believe the Chinese government in Shanghai can be successful in technological innovation, given the past failures in the semiconductor industry. Given what you mentioned to me, you will allow foreign investment only in certain areas, but want strategic partners in all the key areas. That won't work." Jack could see the crestfallen look deepening on Mayor Yang's face with each word he spoke. "You believe the Shanghai government knows better than 5G and cloud companies on where to invest. You're missing the point."

"Okay," Mayor Yang said. "What is the point?"

"If China is the recognized tech leader and has a GDP greater than America—so what? What does that mean?"

"It's important for the nation," Secretary Li said. "It will show the progress the country has made in such a short period of time. China will be looked at as the global leader, because we will be."

"Secretary, you should be worried about per capita income," Jack said. "The average American will still be *six times* wealthier than the average

Chinese. Of course, China will have a larger economy than America, because of its population."

Secretary Li narrowed his eyes. Jack could practically feel the rage emanating off of him. "Yes," the secretary hissed, "but the purchasing power of the Chinese is greater."

"Yes and no," Jack said, shutting his eyes and pinching the bridge of his nose for a moment. He let go and opened his eyes. The mayor and the secretary were no different than any other average Chinese person—they compared their country to America in almost all things. But in this case, they were comparing the wrong things. "Let me explain," Jack said. "When your son graduates, if he moves to Shanghai, what will happen? He'll share an apartment with several other people and make about five thousand RMB a month. That's less than a thousand US dollars a month. It's hard to live on that—especially in Shanghai. Conversely, if someone makes minimum wage in America, they'll make about fifteen dollars an hour, or over twenty-eight thousand a year. This affords a much better standard of living. Comparing GDPs is misleading at best."

"What do you think, then?" Mayor Yang asked. "What would you present?"

Those were the words Jack was waiting to hear—they were about to get into the meat of the meeting. He switched to speaking Chinese so there would be zero miscommunication. "The key is to make Shanghai a more attractive place for companies and people to live. Then there will be more jobs and wages will go up as does demand for labor."

"We've already done that," Secretary Li said. "You're just telling us things that we've already done."

"I beg to differ. Your free trade zones failed, and no one wants to live in Shanghai."

"Excuse me?" Secretary Li said incredulously. "You can't just say that. You offend those of us who have managed Shanghai." He was about to say more, but Mayor Yang put a hand up.

"What do you mean?" the mayor asked. "That people don't want to live here? There are two-hundred thousand foreigners in Shanghai."

Jack nodded. "That's true," he said, "but most of those are teachers and students. The others that matter business-wise constitute about zero percent. Los Angeles and New York have about thirty-seven percent. For Shanghai to be successful, it must not just attract money and companies—it must attract the best and the smartest people in the world. But it hasn't. Shanghai, with twenty-six million people, is absolutely *not* an international city. Do you know why?"

No one said anything. Jack glanced at his assistants to see if they had any ideas, but Susan only gave an almost imperceptible shake of her head.

"Why can't Shanghai attract the best people?" Mayor Yang finally asked.

"Because Shanghai is not cool."

It was the biggest insult anyone could give to a city and those responsible for it, even if it did sound like a middle-school insult. It was like telling someone their baby was ugly. "Shanghai *looks* cool," Jack said, "but it's not. And I'll give you three examples. First, if I lived near the Shanghai Exhibition Center, I'd know it's an underutilized piece of land that I'd much prefer to be a beautiful park that could be utilized by the public. Second, if I lived in the former French Concession, I'd know it's basically a retirement community, as most of those living there are over the age of sixty-five. The insides of the apartments are overcrowded and dilapidated. Third, if I lived near the Bund, I'd know that it is a ghost town, with near zero vibrancy, and that includes the horrible, antiquated streets behind it. Plus, foreigners wouldn't want to live in any of those places, since the internet speed is terribly slow—forget about *industrial strength*."

He stopped speaking so what he just said could sink in.

"What Jack said is all correct." Susan's voice broke the silence. "Though it hurts me to hear it in such stark terms, he is right. In order to attract the world's best, there are changes that need to be made."

"That hurt me to hear, too," Mayor Yang said, looking genuinely wounded. "But . . . I can also understand what Jack has just brought up. And you're right, if we want to attract the best, then yes, changes will be needed."

Jack smiled at Susan, appreciative of her stepping in and softening his message. *Thank you*, he mouthed to her, and she returned his smile with a small one of her own, the color flaring on her cheeks.

"So how do you propose doing that?" Mayor Yang asked. "How do we make Shanghai more attractive?"

"Everyone has the same attitude: if you give a job to a foreigner, you take one from a Chinese, and China has too big of a population to permit this. Everyone needs to get over the fear of a foreigner taking their job.

In fact, they'll help *grow* jobs by making the city more globally competitive. Then, you need to ask yourself a question. Which is: What would motivate a genius programmer from Silicon Valley to move to Shanghai to start a restaurant?"

Mayor Yang blinked, as if Jack were asking him a trick question. "I . . . I don't know," he said.

"This programmer would want cool restaurants to eat at, a decent place to live, a vibrant art, music, and social scene, where they can interact with people from all over the world. In other words, you can't just let in the programmer and expect him to come with all the other components of culture that help make a place *cool*. Desirable. Somewhere that people want to live. So, among other things, Shanghai's visa attitude must change. You have to put the horse before the cart. The good news is that if you can do this, you can get the best businesspeople, doctors, artists, restaurants, teachers, and more. *That* is what will give Shanghai the global standing it deserves. Ultimately, companies, investors, and people, are your customers. You have to constantly ask yourself: *What do they want? Why do they want it?* And: *Why are YOU the best to provide it?* These are imperatives to drive job and wage growth, which in turn, increases consumer spending. Just as you are here to help in these areas so that your economy thrives, the central government is here to help you."

Jack sat back in his chair as Mayor Yang and Secretary Li leaned toward each other and spoke quietly behind their hands. When they pulled apart, Mayor Yang looked at Jack and smiled. The secretary did not smile, but no longer looked as irate as he had been earlier, which Jack took as a good sign.

"Thanks, Jack," Mayor Yang said. "You told it to us like it is. We don't get that honesty often, and, well . . . if you're not used to that, it can be a little overwhelming to hear, especially all at once like that. I can see why President Wang has you in charge of these meetings. Anyway, I think we get the idea and can take it from here. We certainly have a lot of work ahead of us."

From everything Jack had seen living and working in China, the Chinese had difficulty coming up with ideas on their own, but they knew how to execute. They knew the *how* but not the *why*. There were brilliant engineers who could replicate almost anything, but showed little ability in being able to design something new. The same was true here, and why they needed the guidance in order to get to work. Jack thought that it might have to do with how children here were brought up. If you gave a pencil and a piece of paper to a five-year-old in America and asked them to draw a dog, the child would make an attempt, even if the end result ended up looking nothing like a dog. If a child in China were asked to do the same task, the response would almost always be, "We haven't learned that yet."

*   *   *

When they arrived back at the hotel, Jack again thanked his assistants for a good meeting.

"It went better than I thought," Susan said. "Well, Secretary Li acted about as expected, but you handled it so well, Jack. Mayor Yang at least seems to be on board."

"I hope so."

Susan and Jason started toward the elevator, but David hung back, fidgeting with a button on his suit jacket.

"Everything okay?" Jack asked.

David stopped fidgeting and took a deep breath. "I was wondering if I could speak with you for a minute, Mr. Gold? It's important."

"Sure," Jack said. "Let's go over to the lounge." They made their way to the lobby lounge, which was almost empty, as it was still early afternoon and not yet teatime. Davis and another of Jack's guards followed at a polite distance as Jack and David seated themselves on a sofa. Jack placed his two phones on the elegant glass coffee table in front of them.

A waitress approached, with menus in her hand. "What could I get you to drink?" she asked.

David ordered warm water, which, along with tea, were the two most common drinks in China.

"I'd like a latte," Jack said. "A very hot, mouth-burning latte. In a to-go cup, please." He had to be very clear about the temperature of the drink; for some reason, Chinese liked their lattes barely warm and with elaborate foam art. Such a drink would cost over ten dollars, which was an astounding amount for a lukewarm latte.

"So," Jack said, after the waitress left, "David, what's on your mind?"

"I received a call the other night from my uncle. He has a friend who would like to meet with you. I also spoke with my parents, and they are hoping you can meet with him as well. They don't know what it is about, but . . . my uncle's friend is a very important person."

Jack frowned. "Okay, if I'm hearing you correctly . . . You don't know what the meeting would be about and you don't know who it's with?"

"Right," David said, wincing a little, as if to admit he didn't know anything further caused him pain. "I know it's odd and I'm embarrassed to mention it to you. I really don't know anything beyond what I've told you, but, coming from both my uncle and my parents, I could not ignore their request." He glanced up as the waitress appeared with their drinks.

Jack took a tentative sip of his latte, which wasn't quite as hot as he'd like, but close enough.

"I understand," he said to David. "However, I'm not accustomed to going to meetings unless I know more about the person and the topic. There are all sorts of problems that can arise."

"My uncle thought you might say that. He wanted me to give you full assurance that you will *want* to meet with this man, but, for a number of reasons, he feels it's best to communicate the nature of the meeting in person."

Jack looked at David with skepticism. David had done good work so far and was obviously intelligent. Surely David must understand that the work he was doing right now, with the president of China, was "important." Despite the vagueness of the request, Jack couldn't help but feel somewhat intrigued. What would such a meeting be about? Clearly, someone wanted to meet with him and had discovered a possible connection so that could happen.

But why?

He wouldn't know unless he went. He believed that David only knew what he had told him, so there was no point in pressing him for further information. How would it go from a security standpoint? As long as they were there, things would be fine.

"Okay, David," Jack said. "Arrange it. I will be bringing my security, though. I hope you understand that is absolutely essential. And I expect that my security will be the only security there. Does that make sense?"

"Yes," David said. "Of course. Your safety is a top priority. So, um, well . . . now that you've agreed, would you be able to meet tomorrow morning, at eight? Before we leave for the airport?"

"Where did they want to meet?"

"Just around the Corner at Bread Inc., on the second floor. Are you familiar with it?"

"Sure. You can tell them I'll be there."

David smiled. "Thanks, Mr. Gold. I appreciate it."

David finished his water and went to his room, while Jack sipped his latte. He turned and looked behind him, saw Davis sitting at one of the tables. Jack pocketed his phones and carried his latte and his briefcase over to the table and took a seat.

"David wants me to meet with a friend of his uncle's. He doesn't know what it's about, but evidently, the guy is a big shot. I accepted the meeting for tomorrow morning at eight, at Bread Inc. We'll be meeting on the second floor. I'm not expecting any problems."

"That's my job to anticipate the problems," Davis said with a wry half-smile. "A meeting with a big shot friend of the uncle, huh? What do you think it's about?"

"Honestly? I have no idea. But my curiosity is piqued."

"Well, Jack, you seem to have better intuition than most, so hopefully we'll be problem-free, as you anticipate, but we'll get there early to place some extra people. Just in case."

CHAPTER 15

Jack exited his room at 7:45 the next morning. He and Davis took the elevator down and exited right. They crossed one intersection and then it was less than a minute walk to Bread Inc, a popular restaurant and bakery.

Jack checked out the display case and ordered a quiche Lorraine and an Americano. He sat at a table to wait for his food and watched as others entered the bakery. No one looked at him or came over. Unlike in America, there were no guns in China. Jack wasn't sure exactly how they had kept them out, but today, he was thankful.

When they called his name, he collected his plate and coffee and then walked to the back of shop, to a narrow spiral staircase which led to the second floor.

A man sat at a table, his back to the floor-to-ceilings windows. There was no one else there except that man, who immediately stood upon seeing Jack.

"Mr. Gold, it's a pleasure to meet you," he said in Chinese. "I have been following you closely since your broadcast from the CCTV Headquarters. Your passion and dedication to China are commendable."

It had always been a hobby of Jack's to try to tell what region in China people were from, and something he'd become quite good at, though he could not place where this man was from.

They shook hands but the man did not introduce himself and so Jack simply said, "Thank you."

The man wore a light gray suit, clearly tailor-made, by a good tailor. He was fit and tan, not the sort of tan from working in the fields but rather from sitting on a yacht. He seemed fully at ease, both in his expensive suit and speaking with Jack; he was not the sort of man to threaten someone with violence. This put Jack somewhat at ease, though he knew a man like this surely knew plenty of people who spoke the language of violence fluently.

"You're probably wondering why you're here," the man said. "So let's get to it. Your meetings with the municipalities will change the fabric of Chinese civilization. During the dynasties, China was governed centrally. This was essential to keep the country and regions from becoming weak and falling into the hands of local tyrants, or, worse yet—foreigners. You see, China has always been a big country with a disbursed population. Centralization of rule created a nation that could be governed. Previous decentralization always created chaos. And this also made China vulnerable to foreigners. During the beginning of the 1900s, all major countries took advantage of China's weakness and captured a part of its territory." The man smiled and gestured to Jack. "Even your America took China hostage and left only after China agreed to pay thirty-four million taels of silver over time. China was weak then, but consolidation has brought security and prosperity. Your meetings and discussions with municipalities are driving decentralization and thus threaten China at its very core."

Having lived in China for so long, this was not the first time Jack had experienced people trying to make him feel guilty for America's actions. However, having a Jewish mother made him immune to any attempts at guilt mongering.

"I know what you're referring to," Jack said. "The Boxer Rebellion, where Chinese attacked western missionaries, and then slaughtered foreigners." Eight nations then sent forces to China, things escalated, which eventually culminated in the capture of Beijing. Reparations were finally paid to countries for damages, and so they would cease their ambitions of colonializing China. But the man likely knew a different version of the history, a history in which China was the victim who was taken advantage of by the more powerful western countries. There would be no point in arguing with this man. He was completely confident in what he said and believed it to his core. And why shouldn't he? He was clearly prospering. The way things were now worked for him. It was the hundreds of millions of others who had not enjoyed such prosperity that Jack was concerned for.

"What are you hoping for?" Jack asked. "What do you want from me?"

The man slipped a folded cream-colored piece of paper across the table. "Some friends and I have discussed this. We would like you to take a long vacation anywhere else but China. Starting next week. No one will know the reason—no one. You will be doing the country a great service by leaving. I know helping China is something that is important to you, and Jack, please understand—you WILL be helping China by leaving. You might not see it that way now, but trust me, in time you will. Eventually, you will understand that you made the right choice and did the right thing for this country by leaving. That's all."

This man and his friends wanted the meetings to cease, the talks of decentralization to evaporate like mist. Jack reached over and slid the piece of paper toward him. He unfolded it. Written in elegant black calligraphy: US$ 1,000,000,000.

His face remained impassive but inwardly, he ogled the amount. That was a shitload of money! A person could buy their own island with that sort of money.

"We've taken up a collection for you," the man said, "and will send it to any bank account in the world. It will come from accounts all over the globe, but it will all arrive there within twenty-four hours of your missed meeting starting this Monday. All we are asking is for you not to assist the municipalities. And offering you a token of our appreciation for doing so." The man offered him a wide smile and held his hands up. "There is nothing illegal being done here."

"See, now, that's interesting, because usually when someone says something like that, that's exactly what's happening."

"How is this illegal? We are making a simple request, from a man who has clearly shown how deeply he cares about this nation. If your intentions for China are true, and you want what is best for this country, then you will leave."

Now that the money had been offered, everything was business. The decentralization of planning meant provinces would have more control and many decisions would be made at that level. Those in positions close to the central government would be minimalized. Contracts would be lost. That's what had to be driving this, Jack thought: the decentralizing plans brought greater accountability. These people also wanted to see Wang gone, so they could continue to really take advantage of a centralized system.

If that was the case, then one billion US dollars really wasn't that much, in the grand scheme of things.

Jack folded the thick piece of paper and put it inside his jacket pocket. "Thank you for speaking with me today," he said. "Of course, when it comes to matters of money, I never make decisions immediately. That's not a wise negotiation tactic. How do I get in touch with you with a response?"

The man's earnest smile wavered momentarily. "Jack, this is our best and final offer. There will be no negotiation. Just send a message through David's uncle by Sunday evening. He knows how to reach me."

Both stood and shook hands. Jack left his untouched latte and quiche on the table and left. He tried to come up with a law that was being broken, other than that subverting economic development threatened national security. Surely that had to be a crime, never mind the fact that he disagreed with the entire premise the man had put forth. They also knew Wang was his father-in-law, yet they must have assumed one billion dollars would be enough for anyone to turn on a family member.

But he did like the guy's style and his relaxed, confident demeanor. And, Jack thought, *his offer was a good one.* He did not for a moment think that offer was false; concern about what this project could turn the country into was huge amongst some, and they were willing to put up significant money to thwart any forward progress. To keep things exactly the same: those with the connections and in positions of power lived lavishly. It was understandable they would not want to relinquish that, but it was Jack's hope that is exactly what would happen.

"That was not entirely what I was expecting," Jack said to Davis as they climbed into the black SUV to head to the airport.

"Doesn't sound like you'll be winning any popularity contests with that guy's group of friends," Davis said.

Jack pulled his black phone out of his pocket and sent a text to Cooper: *Did you get all that?*

Cooper's reply was almost instantaneous: *Yes, we did.*

Can you please forward the audio confidentially to President Wang, eyes only. Unless I hear from anyone to contrary, I'll decline the offer.

Cooper replied that the audio would be sent immediately. Jack knew they probably had people already looking in to see if they could find out who the person was. Jack had no intention of stepping away from the project, but he also had to consider the ramifications of declining their offer. This was their first attempt, and it was a good one. In their minds, they could not offer a better deal because they likely assumed both sides were getting what they wanted: Jack would receive a billion dollars to fund whatever sort of lifestyle he chose, while they would be able to continue to utilize China as an endless treasure chest to which only a certain few had the ability to access.

And, the man was clear: there would be no negotiating and no other offers. The next step would likely be something far less pleasant for Jack, and could involve his family members. He wasn't concerned about his father or his brother in Sedona, but he had Jojo to think of, and their baby. He couldn't put them in danger, and they would certainly be the next targets for anyone who was trying to get a message through to him.

"That guy in there offered me one billion dollars to leave this project," he told Davis.

Davis caught Jack's eye in the rearview mirror. "US?"

Jack nodded. "Mmm-hmm."

Davis let out a low whistle. "Damn," he said softly.

"I'll be telling them no. I just wanted you to know in case there are any security ramifications. Cooper has the audio which he's going to forward to President Wang."

"A billion dollars if you leave," Davis mused. "I bet they'll also pay someone one hundred million dollars to kill you if you refuse this offer. I'd consider taking the money, Jack. That'd save everyone a lot of trouble."

Davis had resumed looking at the road in front of him, so all Jack could see in the rearview mirror was an eyebrow and his right eye. Yet Jack could hear in Davis's voice that his tone was serious; he wasn't joking.

"It's not bad advice," Jack said. There was certainly a significant element of truth to what Davis said. "I'm going to wait to hear back from Wang and Cooper before rushing into anything."

"Understood," Davis said. "But I'd still think about taking it. There's other people's safety to consider, too, Jack."

"I know," Jack said, thinking about Jojo, who had no idea what had just transpired. What would her reaction be? She'd want him to take the money and be done with this whole thing. What wife wouldn't want that? There seemed to be two irreconcilable feelings channeling through him: He had to do whatever was necessary to make sure his pregnant wife was safe, but he also could not imagine being chased off like this. It seemed an impossible position and he did not want to regret the decision he would make.

Davis drove them to Hongqiao, Shanghai's smaller international airport, and around back, right up to the plane. They would be flying to Chongqing in Sichuan Province. The city was the largest in China, and located right in the middle, which made Jack always think of it like Chicago. It was an industrial city with massive and diverse logistics infrastructure.

Jack sat by himself on the plane, reviewing the five-page briefing. He could hear Susan and Jason discussing something quietly. His interactions with David had been normal; if David had been hoping Jack might elaborate about the nature of the meeting, he did not show it.

He made it through the first page of the document before setting it aside. He just wasn't in the right mindset to review this now; his eyes kept rereading the same sentence over and over. He was tired. His mind was trying to work out what the next step should be—what would be the *right* thing to do, but also what would be the *safe* thing to do. Such things did not often align perfectly. Being away from Jojo and traveling all over to meet with the various municipalities was exhausting enough. Now he feared that no matter what he did, it would be wrong. He would see what Wang and Cooper had to say. Then he'd make a decision. Or should he talk to Jojo? He didn't want to cause her additional stress. But he also didn't want it to seem like he was withholding information from her.

It was more important, he decided, not to stress her out needlessly. Jack sighed and let his eyes close. He'd have to make a decision soon enough, and suffer whatever consequences came of it.

Jack awoke some time later to his black phone beeping. *Wi-fi in the sky*, he thought as he reached for the phone. *There is no escape.*

The text from Cooper read: *You should accept the offer. We will be prepared to trace funds origin. Then you resume meetings the following week. Suggest you visit your dad in Cabo for a few days. Don't worry Jack, we got this.*

Jack read the message again before putting the phone down. The plan made sense. He hoped they would be able to catch them, because if not, Jack was at risk. Jojo and Wang were at risk. And the attack would certainly be far more sophisticated than a drone.

* * *

The plane landed in Chongqing and taxied toward the terminal. There was the sounds of rustling and motion as everyone stood and gathered their things, before moving to the front of the plane to get off. Jack stood up but made no motion to get his stuff.

"So, I need to tell everyone something," he said. "Before you guys leave. A family emergency came up and I need to leave immediately to go be with my father. Sorry to just drop you off like this." Jack looked at David's face as he spoke; David looked as confused as Susan and Jason about this sudden change in plans. "Consider this a well-deserved break, and I'll contact you as soon as I have news."

"I hope everything is okay," Susan said. "We'll be waiting to hear from you."

"Thank you, Susan. I'll be in touch as soon as I can."

Jack hated lying to them, though he supposed it wasn't entirely a lie; he was going to be with his father, after all. He just had to withhold certain information until he himself knew more. He also didn't want to do anything to put his assistants at risk, either. All that would be required was a call to Wang's office and their flights back home would be arranged—his assistants would be just fine.

They exited and the door closed. The plane sat on the tarmac for thirty minutes while they refueled and filed a new flight plan. Then, it was back in the air.

Davis sat down next to Jack. "It's been a long time since you saw your dad," he said. "This could be a good respite for you, too. And hey, maybe you'll reconsider just taking the money and enjoying your life."

"I think it's your turn to go fishing," Jack said. "You'll love it. I'm probably going to spend most of my time figuring out how to present this situa- tion so Jojo isn't mad at me. Which is probably impossible."

"Then let's focus on what should be more easily obtainable: Can we find the best taco in Cabo?"

Whether he was asking as a joke to try to make he feel better or because he really did want to try the best taco in Cabo, Jack appreciated that Davis was here with him.

It was Jojo that Jack was concerned about, mainly how she would react with the latest developments. Did she have to know? There was a part of him that wanted to retain that bit of information, that there were people out there willing to put forth significant sums of money to see him gone. She wouldn't want to hear it. She'd rightly insist that he stop, that he put the safety of her, their baby, at the top of his priorities. And she wouldn't be wrong, he knew, which was probably why he hadn't talked with her yet. They'd traded some messages via WeChat but Jojo sounded like she was having an excellent time and was very busy with the family and friends she hadn't seen in years, and Jack didn't want to be the one to put a damper on that. There was a part of him that felt he was doing the wrong thing, that he was keeping something from her, but it was not like he was out seeing other women or otherwise trying to stray from their marriage.

His black phone beeped. He pulled it out of his pocket and read the message from Cooper.

> We set up an account for you in Luxembourg. Provide this bank account information to the contact:
>
> Name: Jack Gold
> Bank: Deutsche Bank Luxembourg S.A.
> Account: 873876987398765
> SWIFT: DEUTLULL

Jack took out his other phone and opened WeChat to David's contact and sent him a message: Please get word to your uncle's friend that I accept the offer. Also, please provide him this information. He attached the details for the new Luxembourg bank account and then put the phone down.

It was done.

So many things of significance, with potentially massive ramifications, had occurred in such a short period of time. He would talk to Jojo once he got to Cabo, and maybe he'd even know what to say. He reclined his seat and closed his eyes.

CHAPTER 16

He woke up famished, bright sunlight from the plane's window shining on his face. It had been more polluted in Shanghai than he had thought.

Veronica, the flight attendant, came over a few minutes later with an Americano and placed the drink down on the desk next to Jack.

"Ah," he said. "You're a genius."

"Would you like something to eat?"

"Sure. Why don't you surprise me."

Veronica smiled. "Certainly."

Jack pushed the button on his seat to raise the back and then took a tentative sip of the Americano, the temperature right where he liked it.

"We've got five hours to San Diego to refuel," Davis said. "Then it's another two hours to Cabo. We like to refuel there since the fuel for this plane is less reliable than in Cabo. Does your dad know you're visiting?"

"No, not yet. I guess I should tell him."

Davis gave him a wry smile. "Yeah, you probably should."

Jack took another sip of his coffee and then took his iPhone from his pocket.

"Hi, Dad," he said when his father answered.

"Jack—good to hear from you. How are things going?" his dad asked.

"Things are okay," Jack said. "What are you doing today?"

"Right now? Well, it's raining here so I'm staying in and doing some reading. What about you?"

Jack paused. "Actually," he said, "I'm on a flight. On my way to see you. And I'll be there in about seven hours."

If his dad was surprised to hear this, he did not let on. "Okay," he said. "Do you need a lift from the airport?"

"No, I'm all set with that. I just wanted to give you a head's up that I'm coming. I know how short notice this is, so I hope I'm not inconveniencing you."

"Jack. There's always a room for you here, whenever you want. I look forward to seeing you and hearing more about what caused this sudden visit."

"Sure, Dad," Jack said with a smile. "I'll see you soon."

His spirits felt lifted somewhat, after speaking with his father. It was nice to hear that his father was looking forward to this impromptu visit— and maybe his dad would have some good advice to share, after Jack apprised him of the situation.

Veronica appeared a few minutes later, carrying a plate and silverware. She pulled out the small mahogany table that was stored in front of him and placed the plate down. There was steak, crispy hash browns with gravy, and some fresh fruit. It smelled delicious. He thanked Veronica and dug in, feeling his energy revive with each bite. By the time the plate was clear and the Americano gone, Jack felt like a new man. His whole outlook had improved, it would seem—yes, this situation he was currently in had not been anticipated and there was still the matter of how Jojo would take to it, but he no longer felt like it was an insurmountable problem.

He reached for his iPad. It connected to the Starlink wifi system, which gave him high-speed internet access even though he was still on the plane, something Jack still marveled at. He opened WeChat and selected Jojo's icon. *Something came up,* he typed, *and I am on my way to Cabo to see my dad. I'll call you later with more details. I hope you are having a good time. Please don't stress. I love you.*

Her response came right away: *What's going on? What happened?*

He would need to give her the details, but he didn't want to do it over WeChat. If someone knew someone at Tencent, the company that owned WeChat, access to their conversation could be easily obtained. He had probably already written too much.

Turn on your VPN and I'll FaceTime you, he typed. He put his earbuds in.

She texted him a minute later that the VPN was on. He found her icon on FaceTime and seconds later, there she was. He smiled just seeing her face. He missed her.

"Hello, my love," he said. "How are you? How are you feeling?"

She had a worried look on her face. "Jack," she said. "What's going on? Is everything okay?"

"I decided to visit my dad."

"Your dad? Is he all right?"

"He's fine."

"Then . . . what is going on?"

There was no way he could give her only part of the story—he told her the whole thing, about the man and the money, his discussion with Washington, and her father's agreement.

"So," he said, "I'm doing what they have suggested."

Jojo frowned. "I'm glad you're safe," she said, "but Jack, who are those people? What do they want? Are you safe?"

"I am," he said. "I don't want you to stress out. But I wanted to be forthright with you."

"Well, I'm glad you were. And I'm glad to hear you're going to stay with your dad for a little while; it'll be safer. I'm sorry, *mon chéri*. Do you have any idea when you'll be back?"

"I'm not sure. Cooper said next week, so we'll see." He had left China on Friday, which meant it would still be Friday when he arrived in Cabo. Monday, China time, was when the money should arrive. Then they'd be able to trace it. "I'm hoping things will get underway on Monday, and we'll have some more concrete answers then. I will keep you posted, *mon amour*," he added, butchering the French pronunciation.

Jojo grinned. "Best to stick to English or Chinese. I miss you, Jack. I hope you and your dad have a good time. Maybe I could even join you out there? I would love to."

"I would love that, too. Before we plan anything, though, let's wait a few days and just let things settle. This has all been kind of a whirlwind and definitely not what I thought I'd be doing right now."

"Maybe you should just come home," Jojo said, with enough of a smile to let Jack know that she was kidding. Mostly. "It'll be good for you to see your father. You deserve some relaxation right now anyways. Thank you for being upfront with me about everything; it means a lot. I know it would've been just as easy to keep quiet about it."

"I can't keep any secrets from you."

"That's good."

"I don't *want* to keep any secrets from you."

"That's even better." Jack smiled at Jojo, who he was able to talk to as if she were right here with him on the plane. They talked for a little while longer and then said goodbye. Jack promised he'd be in touch soon, and would hopefully have more information to share.

After he got off the call, he Googled "best restaurants in Cabo" and a list of fifteen places immediately popped up. Jack was surprised to see that the Waldorf Astoria had a hotel in Cabo; he checked out some of the photos of one of its restaurants, El Farallon. The restaurant was tucked into the side of a mountain, overlooking the Pacific Ocean. It looked incredibly romantic, with its intimate outdoor seating and stunning ocean view. Jojo would absolutely love it.

* * *

Two black SUVs and one sedan were there to meet them when the plane landed. Jack got into the backseat of the middle vehicle, with Davis, who sat in the front next to the driver.

"These vehicles are on loan to use from the Mexican government," Davis said.

"That was fast," Jack said.

"We flew in people from Mexico City and Los Angeles, and there are ten men and women from China who will meet up with us along the way."

Jack nodded, though really what he wanted to do was let out a low whistle. The window he looked out of was bulletproof glass. He was grateful for the professional protection and the efficiency with which everyone seemed to handle their responsibilities. Still, he couldn't help but feel bad for being such an inconvenience. It seemed a lot for one person.

As the car sped along the modern highway, Jack noticed the overcast sky. The rain had stopped, at least for now, but the pavement had still not dried and the gray clouds suggested more was to come. Usually, Cabo was dry and sunny.

About half an hour later they pulled into Jack's dad's place, a rather generic two-bedroom condo. It was prime real estate, with his backdoor literally opening to the beach, but Jack did wonder why his dad hadn't splurged on a nicer place.

The door to the condo opened and his father appeared. "Jack!" he said. "Welcome. Come on in. Grab a beer." He saw Davis and gave a little wave.

"Dad, I wanted to re-introduce Davis," Jack said, gesturing.

Davis nodded and held a hand out. "Hello, Dr. Gold," he said.

"Good to see you again, Davis. The two of you—come on in, before it starts raining again."

"I'd love to," Davis said, "but I'm not going to stay right now. There's a few things I need to see to, but you guys are secure here, don't worry about anything. Enjoy that beer."

Jack's father looked at him quizzically. "Actually," Jack said, wanting to pivot the conversation, "I was hoping that you might take Davis fishing at some point. Instead of me. I think he'd really enjoy it."

"It would be my pleasure! Davis, just let me know when you've got the availability, and we'll make it happen." His dad nodded to Jack. "This one here's not strong enough to catch some of the larger marlins swimming around these waters, but you look like you'd have no problem at all! Let's just hope this weather clears up and let's do it."

Davis grinned. "I look forward to it."

Jack said goodbye to Davis and made his way inside. He put his briefcase and luggage into his bedroom and then went out to the living room, where his dad was seated on the sofa. There were two beer bottles on the coffee table in front of him.

"Jack," his dad said. "It's good to see you but you're still in dark slacks and a tie. This is Cabo." He paused. "Mexico."

"I'll change later," Jack said. He glanced out one of the big windows and saw an expanse of sandy beach, then the ocean, right there, right in the backyard. The water was gray and the clouds above were gray. His outfit almost felt like the right choice. "Actually, I'll need to buy some more appropriate attire. All I brought was work clothes."

"Have a seat, Jack."

Jack sat in a high-backed armchair, perpendicular to his father. He sighed and tried not to feel like he was ten years old again and about to be reprimanded.

"This is a pretty sudden visit," his dad said. "It's unlike you. You always plan things well in advance."

All true. Never did Jack consider trying to pass this off as a casual visit; he would come clean, just not this very moment.

"Let's go into it tomorrow," he said. "Right now, I need you to divert my attention while I drink a few beers. Which I see are right there."

His father leaned forward and grabbed a beer, passed it to him. "That I can do. An old colleague emailed a bunch of us: Do you know why women prefer obgyns who are over the age of sixty-five?"

Jack took a long sip of the beer, which was ice cold and felt very cleansing. "No, I don't," he said. "And I have a feeling that maybe I don't want to know."

His dad held up a quivering hand, index finger crooked.

Jack groaned and closed his eyes. "No thank you!" he said. His dad laughed.

"I used to get a new joke from my nurse every time I operated. Not anymore. Now I have to rely on forwarded emails from people I haven't talked to in years."

"Surely you've got enough material to last you a while."

He finished the first beer and reached for the second, which his father held out. Jack smothered a yawn. "Here comes the jet lag," he said.

"Finish that beer and just relax," his dad said. "I want to hear about it, but tell me when you're ready."

*   *   *

Jack awoke, disoriented, in a chair he didn't know and a place he didn't remember being in—Oh, Cabo. He sat up, stretching first this way then that. His dad's condo. His father had left a pair of red swimming trunks and a white t-shirt on the coffee table for him. His dad's standard uniform.

He gathered the clothes and followed the aromas coming from the kitchen. Bacon was the most noticeable, but as he got closer he could smell the scrambled eggs and the warming tortillas. His stomach growled and his mouth began to water. Not just because of what had happened, but because of how difficult it was to get such a simple and authentic breakfast in China.

"Good morning," his father said. "You fell asleep not long after you finished that second beer and I figured you'd wake up and move to the bedroom, but you were out cold. How'd you sleep?"

"I guess you could maybe say it was the best sleep of my life," Jack said. Or was it the sight of the breakfast? "Maybe it was that Corona beer; it really does the trick."

Jack's father gave him a little smirk. "I told you that you should move back to America."

"Easier said than done. But, maybe." The fact was, he and Jojo could move anywhere they wanted. And some people would do exactly that—Jack had been compensated generously for what he had done at the Control Center, and even without this one billion dollars, he had the financial wherewithal to go anywhere. He could indeed buy an island, if he so chose, but that sort of lavish lifestyle had never had much pull for him. Sure, he enjoyed nice things and fine dining, but he couldn't imagine only living a life of leisure. It just wasn't in his DNA—He looked at his father, who was plating the eggs. Obviously.

Jack consumed the meal with gusto. There were some places in China that attempted to serve traditional American breakfast fare, but none succeeded, sadly. Not only were there zero percent foreigners in China, but the government would not let in someone who merely wanted to open such a restaurant.

His plate cleared, he took a sip of coffee. Strong, hot, and the perfect complement to his breakfast. He looked at his dad. "You'd make a great wife for somebody."

His father grinned. "Ah, my son, the wise ass. Okay, Jack, you've slept, you've been fed—tell me what's going on."

"Yeah," Jack said. "I will. How about we go for a walk?"

Such an endeavor couldn't be easier—they stepped out the sliding glass door and onto the beach; the water was about a hundred and fifty feet away. As they walked, Jack saw Secret Service agents and Chinese security, both in front, to the back, and the sides of them, though at a distance. Surely his father noticed them, but he did not say anything.

"I was helping the provinces do some planning for their regions. This was on behalf of the president of China. Anyway, someone—or several someones—wanted me stop meeting with the provinces because they don't want to see a decentralized government and they don't want China to change."

"And what did they offer you to stop? Or was it a threat? Are you in danger? Is Jojo?"

"No threats yet. They offered me a lot of money. I consulted the CIA and President Wang, and they told me to stop the meetings and accept the money. Not to keep but so they can trace it."

"How much money are we talking about?"

Jack paused. "One billion dollars."

"China dollars or US dollars?"

"US."

His father looked at him as they continued to walk down the beach. Unlike yesterday, the sun was out and there were only a few fair-weather clouds against the backdrop of a clear blue sky.

"That's an unfathomable amount of money, Jack. Wow. Those people must want you gone."

"They don't want their way of life disrupted, and things have worked out well for them. We figured if I spent some time here, after agreeing to accept the money, they would be able to trace the wire transfers and then I can return to working on the project."

"Hmm." His father frowned. "Let me make sure that I understand. You agreed to stop the meetings in exchange for money, right?" Jack nodded. "Then, you'll receive the money and resume the meetings? All the while China and America are tracking down who made the offer and sent the money?"

"More or less," Jack said. "Except I won't be keeping the money."

"Shit, Jack. One billion dollars isn't a lot of money to some of these people. But if you take their money and they don't get what they thought they were going to, they'll be seriously pissed off. Whoever it is."

"I guess this means we need to switch from beer to whiskey tonight," Jack said, wanting to lighten the mood.

"This is not a good situation," his father said. "What support do you have if anything goes wrong?"

"I have support," Jack said.

"You sound very confident."

"In that regard, I am. Both the US and China are taking this seriously." Jack nodded ahead of them. "Look down there. Behind us. And to both sides." His father did, discreetly.

"Jesus," he said. "They're everywhere. Americans *and* Chinese. They really are taking this seriously."

"Well, I guess I am technically an American *and* Chinese diplomat. Wang gave me a Chinese diplomatic passport."

His father let out a low whistle. "Wow."

"He thought it would help me with my meetings. And he was right—it's proven useful."

"So, how are you going to get out of this situation, then?"

"I'm going to wait and see what happens over the next few days. I'm certainly not going to do anything rash." He paused. "Maybe I'll do one thing."

"Like what?"

"I have this problem, you see. I haven't used any of my credit cards in the last year. I have over fifty million dollars of my own money just sitting around."

"That's quite the problem."

"So I think I'd like to take my father out to an extravagant dinner and get drunk silly with him. Do you think you could help me out with that?"

There was, of course, the chance his father might decline—he rarely ate out and despised lavish spending. But he gave Jack a wry smile and nodded. "Given these dire circumstances you're facing, I'm willing to help you out."

Jack grinned. "Thanks, Dad. I knew I could count on you."

*   *   *

To get to El Farallon, they drove through a privately-owned nine-hundred-foot tunnel. After parking, they walked to the restaurant, tucked into the cliffs. Jack and his father both worse jeans and a t-shirt, which was indeed acceptable attire for the best restaurant in Cabo.

They sat at a small table, both their chairs facing the Pacific Ocean. For the first drink of the evening, Jack ordered a double margarita and his dad got a double Chivas Regal whiskey.

The menu, understandably, was dominated by seafood, boasting the freshest catches from local fish mongers. They ordered the long-leg crab appetizer and the surf and turf with mixed vegetables. The appetizer arrived, the crab shell-less, with a separate bowl of melted butter, garlic, and salt and pepper.

"You know," Jack's father said, "when I don't look at the prices, this menu seems quite nice."

"And they know how to make a good margarita," Jack said, and then took another sip of his drink.

"You should have told me we'd be overlooking the ocean," his dad said. "We could have brought a rod and reel to catch some Rock Cod while eating! The water down there looks deep enough."

Jack laughed. "Leave it to you to think about fishing while you're sitting at a fine dining establishment."

Two agents walked by their table just then, one American, one Chinese. They wore suits and the bulge of the side firearm both wore was visible.

"I still can't get over you've got all these agents following you," his dad said. "I feel like I should keep my voice down. Are they overseeing the cooking of the food?"

Jack winced. "Probably," he said.

"You're taking this all very casually, Jack." His father took a sip of his drink and eyed him. Jack couldn't tell if this last statement was to be complimentary or critical.

He took a sip of his own drink and let his gaze drift out toward the stunning ocean view, dotted here and there by boats, though two were distinctive to Jack: a small fishing boat and then another slightly larger boat, both stationary, both with three people each on board, wearing black bulletproof vests, observing the area to ensure his safety.

"I'm grateful that everyone is being attentive," he said. "And that they seem to take this seriously. Though I admit—it does make me uncomfortable that all of this is happening because, well, because of me. A lot of people and resources are being utilized."

"This is pretty serious," his father said. "Am I in danger?"

"No more than I am. Let's have another drink."

They ordered another round when their waiter delivered their entrees. "I don't think we're in too much danger at this very moment," Jack said. "Because as far as those people who wanted me gone are concerned—I'm gone. I'm not in China and I've told them I've accepted their offer." Jack inhaled the tantalizing aroma from his plate. His father was already digging in, cutting into his steak not as if he were a surgeon, but more like a seasoned fisherman. He took his first bite as Jack cut into his own steak.

His father let out a contended sigh. "They sure don't sell steak like this at Costco."

They had both ordered their steaks medium rare, knowing that cooked any more would kill the meat's flavor. Jack's steak was cooked perfectly, the meat so tender he could almost cut it with the side of his fork.

"Let's have a different conversation with our meal," Jack said. "Tell me a good fishing story." He realized, suddenly, that this was the first time they had gone out to dinner with each other as adults. In a way, he felt like he was getting to know his father anew. It was a nice feeling.

His father told him a few stories, not so much about himself, because his dad never liked talking about himself, but about some of his fishing buddies. There were a number of them, their names blending, their personalities and character traits blurring into a single group, these people that Jack did not know but who his father saw on a regular basis. In a way, Jack thought, these men probably knew his father better than he did.

After their entrees were cleared, Jack asked if his father wanted dessert.

"I don't think so," his dad said. "As it happens, dessert does not go well with whiskey. There is only one thing that goes well with whiskey."

"And what would that be?"

"More whiskey."

More whiskey was ordered, and then it was Jack's turn to regale his father with some stories of China. The drinks kept coming, the stories kept flowing, and by the time the evening was over, Jack was more intoxicated than he'd been in a long time. He was vaguely aware of how amused Davis seemed to find his inebriated state, though really, Jack was just grateful that it was Davis who had driven them there—neither he or his father were in any condition to drive.

He nearly fell out of the car when Davis dropped them back at the condo. "Stay safe tonight, Davis," Jack said, with only a little bit of a slur.

"Yeah, Davis, stay safe," Jack's father said, also with his own bit of slur. "We're on for tomorrow for fishing. Not too early, though, I think."

Davis grinned. "No, not too early I wouldn't think either," he said. "You guys going to make it inside okay?"

"We got this," Jack said. He clapped Davis once on the shoulder. "And I would just like to thank you for being so good at your job. You really are. Thank you."

"Now Jack, you're going to make me blush," Davis said. "You two have a good night. Dr. Gold, I'm looking forward to fishing tomorrow. Not too early."

They stumbled away from the SUV, toward the condo, and somehow made it inside, both still upright.

"I better get to bed," Jack said. The room tilted. He reached out and grasped the counter, steadying himself.

"One more drink," his dad said, going over to the cupboard to get two glasses. He poured a double shot of whiskey into each one. "This is to help you sleep."

Jack took the glass. Right as it touched his lips, his black cell phone beeped. He paused, then threw the drink back before retrieving the phone from his pocket.

Jack, the message read, your cell number was used to create your bank account. It needs to be used to authenticate and register your online account. Can you please log in and then send us your username and password? Then we can access the account details.

"Shit," Jack said. The words on the screen blurred as he tried to re-read the message.

"What?" his dad asked.

"Nothing. I should take care of this, though. I had a good time tonight, Dad. Thanks for letting me take you out."

"It was great, Jack. Thank you."

He made it to his room and took his laptop out and turned on his VPN. Then, he went to the Deutsche Bank Luxembourg website to set up his online access. He input his name and account number with his birthdate and telephone number. Instantly, a code came to his phone, which he entered, and was then prompted to input a username. He typed: *Jack_Gold*.

He squinted, reading the username again to make sure it was right. The letters were blurry. With significant concentration, he typed in a password: *Margaritas4All!*

The registration was complete. He sent a message from his black phone with his username and password.

Jack closed the computer, eager to get into bed. His phone beeped. Had he not entered something in correctly?

Thanks, Jack, I just won $200! read the message from Cooper. *Turns out I'm the only one who thinks you could register after so many drinks.*

* * *

Jack woke up parched. His mouth felt like it was full of sand and his tongue had the texture of a leather strap. Opening his eyes let in a stunningly painful light and his whole head throbbed painfully. Tequila hangovers were the worst.

In the kitchen, he guzzled a glass of water and then looked in the fridge and found a Diet Coke. Everything around him was quiet; his father was out but hadn't left a note. Jack guessed he had already gone fishing—nothing could stop that man from getting out on the water. Jack hoped Davis was having a good time.

Jack sipped the Diet Coke as he went back to his room and climbed into bed. He felt marginally better now that he'd had some water, and the Diet Coke would prevent any caffeine headaches from trying to crash the party.

He awoke a few hours later, got up, got some more water. He reread the messages from last night, barely remembering sending them. That they could all joke and start a betting pool over whether or not he'd register correctly made Jack feel reassured—it would seem they were not terribly worried about the situation. It was Sunday in Cabo; China was sixteen hours ahead. It would be Monday morning in China in about eight hours.

Jack put on his red shorts and white shirt and walked outside. The sand was warm underneath his feet, between his toes. The sun seemed less malevolent now than it had when he first awoke this morning, and the ocean looked like an undulating turquoise gem. He took a deep breath, smelled the salt air, heard the gulls squawking overhead.

The tide was going out, so Jack walked down to a flat area of shore, where the sand was still damp and very compact. He began with jumping jacks, then stretching. From there, he progressed through a series of warm-up exercises and then he did over two hundred different types of punches and kicks, followed by a series of quick kick drills.

He spent about an hour on the beach, doing his workout, and by the time he was done, his shirt was soaked with sweat, his body felt invigorated, and all the fog and fuzz in his brain had cleared. He jogged back to the condo, knowing his appetite would be showing up soon.

His dad's freezer was packed with fish he'd caught. Jack chose a swordfish filet and ran some water in the sink and put the filet in there to thaw while he took a shower.

Ever since Jack was young, he judiciously took liberty with his dad's clothes. Now, freshly scrubbed and clean and in a pair of jeans, he entered the walk-in closet and saw the white and blue button-up shirts that his father used to wear when he was a doctor seeing patients. They were of the highest quality cotton. Jack grabbed one of the shirts and put it on.

Back in the kitchen, he got to work. He cooked the swordfish filet over high heat, in garlic and oil, seasoned generously with salt and pepper. He made scrambled eggs and heated up some tortillas. Once his plate had been assembled, he added a spoonful of salsa fresca and took his meal outside to enjoy.

The food was only halfway gone when he looked down the beach and saw his dad and Davis approaching, both with big smiles on their faces.

"We were wondering if you'd be up," his dad said.

"I managed," Jack said. "Somehow."

"Well, you missed a great morning. Davis here demolished one of the biggest marlins I've seen in a long time."

"Jack, it was amazing," Davis said. Jack could hear an enthrallment in Davis's voice. "It jumped three or four times. We got some great pictures. Your dad is an amazing fisherman."

"That he is," Jack said. "But it sounds like you're not so bad yourself, Davis."

Jack's father looked more closely at him. "I'm just now noticing you're eating my swordfish and wearing my most expensive shirt!"

"What can I say, it's nice to be home," Jack said with a smile. "Can I make some for you and Davis?"

"Yes." Jack's father and Davis said this almost simultaneously.

Twenty-five minutes later, Jack was plating two additional plates of tortillas with swordfish, eggs, and salsa fresca.

"Wow," his dad said after taking his first bite. "Jack, where did you learn to cook like this?"

"I used some Asian cooking secrets," Jack said. Though the reality was, he was not afraid of seasoning, which is something his dad seemed to shy away from in his own cooking.

"I'm impressed," Davis said. "I don't think I've ever tried your cooking, Jack—it's delicious. Probably the best fish I've ever eaten."

Jack glanced at his watch. In three hours, it would be nine am in China. Except Luxembourg was seven hours behind China, so nothing would happen until they opened. These different times zones were giving him a headache. There was also the fact that not all wire transfers went directly through SWIFT, the gold standard for safely facilitating global wire transfers. Some would have to go through intermediary banks. Since they were likely coming from non-US accounts, there shouldn't be any delays due to fraud or terrorist warnings. Jack shook his head, trying to clear the thoughts. It didn't make sense to think about it now, because no amount of thought was going to make things happen any faster. Better to just relax and wait until tomorrow.

"Let me see those pictures," Jack said, taking a seat at the table with his father and Davis.

"Here you go," Davis said, handing Jack his phone. There were dozens of photos, including the ones of the fish jumping out of the water. It was a big fish.

"Let me see your hands," Jack said.

Davis looked at him quizzically. "What?"

"Your hands."

Davis put his fork down and held both hands up. Reeling in a fish of that size would have left Jack's hands shredded and bleeding, but Davis's palms were only a little more red than normal.

"Nice hands," Jack said. "I pity that fish."

Davis grinned and went back to eating. "It put up a good fight. Really makes you respect that survival instinct."

Jack had known Davis for over a year now and could not recall ever seeing him this happy. Granted, most of the situations they'd been in together were not occasions for fun and celebration, but Jack was grateful that Davis got to have this experience. He exuded the energy of a young kid, that pure excitement and enthusiasm for a new experience.

"Your dad sold the fish to some guys at the dock in return for some fish and cash," Davis said. "Then he gave the money to the two deckhands." He glanced at Jack's father. "That was very nice of you, Dr. Gold."

Jack did the dishes after everyone was done eating, which was something he knew his father would appreciate. By the time he was done, the kitchen was clean; perhaps not as clean as an operating room, but close.

Davis left not long after that. "He's a good man," Jack's father said. "Tough as nails but thinks so highly of you. You're very lucky to have someone like that around you, Jack. It was an honor fishing with him today."

Jack's father had always had excellent instincts about his friends, though in the past, Jack hadn't always heeded that advice. In high school Jack's dad had told Jack to get rid of one of his friends because he wasn't the sort of person Jack thought he was. But how could his father know this after only having interacted with his friend that one time he'd come over? Jack had disagreed with his father's assessment, yet weeks later, would catch this friend trying to steal his stereo.

The rest of the afternoon they relaxed, had a few beers, read. Jack's father had suggested *Eye of the Needle* by Ken Follett. "You'll like it," his father said. They sat quietly but in each other's company, and though they weren't doing anything that special, Jack felt it was exactly what he needed.

*   *   *

Jack woke up the next morning, no hangover. It was Tuesday, a little after eight in the morning, which meant the business day in both Asia and Europe was over. He sat up and grabbed his laptop and logged into his Luxembourg account. At the top of the page, the balance was listed: US$ 1,000,000,001.26.

He couldn't help but feel like a kid on Christmas morning, even though he wasn't going to keep this money. Never did he think he'd see his name and an account with that many zeros after it. And the thing was—for the people who had wired the money, this was like pocket change. He reached for his black phone and texted Cooper. *I noticed there is some extra money in my account. Any update?*

We're working on it, Cooper replied. *It may take some time to trace the wire transfers. Maybe a few days. Will be in touch ASAP.*

Jack went out and said good morning to his father, who was sitting at the table, drinking a cup of coffee. Jack poured himself a cup and sat down next to his father.

"How are things looking, Jack? Any updates?"

"Well, the money's there."

His dad looked up from the newspaper in front of him. "All of it?"

"All of it, plus a dollar twenty-six tip. They're tracing the origin of the transfers now. But Cooper said it could take a few days."

"Wow. That's really all I can think of to say, Jack. That's a hell of a lot of money." He let out a low whistle.

"I know. It was a surprise to see, associated with my name, even though I knew it was coming. And that it's not really mine."

"Why the hell not? You ever consider keeping it? Just doing what they wanted? You'd be set for life, Jack. You and Jojo could go anywhere you wanted. Live whatever kind of life suited your fancy. And—best of all—you wouldn't be in danger. Sounds worth it to me."

"Are you telling me that's what you think I should do? That means just giving up. Not seeing it through to completion. Allowing others to get their way, because they had the money to buy me out."

"I'm asking you if that was ever a consideration."

It was tempting, of course. What American had not, at one point, wondered what they'd do with their life if money were no concern?

"Not really," Jack said finally. "Jojo and I already have all the money we need. I realize how fortunate we are. And, I didn't get involve with this because of money. That's not what this is about. If I took that money, I'd be no better than anyone else who is enriching themselves at the expense of others. I can't do it." He didn't add that he simply could not fathom stopping something he'd started before it had been completed. Just like his father. His father had been the one to instill that in him, both through words and actions.

"There's no shame in being a man with morals," his father said. "It's getting to be a rarer and rarer thing these days, I'm afraid. I'm proud of you, Jack. I just don't want to see you get yourself in a dangerous situation. Anyway. Since you don't have any plans to head back to China today, what would you like to do?"

"I was thinking I might take that book you recommended and visit the pool. I'll probably workout this afternoon."

"Sounds good. Tonight, I'll take you out to dinner. I need to pick up a pump for the boat and there's a place nearby."

"Great," Jack said, trying to hide his surprise that his father was offering to take him out to dinner. Though of course there was an errand tied to the outing.

Down at the condo compound's pool, Jack picked one of the lounge chairs with an attached umbrella. It was still early and he was the only one there. He stretched out on the chair and reached for his book. His iPhone beeped.

Jack was surprised to see that it was a text from his Israeli friend, Ari. It had been Ari he had entered the Control Center Building in Beijing with. It was because of Ari that he'd gotten involved with all of this in the first place. Ari was more than a friend, really—he was a brother.

Jack, his message read, *I hope you are someplace safe.*

Jack turned on his VPN and selected an IP in Singapore before replying. *Actually, I'm relaxing in the sun, about to read a book. How are you?*

I'm fine. Things are heating up. Just wanted to let you know that I have your back. More later.

Jack frowned. What was Ari talking about? *Thanks, Ari,* he wrote. *Not sure what you're referring to, but you're my brother and I trust you.*

I'll keep you posted when I can.

Jack put his phone down, puzzled. He assumed this must have *something* to do with his current situation, but what could Ari or Israel have to do with it?

He could puzzle over it all morning, if he chose, and not come up with any answers, so he opened his book and tried to settle back into the story. But reading about a German spy was not the sort of story he wanted right now, so he set the book aside and began swimming laps in the pool.

Twenty-five laps later, he got out and returned to his lounge chair. He stretched out, let his eyes close, and fell asleep.

When he awoke, about an hour had passed. A few of the chairs were now occupied. Jack stretched and then grabbed his book and started to walk back to the condo. Davis was waiting outside for him.

"Jack," he said. "We want you and your dad to stay around here for a while. We can bring you whatever you need."

"Why? What's up?"

"Cooper and others have been pursuing lots of leads. Word is likely getting around about the US government being involved. Cabo has lots of people from many different places. It's hard to track them all, and they may know that you're here."

Jack nodded. "Okay," he said. "I'll let my dad know."

"And, like I said, whatever you need, just let us know."

Back inside, Jack's black phone beeped. He looked at it, eager for any new information that might shed some light onto whatever was happening. *Is this a picture of the man you met with, who offered you the $1bn?*

The photo was most certainly of that same man, with his tanned, smooth features, the easygoing expression on his face.

Yes, Jack replied.

Are you sure?

100%

This was good. They had discovered the man's identity, which was a start. Jack found his father in the living room, reading the *New England Journal of Medicine.* In a way, he was surprised that his father still kept up on the latest medical advances, now that he was retired, but then Jack realized that his father was the sort of person whose inquisitiveness and pursuit of knowledge would not stop just because he was no longer working.

"So, I ran into Davis on my way back," Jack said hesitantly. He wasn't sure how his father would take such news. "He told me that we should stay here for the time being. If we need anything, we just let him know. I guess that means going out to dinner tonight isn't going to happen."

His father put the journal down on his lap. "I see," he said. "I'm sure it's warranted. We'll manage. Do you remember how to play cribbage?"

"I remember all the money you lost to me every time I skunked you."

"Jack, I think you're misremembering, it was the other way around. We'll play later. Bring your checkbook. Money transfers are also accepted."

Jack laughed. He had good memories of playing cribbage with his father. It hadn't happened often; his dad had a grueling work schedule most of Jack's childhood, but the family would always take an annual vacation, and it was during these trips—be it in a tropical island or a Swiss chalet in Aspen—Jack would play cribbage with his father. Jack's brother had little interest in the game, but Jack loved it, and he was good at it. He clearly remembered both his surprise and triumph the first time he beat his father, though he always wondered if his father was letting him win. But he didn't think so, because his dad just wasn't that kind of parent, or man. It's not how he did things.

Jack decided to go to the beach to do his workout again and his father joined him. They were shadowed by security as they headed down toward the shore, to the same spot Jack had previously been in. His father sat in the sand, occasionally looking over at Jack, mostly gazing out at the ocean.

When he was finished with his workout, he sat next to his father, who was still looking out toward the horizon, one hand shielding his eyes from the sun. "I can see some whales out there," he said.

Jack squinted, tried to see what his father had, but just saw the expanse of ocean that seemed to stretch forever. "That's impressive," he said. "I didn't know you'd be able to get a good view of a whale from here."

"It's an art," his father said lightly. "And it's also a good workout," he added with a wry grin.

* * *

Jack spent the next two days reading, working out on the beach, and playing cribbage. He talked with Jojo and afterward, was struck with an overwhelming feeling of cabin fever and homesickness. The waiting was hard, and the restriction on his movement was even harder, despite the fact that he was essentially in paradise.

On the third day, Jack's black phone beeped. He read the message immediately. *We got him. All is clear. You can come back whenever you'd like.*

It was exactly what he wanted to hear, yet now that the message was right before his eyes, he was having trouble believing it. *Provide details, please,* he wrote back.

But the next incoming message was not from Cooper; it came from his iPhone. It was a voice message from Ari. "*We got him, brother. We finally got him. That guy you met with was Chinese and Iranian. He was working with Iran and they wanted China to revert to Communism so they could sell oil again to China. We had wanted to take the guy out for many years, but the US kept saying no. Finally, Israel got the green light after hearing what they were trying to do with you, and China. He was in Tehran when executed.*" There was a pause, and when Ari's voice came back, it was at a much lower decibel. "*Mossad got him. This is a great day. You should be all good now.*"

The message ended. Jack sat back on the couch, stunned. His father, who was seated in his easy chair with his book, seemed to sense that something had happened and was looking over at him.

"Everything all right, Jack?"

"Yeah," Jack said slowly, his brain still trying to process this new information. With all the knowledge, expertise, and contacts that China and the US had, it was Israel's covert operations and counterterrorism unit, Mossad, that had killed the man in Tehran. Iran would not influence

China's development and not be able to sell oil to China; nor would they be able to take profits and fund terrorism. Ari was right—it *was* a good day.

His black phone beeped. *What Ari said is correct,* read Cooper's message. *He communicates faster than we do. Feel free to return to China. Nothing will be reported in the press.*

And just like that—life could resume. It would be like this never happened. "They got the guy," Jack told his father. "Normal life can resume."

He filled his father in with what Ari had told him.

"Real life truly is stranger than fiction," his dad said. "And, I used to think anyone with two phones was an asshole. I've now modified my opinion. You did good, Jack."

"Me? I didn't do anything."

"Sure you did. If you hadn't agreed to meet with the man; if you hadn't said you'd take the money (even though you weren't ultimately going to keep it); if you hadn't gotten out of town—all these things directly resulted in essentially stopping a coup. You did that. My son. I'm proud of you, Jack!"

Jack had never heard his father speak so glowingly about him before. And that, maybe, was the best feeling of all.

*   *   *

The next morning and it was time to go. Jack changed into his slacks and one of his dad's button-up shirts. It was too warm to wear a jacket, so he left that in his luggage.

When he stepped outside of the condo, his father was standing by the SUV, chatting with Davis.

"Sorry that you have to take off, Jack, but I'm so glad you were able to come out. Now you need to get done with everything and get back to Jojo."

"I know," Jack said. "And I will. She was actually hoping to come out here, so we'll try to do that soon, Dad. Despite the circumstances, this was great. Thank you."

"You don't have to keep thanking me. You're my son—you always have a home here. No matter what sort of situation you get yourself in." His father shot a look at Davis. "This one really knows how to get himself into some situations, doesn't he?"

Davis grinned. "That's putting it mildly."

"But I rest easy knowing he's got you watching his back," Jack's father said, extending his hand to Davis.

"Dr. Gold, it was an honor and a pleasure to go fishing with you. An experience I'll never forget."

"Don't let it be your first and only time, Davis. You're a natural out there on the water. Just say the word and we'll go back out on the boat."

Jack knew his father would conclude their visit with a similar handshake, so Jack instead put his briefcase down and gave his father a hug. Though his father was not the hugging type, he returned the gesture, and that was as good a conclusion to his visit as Jack could hope for.

"Bye, Dad," he said. "I'll talk you soon."

He climbed into the SUV, and the security vehicles in the front and back of them formed a convoy to the airport. Time to get back to work.

CHAPTER 17

Jack flew directly back to Chongqing, where he had left off. He checked into his room and then met his three assistants in the lobby lounge downstairs.

"I hope everyone had a nice break," Jack said as he sat down at the table with them. "We have lots of work ahead of us and it'll be non-stop. I know you guys are up for the challenge."

"Is everything okay with your father?" Susan asked.

"Yes, everything is good," Jack said. "Thanks for asking." And everything now, he hoped, was okay; he'd spoken to Wang about keeping David on the team, which Jack had decided to do, after considering David's role, which was negligible, beyond having an uncle who had some questionable associates. "We've looked into the rest of his family," Wang had told him. "I'm told there is no risk, no concerning affiliations. But if you don't feel you have confidence in David's abilities, then just say the word."

Jack glanced over the five-page write up again. "Who has some ideas for tomorrow's meeting?"

No one answered. Jack looked down again at the five-page write-up and felt a little bit overwhelmed. He hadn't been to Chongqing in a long time. Chongqing had a massive population of over thirty million, double the size of Los Angeles. Just looking at their rapid transit system gave Jack a headache. Like other major cities in China, everything revolved around eating, shopping, and working. It was the working Jack focused on.

He reminded himself to simplify things. This always worked. He needed to focus on two things: how to increase revenues or decrease costs. Focus on the high potential big-ticket items to zero in on opportunities. This had worked in the past and forced Jack to quickly identify good potential initiatives.

During China's civil war, much of its industrial production moved to Chongqing. Some military production was moved there in the 1960s and 70s. Today, the city represented a substantial source of manufacturing, ranging from iron, coal, steel, strontium carbonate as well as other advanced materials. It was not just a major manufacturing center, but also a transportation hub and financial center for the region. A good way to think of the city, Jack thought, was like Chicago on steroids.

China's central government was investing heavily to help build new towns, business enterprises, communications and transportation infrastructure. It was like having your dad pay your rent after you graduated from college. Chongqing had grown up and now needed to take care of itself. And, there were a bunch of avenues Jack could now see that could help make the city not just a center for the region, but one for the world. They needed to think bigger, though that was hard to imagine, given the size of the city.

Those living in Chongqing were practical hard-working people. Not arrogant like in Shanghai. After the war with Japan, people had flocked to Chongqing. Much like during America's industrial revolution, all the people were willing and eager to work hard. They could do it. They could bring the city to the next level with the proper assistance and encouragement.

Jack prepared himself for the meeting. They would not speak English, instead they would speak Mandarin with a strong accent. He could handle that.

* * *

Over the next several weeks, they traveled to other cities and provinces, meeting with the officials and hearing their presentations. Though he'd lived in China for many years, Jack felt he was coming to a deeper understanding now of the differences between the people in each region.

Their extensive travel helped paint a clearer picture of China overall. The typical American was likely to think any Asian person was Chinese, and it would certainly come as a very big surprise that within China, there was significant diversity of people, cultures, and languages. It was beyond anything he had ever conceived. Those from Northern China spoke Mandarin and were generally taller, with a slightly longer-shaped face, as compared to those in Guangdong who were shorter, had rounder faces, and spoke Cantonese. There were around two hundred distinct dialects and fifty-five nationally recognized ethnic groups, unbeknownst to most of the world. America's diversity was right there in your face—you didn't need to look far to find it. Despite prevailing Western beliefs, China had its own diversity, that, in some respects, was much greater. You just had to go to greater lengths to see it.

*   *   *

A private home was arranged for them to stay in when they traveled to Xiamen, in the south of China. The property was close to the beach with a view of the water, and it was nice to be in a house, instead of a hotel.

Jack sat outside at the nearby Fat Fat Beer Horse Brewhouse. He had arrived early ordered a beer, enjoying the view of the water. Susan was the second to arrive. When the waitress came over and asked what she'd like to drink, Susan pointed at Jack's beer.

"I'll take one of those," she said.

"This place is so beautiful," Jack said. It's developed so much since I was here last. That was a while ago, but still. I'm very impressed."

"You should see the university," Susan said. She paused to accept the beer the waitress brought over. She took a sip. "I think it's the most beautiful in China. It was my first choice, actually, but my parents forced me to go to Beijing University."

"Are you glad they forced you to go?"

Susan smiled. "I am. At the time, I wasn't, but if they hadn't, I wouldn't be here right now. And, as it turns out, they were right. Beijing University was better academically, and it exposed me to things and people I would not have experienced otherwise."

"I've lived in China a while," Jack said, "but traveling around like this has given me a new perspective."

"How so?"

"It strikes me that Chinese are different geographically. Those from Beijing are different from those in Shanghai. And those in Shanghai are different than those from Anhui . . . and so on. But, there are also commonalities amongst all Chinese. Kind of like Jews carry some common beliefs or values."

"I can see what you mean," Susan said.

"I'm curious," Jack said. "What would you say your top values are?"

He caught her off guard. She paused, the beer bottle almost to her lips. Instead of taking the sip, though, she put the bottle down. "My top values?"

"Yeah. Like what's the most important to you? What do you value?"

"Well . . . number one would be family. Number two would have to be living, like having the basic stuff to survive. Three would be work. And four would be safety. I guess I don't have to explain those last two cause they're self-evident."

Jason and David arrived right as Susan finished speaking. "What's self-evident?" Jason asked.

"I was just asking Susan what things she valued most. She said family, having your basic needs met, work, and safety. What do you guys think?"

"I agree," Jason said.

David nodded. "Me too. What about Americans? How would they prioritize?"

They all looked at Jack. "Good question," he said. "There are many different kinds of people in America, so obviously I can't speak for them all. But I'd have to say, freedom would be number one—all aspects of it. Then family. Third would be education. I guess fourth would be food. Americans do like to eat."

"There are a lot of cultural differences between America and China," David said.

"I can see why you'd think that. But, if you were to go back to the early 1900s, I think the priorities of people would be much closer."

"Really?" Susan asked.

"Sure. If China were at a different economic development stage, and had a different type of government setup, I suspect you'd list different things. That's not cultural."

"So what would be a cultural difference between the two countries?"

Jack looked at Susan with a smile, taking in her the navy pants suit she wore. It was a Western-style of dress, something any American woman who worked in business or government would wear. "What Chinese eat—and wear—are not cultural differences. Americans value their families, too. Maybe the only cultural difference is that Chinese use chopsticks. But there are people in America who use chopsticks. And there are more and more people in China who use a fork and knife. If there are more Western restaurants, Chinese would all use a knife and fork, I bet. Maybe all we have here are historical differences."

His three assistants looked skeptical, which was not surprising, considering none of them had ever been to another country. But he also knew his words were not falling on deaf ears. The Chinese government, up until recently, tightly controlled what its citizens could access online, and there was much that his assistants—and the rest of China's general population—might never have access to because the government previously controlled it; they simply were accustomed to visiting only Chinese websites.

Now that everyone was here, they moved inside to the brewery's main dining area. The building had been converted from an old freezer plant that used to make ice for fishermen, and some of the original equipment, such as the huge mechanical pumps, remained and were somehow seamlessly incorporated as part of the restaurant's décor. They chose a table near the center of the space and a waitress gave them menus and another round of beer.

The menu reflected the restaurant's attempt to represent both the east and west, which made sense since the brewery was located in a popular tourist district. There were such offerings as Thai Spicy Squid Rings and Beef Shish Kebab, as well as pizza and hamburgers.

"Get whatever you want, guys," Jack said, after he'd settled on ordering a pizza. It was hard to go wrong with a pizza, much easier to screw up a burger. "It's Susan's turn to pay for dinner." David and Jason laughed; Susan tried to hide her smile and shook her head. When she looked at Jack, he winked at her; they all knew Susan would expense the meal, as she did every meal they had out.

After they'd placed their orders, Jack held up his beer bottle. "I'd like to thank the three of you," he said. "We're reaching the end of our project here, and we've made excellent progress. It hasn't all gone perfectly smoothly, but what does? I have been most impressed by your diligence, thoroughness, and intelligence throughout this whole endeavor. So thank you. You should be proud of the work you have done."

He toasted them and then took a sip. It would be a relief when they wrapped their visit with the final province, but Jack would miss his assistants.

CHAPTER 18

The final weeks passed at a fast pace. They fell into a routine, where their lives had become consumed with their work. They would study, analyze, meet, get on the airplane, then check into another hotel in a different province. The whole process would repeat. And while there were variables—the level of cooperation or openness from the various officials, for example—Jack and his team's work was largely the same. Doing the same thing again in a new place was their normal, now, and though the schedule was grueling, Jack always had thrived in challenging situations like these. Now that he'd had the practice, he was able to swiftly identify abnormalities within the five-page province summary. The secretaries and governors were always surprised when Jack started each meeting with a few incisive questions and suggestions for consideration.

"You're really in your element, aren't you?" Susan had asked him before they went into the office of the Guangzi secretary and governor.

Jack smiled at her. "I wouldn't be nearly as effective if it wasn't for my great three assistants."

The meeting was going well when Jack felt his iPhone vibrate in his pocket. He discreetly looked at it. It was Jojo.

Most, if not all, of their phone calls had happened after they'd communicated via WeChat first; if Jojo was calling out of the blue like this, something might be wrong. Jack stood up.

"Excuse me, I need to take this," he said. "Susan, please take over for me."

He picked up the call before it went to voicemail but waited until he was out in the hallway to put it up to his ear. "Hi, baby," he said. "Is everything okay? I'm just wrapping up a meeting here."

"Jack," Jojo said. "It's me. Your wife. Your pregnant wife, who you've left for almost two months now. Don't you think this has been long enough?"

He could hear the irritation in her voice. She meant what she was saying—that much was clear—yet he couldn't' help but feel mystified that she would be taking this stance. "Baby, what's wrong?" he said. "I hear that you're upset and you know I don't want you to be, so . . . did something happen? Can I do something?"

"Jack!" she exclaimed. "*Did something happen?* Yes! What happened is, I got pregnant and then my husband decided this would be the perfect time to visit every province in China. And now you're asking if there's something you can do? Yes, yes there is—You can come home!"

"Jojo, I have one more week. That's it. One more week and then this will all be over and I'll be back. We've been killing ourselves going at the pace we have, trying to get this whole thing done and over with. So I *can* get back and be with you. Because that's really what I want."

"You know I grew up with a father who was hardly around because he was so busy. Is that what you want for our child? Is that what kind of husband you want to be? Dedicating all your time and energy to people you'll never meet?"

He paced back and forth as he tried to figure out if there was any way he could get back sooner. Susan could handle doing the remaining province, but not at the level he could. And to stop when there was only a week left—he couldn't do it. It just wasn't in his DNA to not finish something he had started.

"You have a husband and our child will have a father who is there. Who is present. Who is not giving away all his time and energy to strangers, as you say. I can come back tonight, if you want. We can postpone the final meeting. But eventually, I'll have to do it. I need to finish what I've started, Jojo, and the end is in sight, it really is. If you can just hang on a little longer, I'll be home within a week. But if you want, I will come home tonight—just say the word."

"Just hurry up and be done with it." She hung up the phone.

He put the phone back in his pocket but waited a moment before he returned to the meeting. He needed to compose himself. His whole head felt like it was spinning—that sort of call from Jojo was the last thing he expected. He tried to see things from her perspective, to understand that she probably felt lonely, she missed him, she was dealing with a changing body and all sorts of hormones . . . But despite the fact he could understand all of that, he couldn't help but feel upset. He had been running himself ragged trying to get this done so he could get back to her—he thought she realized how important this was. For the countless strangers he would never meet, yes, but also for them, and for her father. She had acted as if he were intentionally doing something wrong, yet that could not be further from the truth.

*   *   *

Their final meeting was complete. They were in Guangzhou, in the south of China. They had traversed the entire country, they met with the head of each province. And now, Jack was treating them all to dinner and margaritas at a Mexican restaurant.

It was the only good one in the city, though Jack was shocked there was even *one*. Just smelling the savory aromas made him miss Los Angeles and its abundance of food trucks. But the menu offerings here looked good, and the place was packed—mostly with foreigners. As soon as they were seated, Jack ordered a pitcher of margaritas.

After everyone had looked over the menu, Jack reached into his inner jacket pocket and pulled out three slender wrapped presents, one for each of his assistants. "I couldn't have done this without you," he said as he handed each of them their gift. "And I mean that. It was a true pleasure to work with you and to get to know you better. Thank you."

He could see they were stunned he had something for them, and they glanced at each other before they began to open the gifts simultaneously. He had purchased Montblanc pens; David and Jason received the classic, one-color version, but Susan's was two-tone, the upper half gold. It had been nearly double the price of the other pens, but when he'd seen it at the store, he just felt drawn to it and knew how much she'd like it.

So much so, it would seem, that she had started to cry, just a little, and she brushed the tears away with the back of her hand. David and Jason looked a little teary, too, which, Jack knew, wasn't simply because of the gift: they were all exhausted, and this exhaustion was certainly contributing to their emotion.

"But you did all the hard work," Susan said after a moment. "We learned so much from you. That was the true gift, Jack."

"I'm glad to hear you learned a lot. I did, too. And I guess that's the way it works sometimes. You have seen all of China and seen its leaders up close. That is a rare experience. Now you have a decent pen to write any stories you might have. I know, I know, a pen is old school, but I also noticed how all three of you used notepads and pens for the duration of this project. So, a nice pen of your own seemed a fitting gift."

As he spoke, and saw how pleased the three were, he realized that it had been a while since he'd bought anything for Jojo. Not that she was the sort who expected to be lavished in gifts, but he would, every so often, buy her something nice, a surprise, a way to say *I was thinking about you.* They had only exchanged a few terse messages via WeChat since she had hung up on him; he thought it would be good to give her her space, because he could tell from her short responses, she was still not happy with him.

He pushed the thoughts out of his mind for now. The waitress had come back with their margaritas and was ready to take their order. Instead of each of them ordering their own thing, they decided to just get an array of crispy tacos, burritos, and nachos for all to share. His three assistants had never had Mexican food before.

Jack poured margaritas and passed out the glasses. "Oh, I thought of one more thing," he said after he took a sip. "We need to prepare eleven booklets of the briefing documents, organized by region, including the sample performance tracking sheet. And there needs to be tabs. Ten should be sent to President Wang, so he can distribute them, and one sent to me. I knew there was one more thing I wanted to tell you after the meeting today, and that was it."

They each took out a notepad and pen and started to write. It was Susan who stopped first, looked at her hand holding a cheap ballpoint pen. A smile crossed her face as she put the old pen down and picked up the new one. Jason and David saw what she had done and did the same.

"Why ten booklets instead of seven?" she asked.

"They will always want to give a copy to a few others, and my guess is that others will attend the meeting. Plus, ten is a better number. You know, better fēngshuǐ."

Susan smiled and shook her head. "This pen is incredible. What a difference! I never would have thought that writing with a pen could feel so . . . effortless. What should be written on the note to President Wang?"

"Something short. *As requested, for distribution prior to presentations. Jack and Team.*"

When the food arrived, Jack showed them how to prepare a taco, the best sauces for the burritos, the nachos needed no real instructions. This would introduce a whole new spectrum of flavors and spices to their palettes, and from the expressions on their faces after the first few bites, they couldn't be happier with the meal.

Satiated, Jack took the last sip of his margarita and leaned back in his chair. He felt good. Davis, who had been waiting outside, suddenly appeared in the doorway, looking right at Jack. Davis gave him a brisk nod and started to approach the table. Jack looked at his assistants.

"Dinner's on me tonight," he said. "I'll take care of the bill and meet you guys outside."

Once they had left, Davis took a seat next to Jack.

"Is the food here too tantalizing to keep you away or is something else going on?" Jack said.

Before Davis could respond, their waitress stopped by and asked if he was ready for the bill. "Yes," Jack said. "But I'd like to add two shots of Patrón to that as well, please." Davis waited until the drinks arrived before he leaned in toward Jack.

"See the two men at the bar?" he asked.

The two men were Chinese, probably in their mid-thirties. Jack hadn't noticed them before. They both wore jackets that looked like they'd seen better days and did not look like the typical patrons of an expensive Mexican restaurants. In fact, they gave off an aura of trying to fit in despite the fact they so clearly did not. The hair rose on the back of Jack's neck.

"Tom and Ricky are sitting at the table over there as a precaution," Davis said. "We think they may have knives on them and are waiting for you to leave or go into the restroom."

"That is not the after-dinner news I was hoping to hear," Jack said. He picked up his shot glass and waited for Davis to do the same. "To a successful knife fight," Jack said.

He paid the bill. The two men were looking around, trying to be subtle but failing. They looked at Davis, then around the crowded restaurant.

"We have no confirmation on these guys, so we cannot approach them," Davis said. "But they entered the restaurant not long after you did and there just seems to be something . . . off about their presence here. Call it a gut instinct. My suggestion is that you go to the bathroom.

Brad Good   141

If they follow you, I'll take out the second one, you take out the first. I'll be right behind to assist if needed. You comfortable with that?"

It was likely not a typical scenario that Jack would be presented with this option. But this would not be the first time he had tangled with those who opposed him, and he was not too out of practice when it came to his martial arts. Jack smiled slowly. "Sounds like fun, actually. Though I can't promise my guy will be able to walk out of the bathroom."

Davis's fingers drummed the tabletop. "Jack, we have to take these guys alive so they can be interrogated. This is the only way to find out who is behind them."

"Okay, okay," Jack said. "I'll play nice." He stood up and walked to the bathroom, looking at his watch as he went. Out of the corner of his eye, he saw both men get off their barstools and follow him. Jack kept walking, taking a right into the men's room. There was no one else in there. Instead of walking over to the wall of urinals, as the two men likely expected, Jack took a few steps in and then stopped, turned and faced the door.

A few seconds later, it opened and one of the men stepped in, brandishing a knife, the blade pointed right at Jack. Despite the fact that Davis was right and he was now being threatened by an unknown man with a knife, Jack felt a bit of relief come over him; this man was not well-trained, this was not some high-level assassin. If he were, he would have held the knife with the sharp part of the blade facing out from his forearm.

That the man was not expecting Jack to be right there—facing him instead of having his back to him—was clear for only a split second when a look of shocked surprise lit up the man's face. It almost immediately morphed into grim determination as he lunged forward, thrusting the knife in the direction of Jack's stomach. Jack threw his arms out and hopped back, easily blocking and then catching the man's wrist that held the knife.

Using his leverage, Jack put immense pressure on the assailant's palm and wrist, bending it forward at an unnatural angle. The hand dropped the knife, and once the knife was not in anyone's possession, Jack let go, stepped back, and kicked the man right in the face. It was a hard, direct kick and the man sprawled on the ground, moaning.

Jack retrieved the knife. It would be so easy to plunge it into the man's neck, he could do it right now and claim self-defense. A part of him wanted to.

"I will kill you if you try to fight back," Jack said to the man's bloodied face. "You now know I can do it." The man only groaned in response.

The second man had not fared any better against Davis. The restaurant was now swarming with agents. One of them bound the hands of each man behind their backs with black zip ties.

Outside, Susan, David, and Jason were standing anxiously on the sidewalk. Jack came out when they escorted the two assailants through the restaurant's front door. He pulled his black phone out of his pocket and handed it to Susan.

"Hold up," he said to one of the agents, before they took the two men away. "Susan, can you please take a picture of us?"

"What happened?" she asked. There was real concern in her voice, fear etched across her face.

"These two men tried to kill me with a knife in the bathroom just now."

She took a bunch of photos and then handed the phone back to Jack. "You're okay, though?" she asked.

"I am," he said. "Better than these two, anyway." He watched as the two men were put into the back of one of the black SUVs. "Can't we just interrogate them now, while they're in the back of the car? Find out who paid them? I'm done waiting. We'll find out who's behind it and I'll take care of them. This has happened one too many times. It's time to send a serious message." Jack took a deep breath, trying to calm his anger. It would be so easy. He could have it done in minutes.

"Jack," Davis said, in a tone not unlike one Jack's own father might take were he trying to talk out of a very bad idea. "I know you want to do that. And you know what? So do I. But—we are on *their* turf and are at a major disadvantage. I'm confident they'll get to the bottom of things, we'll get the answers we need, and justice will be swift and appropriate. Let's let the process work."

Jack gritted his teeth. He knew Davis was right. And he trusted him. It was his emotions getting the better of him, and he didn't want that to happen.

When the police arrived a few moments later, Jack had reined in his anger. One of the officers approached him, asking what happened. After he and Davis relayed their version of events, the officer asked for Jack's ID. Jack took out both his passports and handed them over. The officer's eyes widened when he saw the Chinese diplomatic passport; he shot a look at Jack, one with far more deference than he had previously looked at him with. Just having such a passport was a symbol requiring respect.

"Are either of the two men injured?" the officer asked, handing the passports back.

"Yes," Jack said. "Well, at least one of them is. He's bleeding a little, but nothing life-threatening."

The officer nodded. "We're sorry for the inconvenience. We will take care of this matter from here."

"No," Davis said. He glanced a Jack. "Translate this for me, Jack. *This is not a police matter. What you are suggesting is highly irregular. This is a Ministry of State Security issue. Get the appropriate people down here.*"

As Jack translated, he realized that Davis was correct. State Security dealt with matters involving foreign diplomats and internal Chinese security. This was not a domestic police matter.

It was becoming quite a scene. Jack estimated there were about seventy-five onlookers, trying to get a glimpse of the action, of the two men who had been placed on their stomachs on the ground, their hands still zip-tied behind their backs. The officer Davis had spoken to went back to the other officers and spoke to them. Davis pulled his phone out of his pocket, looked at it, and then put it away.

"They're sending someone now," he said to Jack. "It'll be a few minutes."

As they waited, Davis took a cigarette out of a pack, then handed the pack to Jack.

"Thanks," Jack said. Though he was projecting a calm exterior, his nerves were starting to feel flayed. He took a deep drag, part of him wishing he had disregarded Davis's earlier advice and just taken those two guys out back and gotten the information he needed, concluding with sending that serious message to whomever was behind this.

Jack was almost finished with his cigarette when a car with official markings pulled up. The driver got out. He wore a dark blue uniform and had an official military hat on his head. Unlike the police, he carried a firearm.

"Who's this guy," Jack murmured. Davis was watching the man intently as he approached.

The man extended his arm, offering his hand, and Jack shook it. "I was sent here to pick up the two men who attacked you," he said.

"Excellent," Davis said. "Can we see your identification?"

As the man reached into his back pocket, Davis took out his phone. The man opened his wallet and showed them a Ministry of State Security ID. Davis took a picture of it. "You're not the right man to pick up these two men," he said, pocketing his phone. "We have been informed by the US Embassy that another person will pick them up."

"Yes, yes," the man said. "That's my partner. He asked me to get them, since I was closer. Don't worry, they will go where they are supposed to."

"That's not the way things work," Davis said. "These men are not being released to you."

"I'm sorry," the man said, his brow creasing. "I must insist that I take these men with me for questioning. I understand if this is not exactly how you anticipated things, but it is the correct protocol, I assure you."

Davis looked amused, or maybe annoyed. "The only way you are taking these men is by going through me. But if you touch me, you will be prosecuted for a crime against a diplomat."

"I see." The man wiped his nose with the back of his hand.

Jack knew what that meant—it was a telltale sign he was about to do something. As if right on cue, the man's hand moved toward his gun. He was going to take it out and threaten them with it, demand that they release the two men or they'd be shot.

Davis wasn't taking any chances. The moment the man's hand moved toward his gun, Davis lunged forward, thrusting his forearm into the man's throat. He grabbed the man's gun with his other hand, and before anyone could say or do anything, Davis used a zip tie to secure the man's arms behind his back. He put the man in the backseat of one of the police cars and put his gun on the dashboard. That was smart. Jack knew the people on scene would be nervous if a white person was holding a gun.

The officers had watched everything. Jack had kept one eye on them while Davis had subdued the man claiming to be from the Ministry of State. Though the officers all had neutral expressions on their faces, Jack knew that it was offensive for them to see a white man treat a fellow Chinese official in such a way.

Jack's black phone beeped. He took the phone out of his pocket and read the message from Cooper: *It's being taken care of. They are sending in a chopper.* He put the phone away right as another car pulled up. This time, two men got out, both in uniform with military hats.

"Hi," one of the men said. "We are here to pick up the two men who assaulted you."

"They tried to assassinate me, not assault me," Jack said.

"Well, whatever they tried, we're here to take them. We are from the State Security Bureau." The man turned and looked at the police cars. "Is that our colleague in the car?" he asked, obvious disdain in his voice.

"You are not taking those men anywhere," Davis said.

"I do not take orders from you," the man snapped. "So now if you would—"

His words were drowned out as the helicopter approached. Davis pointed. "They'll be taking the two wannabe assassins!" he yelled over the noise from the rotary blades.

Jack stared at the two men. Would they leave? Or would they try to insist they were taking the men?

"Why don't you two also stay so you can tell your side of the story," Davis said. He had his phone back out and took a picture of the two men, who flinched and shielded their faces with their arms, even though it was too late.

By the time the helicopter landed in a large, empty lot nearby, an even larger crowd had formed. Unlike in America, here it was uncommon to see a helicopter. Jack estimated there were at least a few hundred people there, maybe more. Almost all of them had their phones out, taking videos of the helicopter, the police, the men on the ground, the two white men. Chances were good this was something that would get posted on social media and Jojo would see. He needed to talk to her before that happened.

The men from the helicopter wore the dark green uniforms of the Chinese Central Security Bureau. There were four of them, and they were all tall, burly-looking men, each with a handgun strapped to his chest and a sub-machine gun in his hands. Such men were rarely seen in China except in parades. Jack was relieved to see them and also couldn't help but be astounded at the stark contrast between the unarmed police and this elite force.

One of the men walked right up to Jack. "Hello, Mr. Gold," he said, shaking his hand. "I'm General Ma. Please tell us what happened."

Jack and Davis again explained what had transpired. The police officers corroborated what was said. Then, the assailants, the man in the car, and the other two supposedly from the Ministry of State Security were put into handcuffs, real ones, this time, and escorted onto the helicopter.

"Sorry about all of this," General Ma said to Jack and Davis. "We'll sort through everything and get to the bottom of what really happened. And we'll let you know as soon as we do." The general shook Jack's hand, then Davis's hand again before he left.

Jack watched him go and then turned to Davis. "Can't even go to the bathroom in a Mexican restaurant without getting in trouble."

Davis grinned. "It seems to be a common occurrence with you."

"Hey, I was just minding my own business."

They headed over to their SUV. "Jack," Davis said, lowering his voice, "I'm not sure of what just happened, but they obviously had a backup plan in case things didn't work out. They may have even had a backup to their backup. They were in real-time communication with each other. This level of coordination with people, cars, and uniforms is a big deal. This is the work of people with resources. I'm glad this journey around the country is over. I think I have seen enough."

"I agree, Davis," Jack said. "Let's hope Wang Yang gets to the bottom of this and finds out who is behind everything. He needs to make an example of them. I'm getting tired of things like this."

The crowd was starting to disperse. Susan, Jason, and David were still there, and as the crowd thinned, they made their way over to Jack. The difference in the expressions on their faces—earlier, when they'd been enjoying the cuisine, carefree and happy, compared to now, after witnessing everything they did. They looked stressed and worried.

"Are you okay?" Susan asked.

"I'm okay," Jack said. "Thanks for asking. I'm sorry that had to be the conclusion to our lovely meal tonight. Anyway, the show is over; time for a luxury flight back to Beijing."

*   *   *

Jack knew he needed to get in touch with Jojo, but now he was thinking maybe it would be better to do all his explaining in person. He didn't want any conflict with her, and he didn't want her to be upset with him; their travel around the country was over and he was heading back home.

That was what she wanted, and really, he wanted to be right there with her, too.

On the flight back, he checked the news. There had been no reporting of the incident on any major networks, which wasn't surprising. However, there was something about China, reported by CNN: *Almost 40 Chinese warplanes breach Taiwan Strait median line; Taiwan President calls it a "threat of force."*

Shit, Jack thought. That wasn't good. China was sending a message that it could take Taiwan at any time.

China had never done anything like that before, and Jack couldn't understand what rationale Wang had for doing it *now*. The situation seemed contrary to everything Jack knew.

He leaned his head back and rubbed his eyes. He was too tired to try to look into anything now; he'd find out Wang's reasoning soon enough.

"You seen enough of China yet?" he asked Davis, who was sitting across the aisle from him, writing in black notebook. Davis put the pen down and gave him a wry smile.

"I can't believe we visited all the municipalities. I have definitely seen enough of China. We're all exhausted. You were pushing everyone pretty hard, not just yourself."

"I know," Jack said. "But we had to get it done. And it was more efficient than returning back to Beijing every week. Get the pain over as fast as possible."

"That's one way of putting it."

"So, what's your overall sense of China, now that you've seen more cities than you care to?"

Davis shrugged. "Honestly? They all seemed pretty much the same. The majority of people are living on the edge of poverty. Yet they seemed okay with it, since this situation is better than their previous one. It reminded me of this famous story about two black kids who were caught right near a gun that was used to shoot and kill a white man. The NYPD arrested the kids. The downtown PD were pushing to prosecute the kids, one of which was about to enroll in college. One newspaper hounded the uptown police department about the story and eventually got a quote that the kids' prints weren't even on the gun. They ran the story, and the next day, the kids were released. I guess my point is that the free press made the police honest. The Chinese are not accustomed to free speech or freedom of the press. In America, these concepts are institutionalized. But here, they need to evolve substantially."

Jack nodded toward Davis's black notebook. "Are you writing reports for the State Department now? That's pretty insightful."

"Nah," Davis said, shaking his head. "Nothing for the State Department. This my own journal. Figured it wasn't a bad idea to jot some of this down. What about you, though, Jack? You've seen more of China and talked to more people than anyone. What do *you* think?"

"You really want to know?"

"I do."

"Well, the real harm the Chinese government caused was not in Hong Kong, Xinjiang, or Tibet. The danger the government presented was not because of stealing secrets or intellectual property, or the buying of Iranian oil that funded terrorism. What the Chinese Communist Party did over the years was subjugate and keep 1.4 billion Chinese in the dark."

Davis frowned. "What do you mean?"

"Chinese were never allowed to have free speech or access *real* information. They became naïve because of a closed ecosystem, exacerbated by inferior education and little interaction with foreigners and other countries. The people were controlled through censorship. Zero percent of the Chinese population know Mao Zedong was responsible for the deaths of over fifty million people. His face is still on every single dollar bill. They even adopted his image for China's digital currency. And why is he still held in such high regard? Because of censorship."

"But you addressed that when you spoke to everyone at the Control Center. Why don't people want to wake up? You know the saying, Jack: *You can lead a horse to water . . .*"

"Right," Jack said. "*But you can't make it take a drink.* We can't force people to wake up, if they don't want to. The Chinese are still like a prince and a princess, living in a caste, thinking all is great, never having seen the outside world, never knowing that their government has been keeping them in a proverbial cave. They might now have some measure of freedom and increased economic comfort, but their minds might be irreparably impaired. It's a travesty against humanity. And for what? Control."

"It doesn't sound great at all," Davis said. "You've done a lot, Jack. More than any one person should be expected, to, maybe. Can I ask you a question?"

"Of course."

"You have a kid on the way. A family to take care of. Ever think about getting a regular nine to five job?"

Jack suppressed his smile. "Davis, you sound like my dad. I know Jojo would certainly like that. Well, that is, if she's still speaking to me. I'll find out soon enough. Oh, that reminds me." Jack leaned down and reached into his briefcase, retrieving a rectangular gift-wrapped box. He handed it to Davis, who took it, a look of genuine surprise on his face.

"Jack, this is completely unnecessary," he said as he opened the present. It was a Waterman Diamond Black Fountain Pen, and matching Roller-ball Pen. The Montblac pens Jack got for his assistants were excellent, but Waterman pens were even better. Seeing that Davis was keeping a journal made Jack feel the gift was all the more perfect.

"This is extraordinary," Davis said, admiring the pens. "I think I might have to report this gift to the State Department."

Doing so would be a pain, so Jack winked at Davis. "No need to," he said. "They're fakes. I bought them in Hangzhou for five dollars each. That's below the threshold of having to report. The reason you have a ballpoint *and* a fountain pen is that I didn't have the slightest idea which you might prefer."

"You know, I'm not sure either. I guess I'll have to try them out. Thank you, Jack. This is truly appreciated."

Davis opened his journal again and began testing both pens out. Jack took out his laptop and went on to Cartier China. The site was easy to navigate despite his limited ability to read Chinese. He scrolled through until he found what he wanted: a diamond platinum Love Bracelet. It would go perfectly with Jojo's black tungsten ring. He hoped she would love it.

CHAPTER 19

It felt both surreal and exciting to finally be back home. He paused outside of the boutique hotel before entering; he was also exhausted. And apprehensive about how welcome Jojo's reception would be.

He entered.

Right away, he noticed the paintings, in all different sizes, that were affixed to the walls, transforming the place's original industrial feel to something softer, more inviting. He knew without needing to ask that Jojo had painted all of them, and just the sight of them put a smile on Jack's face.

"I'm home," he called. He walked over to where she was sitting on the sofa. She was using her iPad but set it aside. He sat down next to her, put his hand on her growing stomach. There was no hiding that she was pregnant now. "Hi, baby," he said.

She glowered at him. Her facial features remained impassive; it was her eyes. Jack leaned closer, his face just a few inches from hers. He was waiting for a kiss, which she would have given him without hesitation if she were not still upset. But instead, she simply stared straight ahead.

So he gently turned her head toward his, his fingertips pressing against her lower cheek. He felt her resistance but continued to turn her head until he could look her in the eye. He gave her a kiss, which she did not reciprocate. He pulled back. They sat there in silence for several long moments.

Finally, Jack barked like a dog. He did it again, then a few more times once he saw that Jojo was fighting mightily against letting a smile break through. He had only been trying to illustrate the fact that everything they were arguing about was really no more than two dogs barking at each other. He barked one more time and that did it—the smile broke free and Jojo burst into laughter.

"I can't stay mad at you," she said, holding her arms out. He leaned into her embrace, relief flooding him that he was back, that he was where she wanted him to be. Now he could focus on his family.

He leaned down and spoke to her stomach. "We can't wait until we get to meet you," he said. "You have two crazy and emotionally exhausted parents here."

Jojo laughed. "That doesn't sound so good, considering the baby isn't even here yet!"

"Okay, Xiǎo Chūn Juǎn'er," Jack said, using the "little spring roll" nickname her father had given her. "Something I have been dreaming of asking you ever since I left: Shàng chuáng ma?"

*　*　*

A few hours later, they were downstairs, waiting for their takeout order of dumplings to arrive. There was a large box in the corner of the room that Jack hadn't noticed until now.

"What's that?" he asked.

Jojo glanced at the box and shrugged. "I'm not sure. I haven't opened it; it's addressed to you. There's a note on top of it."

Jack went over to the box and picked up the envelope, opened it. *Thank you for your service to the country.* It was signed with the Chinese character 王, Wang in pinyin.

Inside was a case of Maotai. This would be the perfect beverage to celebrate his arrival home. "Hey, babe," he called to Jojo. "You feel like a glass of Maotai?"

"We don't have anymore," she said. Then she turned and saw what he held. "Hey, what's that?" She got up off the couch and went over and Jack handed her one of the bottles. "Wow. A whole case of my favorite Maotai? Who sent it?"

"Your dad," Jack showed her the Chinese character. "He had originally offered to pay me for my services, but that could look inappropriate. So, I requested the money go to charity. But—I did say, if they wanted to share a small gift of Maotai, I would certainly appreciate it."

Jojo looked at the bottle again and then back to Jack, laughing. "So you basically worked for rare and expensive Maotai that no longer exists. Let me see, one bottle of this stuff would go for a quarter million dollars.

Which would make that case worth . . . three million dollars? My husband is a good negotiator. Let me go get some glasses so we can enjoy this properly. Oh, and something else arrived for you; I put it on your desk."

"Great," Jack said. That had to be her Cartier bracelet. He considered giving it to her now, but he decided to wait. "I'll have to thank your father," Jack said. It had been a while since he'd last spoken directly to Wang. He had a meeting set with him for next week to give him a briefing about how he felt the whole project went.

Jojo brought out a small traditional Maotai glass for herself and an elegant glass teacup for Jack. She poured a small amount for herself, slightly more for Jack. As she poured, he watched her, taking in her new shape, which really was just a pleasant roundness in her midsection where it had before been flat.

"You look great," Jack said. "Pregnancy suits you."

"It's definitely noticeable now," Jojo said. She handed him his teacup. "I've gained a little bit of weight."

"You carry it well. Have you told your dad about the baby yet?"

"No, I thought we should do that together. He texted me earlier about us going over there for dinner on Thursday. You up for that? He mentioned he has a meeting with you the following week."

"Of course I'm up for that. We can tell him then." Jack paused, a smile coming to his face. "Actually, we wouldn't even need to say anything—he'd be able to tell just by looking at you. That would be an interesting way to convey the news!" Jack raised his glass. "To family," he said, gently toasting Jojo's cup.

"To family," she repeated, smiling up at him before they both took a sip.

*   *   *

For dinner with Wang, Jack wore a dark blue suit, no tie, which was his standard conservative dress when going to Zhongnanhai for a casual dinner. He sat on the couch with his iPad, scrolling through the news from America, where it was five-thirty in the morning, Washington DC time.

When he heard Jojo coming down the stairs, he put his iPad away and looked up; his jaw dropped. She looked stunning in a form-fitting, full-length orange dress, her baby bump prominently displayed. Her hair was up in an elegant twist, with tendrils framing her face. A smile spread across his face just at the sight of her; he was enchanted. How could he not be?

It was getting cold in Beijing, so they put on overcoats before they left. On the drive over, they both fidgeted in excitement. "When we enter, we can't smile," Jack said. "We have to try to act normal."

Jojo laughed. "What if he doesn't say anything?"

"How could he not?"

"I don't know, but it would be pretty funny if he didn't, and then what? We just act like everything is normal?"

"There's no way he's not going to notice. We have to try to keep straight faces, though. The first one to mess up has to do a favor for the other."

Jojo grinned, narrowing her eyes. "You're on."

When they arrived, Wang Yang was speaking to an attendant, and Mini was right by his side.

"I think the dog's adopted your father," Jack whispered. Jojo smiled.

"Hi, Mini, come!" she said, and the dog trotted over. Jack gave him a pat; the dog seemed glad to see them but not like he had missed them, which Jack found reassuring.

Wang turned and came over to them, a smile on his face. "Jack, Jojo," he said, taking his daughter's hands. "I feel like it's been a long time since we last got together. Far too long! Come in, come in, let's get your coats off. Mini and I have been quite enjoying ourselves, he's been the perfect house guest."

"May I get your coat?" Jack asked, turning his face away from Wang, trying to bite back his smile.

"No, I've got it, thanks," Jojo said, who, from the looks of it, was trying to suppress her laughter as mightily as Jack was. She turned and went over to the standing coat rack in the corner and removed her coat, her back to them. Once it was hung up, she turned and walked back over, her expression perfectly neutral.

Jack watched his father-in-law, first the shock on his face, which quickly transformed into unbridled joy. Then he began speaking in Suzhou dialect, which Jack couldn't understand, though he thought it was something along the lines of *How come you didn't tell I am going to be a grandfather, how could you do this to me?* Yet all of this was said with the biggest grin Jack had ever seen on Wang's face.

They went and sat down at the table and Wang asked one of the attendants to bring in some hot water and lemon.

"Congratulations to you both," Wang said, now in Mandarin so Jack could understand. "This is incredible news! Have you seen a doctor?"

"Not yet," Jojo said. "I've felt completely fine this whole pregnancy, but I know we should see someone. Do you know of a good Fùkēdàifu?" Fùkēdàifu was the Chinese word of ob-gyn.

"Yes, yes, of course," Wang said. "I'll get you a name and number before you leave."

"Thanks, Dad. I think this calls for a toast!"

Wang gave his daughter a skeptical look. "You should not drink when you are pregnant."

"A half glass is okay," Jojo said. "Jack and I have both done plenty of reading. Things in moderation are fine."

Wang looked at Jack, who nodded. "Okay," Wang said. "Perhaps I am wrong about that. Then yes, let's celebrate with a toast."

One of the attendants brought out a bottle of Maotai, identical to the ones that they had just received a case of.

"Thank you for the case you sent over," Jack said to Wang. "We appreciate it."

"You deserve about twenty more cases for the work you did," Wang said. "Which we'll be discussing later. But right now . . ." Wang looked at Jojo. "Have you had any strange food cravings? Your mom used to crave spicy eggplant when she was pregnant with you."

"Did she?" Jojo said. "I didn't know that. I've been craving Mexican food and Thai food. Anything spicy, really. Luckily, Jack can make really good Mexican cuisine. Thai food . . . not so much."

When the Maotai arrived, Jack reached over and took Jojo's glass, drank half of it. "Just trying to help out," he said with a wink, when Jojo made a face at him. Then he stood up, holding his own glass. "Yùe fù," he said, using the respectful term to address a father-in-law, "please sit next to your daughter and your grandchild." He stepped back from his seat so Wang could sit. A picture-perfect moment. Except, he didn't have his phone on him.

"Hold, please," he said. "Stay right there."

He hurried out of the room, back to where Jojo had hung up her jacket when they first arrived. He reached into her pocket and got her phone.

"This is too good a moment not to take a picture," he said. He tapped the code to unlock her phone, then opened the camera app. "Ready?" he said. "Say *eggplant!*" Jojo and Wang both smiled; Jack had always thought *eggplant* was a funnier and more appropriate term to get a smile for a photograph than *Say cheese!*

Jack took several photos, knowing at least a few of them would be good. Wang looked genuinely thrilled, happier than Jack had ever recalled seeing him.

The attendants started bringing out plates of food, mostly northern Chinese dishes: sliced duck, fried chili chicken, watercress with garlic, fried eggplant, steamed fish, lightly seasoned noodles. There was also spicy Sichuan pork. "This was something else your mother loved when she was pregnant with you," Wang said, as Jojo scooped some of the pork into her rice bowl.

"It's delicious," she said after trying the first bite. "Actually, it's perfect—just spicy enough and I've definitely been craving pork."

"I'm glad you enjoy it," Wang said. "Whatever you find you're craving, we'll try to get it for you. It's the least I can do. I had no idea you were pregnant and now I feel bad asking Jack to be away from you for so long. I'm sorry."

"You don't have to apologize, Dad," Jojo said. "You didn't know. It was a bit of a challenge, yes, but we made it through. And it's better that Jack be away in the beginning of the pregnancy than at the end of it."

Jack felt relieved to hear her say that. Her anger at him, or about the situation he was in, rather, were valid. Of course he could never entirely put himself in her shoes and imagine how it would feel to be pregnant, but he knew what it was like to feel vulnerable, and also alone.

"We were very impressed when we learned about the first province's plans," Wang said. "We haven't seen the provincial secretaries and governors' presentations yet. But Jack's summary of findings and national recommendations are both insightful and profound." Wang beamed at him. "Jack has once again done a great service for this country."

"That's my Lǎo Gōng," Jojo said. Lǎo Gōng was the traditional term for husband, which Jojo seldom used, since Jack didn't particularly like it; though the term was used by all ages, *lǎo* meant *old*, which was not a term any man he knew enjoyed being referred to. He preferred the other word for husband, *xiansheng*, which translated to "Mr."

"I spoke with your assistants," Wang said to Jack. "And, they had lots to say about you. All very good. Anyway, the Standing Committee and I agree that a case of Maotai is an insufficient expression of gratitude from the nation. It's the least we could do."

Jack took another sip of his Maotai. "I'm glad I could help," he said. "It was a very important assignment, and we took it seriously."

"We know," Wang said. "The problem is that it is difficult to find other people like you."

"I'm sure they're out there," Jack said. "But, thank you. It is nice to be appreciated."

"And I wanted to give you an update about the issue in Guangzhou."

Jojo looked quizzically at her father, then Jack. "What happened in Guangzhou?" she asked.

"Two men tried to attack him with knives, in a restroom. Jack disabled one of them, and his guard took care of the other. But the real problem occurred when an impersonator from the Ministry of State Security arrived and tried to take the assailants away."

Jojo's jaw dropped. "What? When was this?" Her head swiveled to Jack. "You weren't going to tell me?"

"We interrogated everyone," Wang said. "Two provincial secretaries, along with a wealthy businessman, and a few others, have been rounded up. They will be sentenced shortly for their crimes, and the punishment will be made public as a clear warning to others that such lawlessness with never be permitted."

"I was going to tell you," Jack said. "But I was going to do so in person, but by the time I got back and saw you, well . . . There were other things that I wanted to talk about. I wasn't trying to hide anything from you. But I also don't want to stress you out."

"Jack is no longer in any danger," Wang said. "And neither are you. The punishment will be death. We will be sending a very clear message."

Jack raised his Maotai glass. "To justice." While the sentence might sound extreme to some, Jack was pleased to hear it, and knew that Davis would be as well. Other people who might be inclined to try something similar would be discouraged—they had tried to kill him and were caught in the act. If this were in America, such punishment would not be administered.

"But enough of this conversation," Wang said. "No more talk of unpleasant things, at least not this evening. Tell me, how did you find Dali?"

"We loved it," Jojo said. "We went to the lake, which was beautiful, but no swimming is allowed. We hiked around Dali University. Which reminds me—how come they don't let anyone into the university? Tsinghua was never like that."

"I don't think you'll have a problem going into Dali University soon, thanks to Jack," Wang said. "I expect the same for the lake."

Jack was pleased to hear that Wang had obviously started reading through the booklets they'd prepared. He thought of Governor Bo, and he looked forward to hearing whatever he had come up with to present to the Standing Committee.

"You know," Wang said, "if you liked Dali so much, there's a house there that's available, not too big, excellent views. You two could spend a few weeks or even months out there, if you'd like."

"Really?" Jojo asked. She glanced at Jack. "What do you think? That sounds excellent to me. I've been getting back into painting and there's so much inspiration there."

After his months of travel and meetings, living in Dali for a time sounded like the perfect respite. "That sounds like a wonderful idea," he said.

"I'm sure Mini would love it there, but . . ." Wang paused. "He's also more than welcome to stay here with me."

Jack glanced at Jojo, suppressing his smile. It was clear how much of a liking Wang had taken to the dog, but whether he stayed with Wang or went with them was really up to Jojo—he was hers, after all.

"He's not really left your side all night," Jojo said.

"It's no trouble at all. I've quite enjoyed having him around."

So it was decided that Mini would stay with Wang while they went to Dali. At the end of the evening, Wang walked them out to the car. He held Jojo's hand, the sight of which Jack found incredibly sweet. It was like Wang was already bonding with his grandchild, and Jack couldn't help but notice how diametrically opposed Wang's reaction was to his impending grandfatherhood as compared to Jack's father's.

"You have made my night with this good news," Wang said. He handed Mini's leash to Jack. "Any time this guy needs a place to stay, just let me know." He looked at Jojo's stomach. "May I?"

"Of course," she said, and her father put his hand on her stomach.

"I think I felt a kick!" he exclaimed after a moment. Jack had never seen him so happy.

Jojo echoed the sentiment once they were in the car, driving away from Zhongnanhai. "I have never seen my father so excited," she said. Her own eyes were bright with happiness. "And he seldom gives out praise, Jack, at least not the way he did tonight. I'm sorry for getting so upset with you. It was selfish."

"It wasn't," he said. "Your feelings were entirely valid. And I'm going to make up for all the lost time in Dali. I think it'll be really good for us to have some time away."

Jojo leaned over and gave Jack a kiss. "I think I won the bet tonight," she said.

He smiled. "You did keep a straight face longer than I did."

"I'll have to think about what you're going to do for me."

She gave him another kiss. He let his eyes fall shut. "I've got a few ideas," he said.

CHAPTER 20

The day of the presentations, Jack found himself back at the Great Hall of the People, in a special meeting room meant for the Standing Committee, with a large Chinese flag as the central focus of the room. Jack's seat was next to Wang Yang, which was an honor, since all Standing Committee members sat in a hierarchical order, strictly in accordance with their seniority. Jack looked at each member and was relieved none of them appeared upset about where his seat was. The Standing Committee members served at the will of the president, and all present looked eager to begin and hear the first of the presentations.

The first to present were Secretary Hu and Governor Bo, from the Yunnan Province, the first province Jack had met with. Governor Bo looked decidedly more nervous than Secretary Hu and Jack wished he could take the younger man aside for a moment and give him a few words of encouragement. It was an intimidating situation, being in this room with the entire Standing Committee and President Wang, the enormous red flag looming. Everything was there on purpose, Jack knew, to invoke a sense of supreme importance.

"Thank you for the opportunity to present to you our plan for the Yunnan Province," Secretary Hu started.

Wang held up a hand. "Actually, we would like to hear from Governor Bo."

The secretary's eyebrows shot up but he said nothing, only looked to his left at the governor.

Bo looked even more nervous now, but he took a deep breath, let his gaze land on Jack for a moment, and then began to speak. "There are five key actions we should immediately take in Yunnan Province. First, open up Erhai Lake in Dali to swimmers and other water sports. Zero percent of Chinese in the province can swim. Yet swimming, sailing, and water polo are all Olympic sports. We can protect the water quality and *also* allow people to swim and boat. An open lake will draw more tourists and increase property values and tax revenues." Bo paused, his gaze again landing on Jack, who gave the slightest, almost imperceptible nod. The young governor was doing an excellent job so far.

"Second," Bo continued, "Dali University must be transformed. There are only ten thousand students on a 410-acre campus. There needs to be subject realignment and teacher adjustment. Most teachers are there through connections. Third, the government-owned commercial buildings will be sold within the year, and Yunnan Province will not, moving forward own such real estate." Bo paused. "Returns to province coffers are estimated to be at fifty-five million dollars."

Several of the committee members raised their eyebrows at the price. Jack was pleased with how well Bo was doing.

"The fourth thing is that all government personnel occupying office space or government-owned property will pay market rent. We want to allocate all costs clearly so we can understand where revenues and costs are, and so that everyone appreciates the costs of things. And finally, we would like to re-zone property around Lake Ehai for the building of three-story commercial structures, which would adhere to current architecture requirements, to maintain cultural heritage. That is important. But so is making progress. This will attract high tech companies, much like what is built in Silicon Valley. The land is now otherwise unused. It's estimated that this will add seventy-five million dollars in property and tax revenue."

"Seventy-five million over how many years?" a committee member asked.

"Three to five," Bo said. His gaze landed briefly on Jack; Jack wished he could applaud but he refrained. Bo had done an excellent job, and the longer he stood up there speaking, the more at ease he seemed.

"I have a question for the secretary." This was Zhang Li, who Jack recalled meeting when he'd come to the Great Hall previously. "Were you discourteous to Mr. Gold?"

Secretary Hu shook his head vehemently. "No. Absolutely not. I was in no way discourteous. In fact, I gave him a warm welcome when he arrived to meet my staff."

Li nodded to one of the assistants who was seated at the other side of the table, in front of a laptop.

Everyone turned to look at the projected video on the wall. A video of the secretary, speaking to Jack, started to play. Jack frowned, and then realized that all the times he had thought Jason had been taking photographs, he had actually been *filming*.

"*You are a foreigner,*" the secretary said in the video. "*You're not Chinese. How could you know anything of China? Why don't you just go away.*"

There was a heavy silence in the room. Jack was still trying to get over his disbelief that the interaction had been filmed. From the look on Secretary Hu's face, he couldn't believe that the interaction had been documented, either.

"I would not call that 'active participation,'" Li said. He glanced at Jack and then back to Secretary Hu. "You were disrespectful to this office by insulting our representative. On behalf of the Standing Committee, I hereby notify you that you are immediately dismissed from all of your duties, and all of your positions and titles are hereby rescinded."

Secretary Hu would not be the only official to be dismissed from his post because of an unwillingness to move forward with the bottom-up plan, but it was still an uncomfortable thing to have to witness. The secretary had no choice but to accept what he was just told, though the crimson color his face turned before he was escorted from the room gave Jack plenty of clues to the depth of the man's anger.

"Now, Governor Bo," Li continued, "we thank you for your presentation. Your plan is tentatively approved. We'll be sending you a form to fill out to formalize the approval. Also, we have some potential ideas we'd like to talk with you about, regarding the university. As you implement your plan, if you encounter any resistance, please let us know. Your plan is important to the nation."

Governor Bo still had a shocked look on his face after seeing the dismissal of Secretary Hu, but he nodded deeply. "Thank you, thank you," he said. He caught Jack's eye and gave him a nod of appreciation.

When Governor Bo left, Wang Yang turned to Jack. "We've been doing our homework to supplement your work," he said. "I wanted you to see this first meeting so you'd have an idea as to how all of these meetings will go. We can take it from here. You injected a new perspective, which ignited and spread throughout the provinces. It's quite a thing to see. And yes, there will be holdouts like Secretary Hu, who think they ultimately know what is best, but you've now seen how we plan to deal with that. You've done a great job, Jack. Once again really coming through for the people of this country. We'll take it from here. You can go home."

The committee members nodded and smiled, a few of the murmuring their thanks. Wang stood and shook Jack's hand.

"Thank you again," he said. "I will see you soon."

Jack said goodbye and exited the room, relieved that he was finished, but also a little disappointed he wasn't going to stick around and hear what Shanghai had to present. His disappointment was short-lived, though; he'd be able to easily find out how the presentation went.

Outside, Jack got into the SUV that Davis had been waiting with. "That was fast," Davis said, glancing at him in the rearview mirror. "I was expecting you to be in there at least a few more hours."

Jack stretched, leaned his head toward one shoulder, then the other, felt a few pleasant cracks in his cervical spine. "They don't need me now. I'm officially done with the assignment." Saying it out loud felt better than he would have expected.

CHAPTER 21

Jack woke up early the next morning, Jojo still slumbering peacefully beside him. They'd had a good day yesterday, when he returned home from the Great Hall. They'd taken Mini for a walk and then spent a quiet evening in; Jack had cooked, they relaxed after dinner, and then they'd gone to bed and fallen asleep in each other's arms.

But now Jack was up and saw that he'd received a text late in the night from Cooper: *Significant amounts of money are flowing out of China.* Jack took a sip of his coffee as he scrolled through the usual websites—BBC, FOX, Google News—and found nothing of substance about China.

What's up? he texted Cooper. *What's the cause of the outflow?*

Not sure, Cooper replied.

Jack frowned. It was implausible that Cooper and the CIA wouldn't know why there was a significant outflow of money from China. He continued his online search, looking at all China-related development. If cash was moving out of China, that meant someone—or several someones—wanted to get their money out. Because they were worried.

But how would they know? Jack wondered. *How could they predict it?*

He typed in *predicting events* to the search bar and several articles appeared. He clicked one entitled "Joint Artificial Intelligence Center Keeps Branching Out."

The article was from the *National Defense Magazine*. Jack began reading. One of the sentences stood out: "Today, more than 200 talented civil service and military professionals work diligently to accelerate AI solutions and deliver these capabilities to the warfighter."

AI solutions were certainly being used in other areas, too, and he wondered if AI's prediction abilities were perhaps the reason for this sudden outflow of money. But the truth of it was—Jack simply did not understand AI well enough to know if this were even possible.

He called his friend, the Stanford professor, Jeff Hern, on FaceTime. "Hello, Jack," Jeff said, when his face appeared onscreen. "This is the second time I've heard from you recently. Something must be going on. What's on your mind?"

"Nice to see you again, Jeff," Jack said. "And yes, I've got a few things on my mind. One of which I was hoping you might be able to help me with."

"Ask away."

Jack paused. He'd called Jeff up without first considering how he might word things. "Well," he started, "I just got done with a pretty big project that should help China economically. Then, a day after that, I get word that there is a lot of money flowing out of China. It seems highly unlikely to me that this is just a mere coincidence. What do you think?"

"Money leaves a country when something bad is going to happen," Jeff said. "It happens when people want their money in a safer place. But you didn't need me to tell you that."

"What would you consider a *bad thing*?"

Jeff shifted in his chair, reached for his cup of coffee. Jack held his own cup up. "Cheers," he said.

Jeff smiled. "I shouldn't be drinking coffee this late in the day. So, when AI scenarios are run, there are all sorts of things that can be influenced. For example, a serious drop in the stock market, or prediction of a major environmental disaster. Even a coup. The list is very long. The key is that when multiple events occur, it can affect people's beliefs about the future and exacerbate a fear that life will end, or at least *normal* life as we are all used to. Reactions to such things include anxiety, agitation, and confusion. In such situations, people are vulnerable emotionally."

"What you're saying makes sense," Jack said. "But keep going."

"Sure. So, think about people who have experienced trauma. Some of them have a hard time regulating emotions, such as anger. However, studies show that once key stress is removed, emotional stability can be reinstated. There have been some great studies performed in South Africa about the impact of multiple trauma events. Want me to send you one of them?"

"Thanks, Jeff, but no." Jack pressed his fingers to his temple. "I'm trying to absorb everything you've just said. So you can run scenarios involving this sort of stuff using AI?"

"Me, personally? No. Computers run them themselves and make calculations. We see the outcomes. With AI, there is constantly out-of-the-box thinking. Human beings think in a linear way and constantly see boundaries. Computers are instead playing three-dimensional chess, and the world is their board."

"I see," Jack said. "I appreciate it, Jeff. You haven't heard the last from me on this, I'm sure. And hey, if you hear anything about China, will you give me a call?"

"Absolutely," Jeff said. "Take care."

Jack sat there for several moments after the call ended, trying to recall exactly what Wang had said weeks ago about some resisting change and wanting a more aggressive stance toward Taiwan. But so much had happened in between that he was having a difficult time recalling most of the conversation.

"Good morning."

He swiveled in his chair at the sound of Jojo's voice. She walked over to him and Jack held his arms out. She sat down in his lap, gave him a kiss. "Good morning," he said. "Can I get you something to eat? We have bagels and salmon."

Jojo wrinkled her nose. "Gross. No thank you. You know what I really want?"

"What?"

"It might sound totally weird, but what I really want is an egg and sausage breakfast sandwich from McDonald's with some salty hash browns."

Jack smiled broadly. It *did* sound a little strange; he couldn't recall Jojo ever requesting McDonald's, but then again, maybe it wasn't so odd. "That is definitely my child inside of you," he said. "I'll order and have it delivered. I do have one question for you."

"And what would that be?"

"Did you have a preference as to when we left for Dali?"

Jojo shrugged. "No. Did you?"

"I was thinking tomorrow. I know it might seem kind of soon, but it was also so nice and tranquil there, I'd like nothing more than to go back. Why wait?" He did not add that if something was going to happen, it would be good to be far away from Beijing.

"Sounds good to me," Jojo said. "I'll let my dad know. And I'll ask my dad about a doctor there. But *most* importantly right now is that break-fast sandwich."

Jack winked and gave her another kiss before she slid off his lap. "I'll get right to it," he said. He opened the app to order for both of them, trying to ignore the feelings of worry that had settled over him.

*   *   *

They arrived at the Dali airport the next day, with Davis and Rio in tow. Outside the airport, waiting to greet them, a small crowd of people had assembled, with Governor Bo front and center, holding a dozen yellow lilies, which he gave to Jojo.

"These are beautiful, Governor Bo, thank you," she said.

"Good to see you again," Jack said, shaking his hand.

The governor smiled broadly. "Welcome to Dali," he said. "We are so happy to have you here, and if there's anything that you need or we can do for you, please don't hesitate to ask. We are honored to have you with us."

"Thank you," Jack said. "We're really happy to be able to return to your lovely city; I hope this time will have more relaxing and getting to know the place better."

"I've got a list of places I thought you might like to visit. More private visits can also be arranged, and I'd be happy to do that for you. But you probably want to get settled in first before we get into all of that."

"Your hospitality is much appreciated, Governor," Jack said. "We'll certainly be in touch soon."

They climbed into the back of the waiting SUV and made their way down the highway. The roads, Jack noticed, were noticeably empty. It was likely this was Governor Bo's doing, to make their travel smoother.

Just north of Dali Old Town, they pulled up to a large, picturesque four-story home. The exterior was modern, with big windows and a red Chinese tiled roof. They entered through the first floor and found themselves in a pristine garage with a tile floor, housing a red convertible Targa Porsche, a Ducati, and a gas-powered Vespa.

Jack grinned. "I like this place already," he said. He pointed to the Ducati. "That one's mine."

"It looks like someone designed a playroom for you," Jojo said, laughing. "Smart move. Okay, well, I'll take the Vespa. The Porsche can be for our Sunday drives."

On the second floor, they found the kitchen, dining area, and living space. The main feature of the dining room was a large, antique-looking wooden table, long enough to comfortably seat eight.

"That's a great table," Jojo said.

"We could eat at one end and work at the other." Jack put his hand down on the table's surface, felt the smooth grain of the wood. He wondered about who had sat at this table before them.

There were plenty of windows throughout, letting in an abundance of light. The living room was furnished with a sofa, a loveseat, and two easy chairs. In the kitchen, there was an oven, a dishwasher, and a washing machine *and* dryer, which was a luxury, as most homes in China only had a washing machine.

There was a door off the kitchen which led to a large outside deck with a swimming pool, lounge chairs, and a Weber grill.

"We definitely made the right choice coming here," Jack said. "I feel like we've just arrived at some retreat tailored specifically to what we like. This is great!"

On the third floor they found the bedrooms; the master bedroom featured three huge windows that looked right out onto Lake Erhai and the farms below. The view was stunning, and not obstructed by any drapes or curtains. Instead, there was a button on the wall near the light switch that could be pressed to tint the windows. "Fancy," Jack said. Connected to the bedroom was a large bathroom with a deep soaking tub, a glassed-in shower, and two sinks. The rest of the upstairs was dedicated to two additional bedrooms with their own bathrooms.

"Plenty of spare rooms for that awesome party we're going to have to host," Jack said.

They were about to head up to the fourth floor when Jack thought he heard something far below. He listened—it sounded like someone was knocking.

"I think someone's at the door," he said. "I'll go check."

He went down and found a woman standing at the doorstep; she was in her thirties and wore a backpack, had a pleasant smile on her face. For a moment, Jack thought maybe she had knocked at the wrong door.

"Hi," she said, in American English. "I'm Dr. Song. Mr. Wang's office sent me over. I'm an obgyn. You must be Jack Gold?"

"Well hello," Jack said, extending his hand. "Nice to meet you. Come on in."

Jojo had made her way back down to the second floor. Jack introduced her to Dr. Song and then said he would go make some tea, so they could chat at the dining room table. While he was in the kitchen, he heard Dr. Song tell Jojo she had gone to Harvard Medical School, then served as an intern at Georgetown University. She was in practice in San Francisco for a number of years before getting recruited to return back to Beijing, where she now worked mostly for the wives of government officials. Everything she said reassured Jack that Jojo was in good hands.

Jojo laughed. "I guess that's me, huh? A wife of a government official."

When the tea was ready, Jack put everything on a tray and brought it out. Jojo gave him an appreciative look. Not every husband in China would make tea, as some saw it as just one of the many duties of a wife.

"We're sorry that you had to make the trip all the way out here," Jack said as he poured tea for the three of them.

Dr. Song waved him off. "Oh, please don't be sorry. I've actually moved in down the street. It's a wonderful break to be here and away from Beijing. I wanted to be close so you could reach me at any time. Babies often don't adhere to the typical working hours! Why don't we exchange WeChat."

After Jojo scanned the code, Dr. Song outlined what she was going to do for her visit today, which included an exam, an ultrasound, and some standard blood tests.

"These tests are usually done in the first trimester, so we'll be doing a few more today than normal," she told Jojo.

"What types of tests?" Jack asked.

"Mostly to make sure the placenta and abdominal wall are healthy." Dr. Song looked at Jojo. "How have you been feeling?"

"Pretty good, for the most part, though I'd say I've noticed being more tired this past week or so."

"You're probably low on iron, which is common. Try to eat more things rich in iron, like steak and spinach. I'll also leave you with some iron tablets. Is there a place we can go so you can lie down for the exam?"

"We can go upstairs," Jojo said. "Jack and I were just exploring up there and discovered the numerous bedrooms."

"That sounds perfect," Dr. Song said, shouldering her larger than normal backpack. She gave Jack another smile. "Dad, sit tight, we'll be right back."

"What's in the backpack?"

"Oh, I brought an ultrasound device, along with some other things."

Jack remained sitting and finished his tea. He wasn't sure what to do with himself. He knew medical devices had modernized, but still found it surprising that ultrasound equipment would be so small that it could fit in a backpack.

He brought his teacup out to the kitchen and rinsed it out, set it to dry. He couldn't hear anything from upstairs and was curious what was happening, but he didn't want to intrude. He liked Dr. Song and was glad that Jojo would be under her care for the rest of the pregnancy.

Jack retrieved his laptop from his briefcase and sat at the dining table. He connected to the wifi and then checked that his VPN worked. He still needed it; not to access overseas websites but for enhanced security. He considered looking at the news, but he didn't feel like it just yet. It would likely only cause stress, and at least on their first day here, he wanted to avoid that. He was realizing, even though they'd been here just a short while, that he was ready to stay put. The last several months had been change, day after day. His mind had gotten used to it. He was looking forward to staying relatively stationary.

A WeChat call came through, from Ari. Jack answered the call, a smile already on his face. "Ari!" he said when his jovial, heavyset friend's face came into view.

"Hello, Jack!" Ari said. "I've been meaning to get in touch. I heard about the project you did, visiting all the provinces. You've got to tell me how it went!"

"I learned a lot," Jack said. "Too much to get into right now, though. Maybe in person, though? Jojo and I just got to Dali, we're going to be staying here for a few months."

"Dali? I've been wanting to go there. Mary, too."

"We've got plenty of spare rooms."

"We're going to take you up on that offer, Jack. Anything else new?"

"Well . . . I'm going to be a father," Jack said.

Ari's eyes widened. "Jack!" he exclaimed. "Wow! Congratulations. And to think that I met you when you were on a date with another woman! Ha. Mary will be so excited to hear this excellent news!"

"Everything with you good?"

"Can't complain. I've been busy. Mary has too. So a little vacation to visit our friends in Dali might be just what we need."

"We do have some things to talk about," Jack said. It would be good to catch up with Ari, but Jack was also curious to find out more about Israel's involvement with the Chinese/Iranian guy who had offered Jack all that money if he stopped working on the project.

Jack chatted with Ari a little longer, but then ended the call when he heard Jojo and Dr. Song coming down the stairs.

"All looks good, Mr. Gold," Dr. Song said. "I encourage a normal life for Jojo. That means exercising, getting fresh air, also sex is fine, right up to the ninth month. Moderation when it comes to coffee, tea, and alcohol."

"I'm so glad to hear all of that," Jack said. He could tell by the expression Jojo had on her face that she was happy with Dr. Song as well.

CHAPTER 22

Over the next two weeks, Jack and Jojo explored Dali, both by foot and by moped. They found one Starbucks and one McDonald's. They came to appreciate that Dali was a place for travelers, as it always had been. There were barely any foreigners, just visitors from other parts of China. Jack quickly learned to carry a packet of tissue with him on their long outings, as most public restrooms did not have any toilet paper. These restrooms also featured squat toilets instead of a toilet to sit on, which meant Jack had to get comfortable squatting, a position that he was not accustomed to using.

The food in Dali was inexpensive compared to Beijing or Shanghai, as was the fare for a taxi. They found a local open air market which went on for blocks, featuring stall after stall selling a cornucopia of flowers, fruit, and other fresh food.

"This place is incredible," Jojo said. "We should be able to find every-thing we need here for tonight. What were you thinking?" That evening, they planned to host a small dinner for Governor Bo and Dr. Song.

"I was thinking they might enjoy an American meal. Steak and potatoes," Jack said. "I'll make some spinach, too. We've got the steaks from the Shanghai Costco and I bet we can find everything else we need here."

There were three types of potatoes. Jack tried to select the ones that most looked like the russet potato from Idaho, his favorite. He bought fresh purple garlic for the steaks and then he followed Jojo to a stall selling ginger, both fresh and dried.

"Which one has the stronger flavor?" Jack asked the woman behind the counter.

"The fresh," she said. "The fresh ginger is stronger."

"Interesting," he said. He was surprised; he thought the dried would have had the stronger flavor.

He picked up a piece of fresh ginger and asked how much. The woman looked at it, then looked at him, and waved him off. "Just take it," Jojo said. "No one buys such a small amount of ginger. Except you!" She smiled and then turned to help the next customer. Jack shrugged and slipped the ginger into the bag with the potatoes.

When they were done, they walked the four blocks over cobblestone streets to get back to their house. Jack put some music on, the "Classic Road Trip Songs" playlist on Spotify, and "Splish Splash" by Bobby Darin came on. Jack liked that he was here in Dali, which came to be in the 1300s, listening to classic American music.

"I'm already starving," Jojo said, coming up behind him.

"I'll start prepping now," Jack said. "They should be arriving at six. Can you make it?"

"I'll have a little snack. I want to save room for steak. Dr. Song will be glad to see that I'm taking her advice and having some red meat." Jojo gave his arm a light squeeze. "I have to say, Jack, you're so much more relaxed here. It's really nice to see."

Jack smiled and gave her a kiss. "The laidback lifestyle suits me," he said. "In fact, I'll get this stuff prepped now and then maybe join you on the sofa for some relaxing."

"I'll see you out there," Jojo said.

There was about an hour and a half for relaxing on the sofa after Jack had finished prepping the meal. He had just put the potatoes into boiling water when the doorbell rang. He roused himself, stretching. He was excited to host their dinner guests but also partially wished the relaxing with Jojo could have continued straight through the night. There would be other evenings for that, he reasoned, as he went and answered the door.

It was Governor Bo, who showed up alone, without his wife, because she had to work late. "She was very disappointed not to be able to make it," the governor said.

"It's not a problem," Jack said. "We'll have another get together at a time we know she can come. And we invited another friend. Oh, here she comes." Dr. Song was a few paces behind Governor Bo, though Jack almost didn't recognize her because she had traded the backpack and plain clothing for makeup, high heels, and a brightly colored dress.

"Good evening, Dr. Song," Jack said. "May I introduce Governor Bo."

The two shook hands, made their introductions. Jack led them into the house and up to the second floor. While Jojo talked with Bo and Dr. Song, Jack poured everyone a glass of red wine. Jojo got a half glass.

"We're going to take this out on the deck," Jojo said.

Jack nodded. "I'll be right out. I just want to wash this spinach."

Governor Bo hung back in the kitchen. "How are you enjoying Dali so far?" he asked.

"It's really good," Jack said as he rinsed the spinach leaves. "As you can see, we've been set up pretty well. It's lovely here, especially now that I can take my time to enjoy it. How are you doing?"

"Things are really good." Bo smiled. His self-confidence had grown significantly since the first time Jack had met him, Jack could sense it just in his stance, the way he spoke. "I still can't believe I presented a plan that was approved. Talk about nerve-wracking! But they really are providing support. To be honest, it's been one of the most rewarding experiences in my life."

"That's great to hear," Jack said. "In my eyes, that's the job of central government. To assist the municipalities."

"That's what everyone used to think," Bo said. "And now I get to witness it for real. It's incredible!"

Jack turned the burner off on the potatoes and drained them. "I appreciate your enthusiasm. It seems to me that all companies and governments have deficiencies, they just vary in degree. Look at all of America's political disagreements. It's exhausting. Anyway." Jack shook his head, smiling. "We don't have to get into all that right now, or at all tonight, really. I wanted everyone to enjoy themselves tonight, and discussing politics is probably not the way to make it happen. Why don't we bring the wine out and I'll get these steaks on the grill."

On the deck, Jojo and Dr. Song were engaged in a lively discussion about all the places they'd been discovering in their locale. Jojo was telling Dr. Song about the bakery they had stopped at when they'd come here the first time, Simple Stone.

Only Bo was truly familiar with Dali, but Jack could see the pleasure on his face as he listened to the two women share details about what they liked about Dali.

"I found a great path on the other side of the university," Dr. Song said after she had input the Simple Stone info into her phone.

"Is that the one that hugs the university wall?" Jojo asked.

"No. You have to go further over the bridge. It's past that, and the trail goes up by a tea factory. The scenery is beautiful."

"We'll have to check it out," Jojo said to Jack.

"Have you been there?" Jack asked Bo once he'd got the grill going.

Bo gave them a chagrinned look and held his hands up. "You guys probably know more about Dali than me."

When the grill was hot, Jack used tongs and laid out each steak on the rack. He held the tongs out to Bo. "Can I put you on grill duty for the time being? I've got to run inside and take care of the potatoes."

"Gladly," Bo said.

Jack hurried inside and put the pan on to sauté the spinach. While that was cooking, he mashed the potatoes, generously adding butter, milk, and salt and pepper. He transferred the potatoes to a serving bowl, put the cooked spinach in another bowl, and brought them both out and set them on the table.

"How are those steaks looking?" he asked Bo.

"I think they're almost there," Bo said. He handed Jack the tongs. "But I'll let you make the final call."

Bo was right, the steaks were done, all they needed to do was rest a few minutes. He turned the heat off and put the steaks on a plate. "Almost ready," he told everyone.

"Jack, I am so looking forward to this," Dr. Song said. "I was just telling Jojo that it's been a long time since I last had a homecooked Western meal. Thank you."

The meal was simple but delicious, and Jack was pleased that everyone seemed to enjoy it thoroughly.

"The spinach is delicious," Bo said. "Jack, how did you cook it?"

Jojo grinned. "It's a secret," she said. "He won't even tell me. I think it's a special combination of special oil, garlic, red chilis, and soy sauce."

"It's as good as anything I'd get from a restaurant."

When everyone was done eating, Jojo and Dr. Song volunteered to clear the dishes since Jack had prepared and served everything. Jack poured himself and Governor Bo another glass of wine and then sat back in his chair, satisfied and satiated.

"This sort of evening is just what I needed," Jack said. "It's nice to slow down and be able to enjoy good food and good company."

"I thank you for your hospitality and tremendous culinary skills," Bo said. "Truly, that meals was fantastic. Now . . ." He paused, glancing over his shoulder toward the house. "I don't want to sour the evening, but . . . there is something I wanted to briefly mention."

"Sure," Jack said. "Go for it."

"Well . . . I think you should know that some things are going on."

"What sorts of things?"

"Your project resulted in many senior officials getting replaced or removed. You . . . you didn't hear this from me, but they're angry. Very angry. Many think the country is going in the wrong direction, away from traditional communism. In the past, senior officials have all been strong believers of communism and Mao. That's partly why they were picked for their positions. Now, private enterprise, given the opening of China, is taking over to the point that others can no longer deny it, but they also cannot accept it. Or they think they can't. There's also another fraction of people, I'd say mostly businessmen, who believe the past is better. For those people, it was easier to make money when State-owned enterprises dominated, and they had relationships to easily get business contracts. These two groups have come together and I would imagine working in overdrive to try to change things back."

This was not surprising. Jack hadn't wanted to discuss politics, but he also wanted to stay on top of any developments that could affect him and Jojo. "What sort of things are they considering?"

"I don't know specifics. They approached me to see if I was interested in joining their efforts. Once I declined, they understandably did not want to share anything further with me. But I know these types of people. You have some before, like Secretary Hu. Jack, you need to remember China's government is Yī dǎng zhízhèng."

The phrase referred to China as a one-party dictatorship that had a monopoly on political and military power. Such a system did have its benefits: the centralized control could help focus momentum to change and evolve the economy and related mechanisms, that is, if the leaders within the party did not hamper progress.

"I did hear one thing that surprised me," Bo said. "And that was *Olympics*. They may attempt to sabotage China's hosting of the games next year. I'm not sure. I just thought you should know, considering what you have done for the country. Although planning has always been done top-down, this new bottom-up approach could herald in a welcome tide of change."

Jack took a sip of his wine and looked at the turquoise water of the pool. It was perhaps a bit naïve to think that he could complete his end of the project and then go back to his regular life, though at this point, he was sometimes uncertain if he even knew that that meant. But *this*, being here in Dali, spending time with Jojo, having friends over for dinner—this was the kind of life he wanted to return to. "I appreciate you letting me know," he said. "I don't know if you saw it in the papers, but two men did try to attack me in a restaurant. They're taking things very personally."

"I did see that," Bo said. "I was also glad you were not hurt. But . . . I'm sure they have other things in mind."

"Who has other things in mind?" Jojo asked as she and Dr. Song came back out.

Bo shot a look at Jack. "Um . . ."

"There are some people who aren't as eager about opening Lake Erhai for recreational use," Jack said.

"Yes," Bo said quickly. "Yes, that's what we were discussing. More ruralization is taking place, so we have to provide more infrastructure. And the University is also being transformed. We've been busy. Most are excited about it, but of course there are some who will always complain and want to be contrary, no matter what you do. But, visitors to Dali are projected to reach an all-time high."

Jojo had come out and heard the last of what Bo had said. "That's great!" she said. "And I wanted to ask you: What's going on with the art scene here?"

Jack listened while Bo descried the Dali Art Factory and the Dali Museum, and an art scene that existed but was not what you would refer to as vibrant. If Jack felt any guilt for the dishonesty just now to Jojo, it was eclipsed by his desire to not add any more stress to her life, to try to keep things as even keeled and pleasant for her as possible. She deserved that, at the very least.

CHAPTER 23

Jack had just woken up but was still lying in bed when he heard something he hadn't in a while: his black phone beeping. Which meant an incoming message from Cooper. Jack reached over to the bedside table and picked up the phone.

President Sutton and the First Lady would like you and Jojo to join them for dinner and an important briefing.

Jack glanced at Jojo, who was still asleep. *Is it important?* he texted back. *We're in an isolated part of China, very much enjoying ourselves.* He was hoping what the president had to communicate could be done a different way. Jojo would probably not be thrilled to hear they would have to leave—even if it *were* to go to DC and have dinner with the president. Jack felt likewise.

Yes, came Cooper's immediate response. *It is important for both you and Jojo. And China. Your flight leaves Dali Airport at 2pm. We arranged a nice plane for you this time.*

We'll be there. Jack set the phone down. Jojo was beginning to stir. She yawned, stretched, opened her eyes and looked at Jack.

"Good morning," she said. She looked at him more closely. "What's wrong?"

There was no way to sugarcoat things. "The president and First Lady want to have dinner with us," Jack said. "And they want to talk about something important that relates to China." He paused. "I got the message from Cooper, who I trust completely. If he says it's important and needs to happen, then . . . I believe him. I did tell him where we were right now and that we didn't want to go."

Jojo was quiet for a moment. "Well," she said. "If the president of the United States wants to meet with you, then . . . I guess you really can't say no, can you? When do we have to leave?"

"Errr . . . this afternoon at two."

"Oh." She frowned. "That's rather . . . soon."

"I know. And I'm sorry. Now that we've been here a little while, the thought of traveling anywhere sounds like the last thing I want to do, but . . ."

"It's okay, Jack. Do you think we should bring Dr. Song?"

"I'm not sure. I think that should really be your call. Or maybe ask Dr. Song what she thinks? I don't anticipate that we'll be there for much more than a day or two. Plus, I'm pretty sure if we need a doctor in America, we'll be able to find an excellent one."

"I'll call Dr. Song in a little while," Jojo said. "I guess I better get up and start getting ready. Food first, though."

"I'll make you something," Jack said. He felt bad. It had only been a few nights ago when Dr. Song and Bo had been over for dinner, when Jack had not told Jojo what Bo had told him about a few "things going on." He had withheld that part of the conversation from her to protect her from the stress and worry, and because they were here in Dali and he wanted the tranquility they both felt here to continue uninterrupted.

Whatever President Sutton wanted to meet about, it likely had to do with whatever Bo told him. Which meant that Jack's life—and Jojo's—might still be very much in danger.

*   *   *

When Davis pulled into the private section of the airport and Jack saw the plane they would be flying on, he let out a low whistle. The aircraft was a sleek black and gray, its wings tipped up on their ends.

"Now that's a good-looking plane," Davis said. "A new Gulfstream 700. That thing travels at Mach 0.9. Traveling in style."

"That is quite the plane," Jojo said.

Jack smiled. "Shàng Chuáng ma?" He and Jojo were platinum members of the mile-high club; he had lost track of how many times they'd made love on an airplane.

"The chances are good," Jojo said with a wry smile.

The interior of the plane was as impressive as the exterior, Jack saw as he, Jojo, Davis, and Rio, who would be joining them for the trip, boarded. The floor was covered in a tan and black striped carpet and there was a large sofa facing the right-side windows. Jack looked to his left and saw into the cockpit, which came equipped with multiple flat screens instead of the usual manual switches. It looked more like a set of gaming panels meant for a teenager's home video game system.

The pilot turned and said hello, he was probably a few years older than Jack. "This is quite the plane," Jack said. "I'm wondering if you can show us what it can do on takeoff?"

The pilot said nothing. "I know the governor," Jack continued. "I'm certain we won't get in trouble."

He smiled and did not wait for the answer; instead he followed Jojo and took his seat.

"Did I just hear you ask the pilot to show you what the plane can do on takeoff?"

He raised his eyebrows and shrugged. "Maybe . . ."

She laughed and hit him lightly on the shoulder. "You are such a little boy sometimes! But it's adorable."

Once everyone was seated, the pilot swiftly made his way to the takeoff runway. There were no other planes in sight at the small airport. The plane was soundproof, so Jack could barely hear the engines, but he could certainly feel the vibration. The plane picked up speed as it shot down the runway. It stayed on the runway longer than Jack would have expected; right when Jack was certain the runway would end the nose of the plane went up nearly vertical and they were airborne, a straight shot until they reached above the clouds and leveled off.

"Okay, Jack!" Jojo said. She released his hand. "I wasn't expecting an amusement park ride as part of the flight itinerary!"

"I'm sorry," he said, unable to wipe the smile off his face. "But you have to admit, that was pretty cool." He put a hand on her stomach. "We'll keep things calm and mellow for the rest of the trip."

It would be about a twenty-nine-hour flight, with a stop to refuel in San Francisco. "We need to get something to wear," Jojo said. Neither she or Jack had brought the right sort of attire to dine with the president; they would be able to get something online, since the plane was equipped with high-speed wifi connected to the Starlink satellites.

Jojo already had her laptop out and was going onto Chanel's website. "I've been wanting to get a dress and some shoes from Chanel," she said as she scrolled through pages. "Now is a great time."

Jack was no fan of shopping, but being able to do so from thirty-thousand feet in the air and have the goods delivered the following morning made the whole process seem as painless as it could. He took his laptop out and went on to Armani and picked out a single-breasted jacket in printed velvet that came with matching slacks. Then he found some durable Crocket & Jones boots made in England.

Less than thirty minutes later, both Jack and Jojo put their screens away, their outfits procured, all shopping completed. That was one of the things Jack truly appreciated about Jojo: she did not feel compelled to spend hours shopping. She did not just buy things compulsively, rather, she knew what she liked, and she would get it.

*   *   *

Jack and Jojo spent the next seven hours asleep in the bedroom located at the back of the plane. When they woke up, they were famished. The flight attendant, Stephanie, took Jojo's order for steak and spinach and Jack's for steak, eggs, and corn tortillas.

"And coffee, please," Jack added. He'd just had quite a decent sleep for being on a plane, but he also felt in desperate need for some coffee.

Jojo was chatting with Rio, so Jack took his laptop out and started to browse the news websites. The Starlink internet connection was lightning fast. "Uyghur protests in Xinjiang occurred yesterday," he read on the BBC's website. "Those outside the re-education camps refused to eat. Protests were in response to the detention of relatives and others. There were no altercations with the police or authorities." The next article Jack read was about Mongolia, where there were plans to make Mandarin Chinese language the main language taught in schools had parents keeping their children at home. "Classes," the article stated, "for the past three days have been empty. There is concern that the lack of teaching of the local language will result in the slow disintegration of the local culture."

The final article Jack read was about cadmium tainted rice that poisoned six hundred people in Hunan. The grain stockpile had been tested and was found to be highly contaminated. Fifteen people were arrested after protesting and the local head of the Environment Protection Bureau had been dismissed.

Jack frowned and closed his computer. He couldn't recall so many incidents occurring at the same time like this—it seemed too coincidental. He tried to recall some of the things that Jeff had told him about AI. There were definitely forces at work that Jack did not fully comprehend.

Several hours later, the plane landed in San Francisco to refuel. While they waited, Jack decided to FaceTime his father.

"Greetings from San Francisco," Jack said when his father's face appeared.

"Hi Jack, hi Jojo," Dr. Gold said. "I didn't know you were back in the States."

"Just briefly," Jack said. "And we didn't know until last minute, either. We've got a meeting with the president."

"Wow, Jack. Does this mean you're staying out of trouble or getting into more trouble?"

"Trying to stay *out* of trouble," Jack said. "But we'll see how it goes."

"Jojo, how are you feeling?" Dr. Gold asked. "How is my grandson?"

Jojo smiled and stood up, turned to the side. "Growing, as you can see!" Jojo said. "I'm feeling pretty good."

"Glad to hear it. You look great. I thought Jack was going to be settling things down once he was done with that project of his, but it doesn't sound like it. Jack, have you ever thought of taking up a different profession? A teacher? Mentor? Anything, really, other than what you're doing?"

His father said it jokingly, but Jack could hear see the seriousness in his expression. He was concerned and, in a way, that did make Jack feel good.

"I'll consider it," Jack said. "I've got plenty of time for that. For now, I just want to be with Jojo as much as I can."

"I'm proud of you, Jack. I just want to see you stay safe. Maybe consider visiting me on the way back. Jojo, keep an eye on him, will you? Make sure he stays out of trouble."

When the call ended, Jojo reached over and took Jack's hand. "Your dad seems pretty worried about you," she said. "I'll have to do my best to keep you out of trouble."

"He's right," Jack said. "I really should think about other things to do. Teaching actually wouldn't be that bad. I could see myself doing something like that."

"You'd be great at it. But, like you said, you've got plenty of time to think about that. I think the more immediate thing you should focus on is the fact that you're going to be a father rather soon."

Jack smiled and gave Jojo a kiss. He liked the sound of that.

*   *   *

Around nine pm they finally landed in Washington DC. They went directly to the Mandarin Oriental, and Davis and Rio escorted them up to their Diplomatic Suite. Two additional agents—one American, one Chinese—were stationed outside the door. The American introduced himself as Tom. The Chinese agent was Clint.

Jack felt reassured seeing them there, and he knew there were other agents nearby. Their suite was a far cry from the hotel rooms Jack had grown accustomed to staying in during his trek across China; the suite was essentially one large, long room with many windows that overlooked the marina. The furniture was elegant and tastefully appointed.

They showered and went to bed early. The morning sun through the windows they did not close the curtains which woke them the next day. For breakfast, they ordered room service and when the meal cart came up, along with it were the packages of clothing they'd ordered on the flight over. After eating, they relaxed for a little while and then Jojo decided to take a swim in the hotel pool while Jack worked out. He was out of practice, but it felt good to move his body, especially after being on a plane for nearly thirty hours.

Davis came to pick them up at four-forty-five. Jack had changed into his Armani suit with the printed velvet. Jojo looked stunning in her Chanel dress and very light makeup. Her hair was down and flowed past her shoulders.

Davis did a double take when he saw them. "You both look immeasurably better than when I saw you last."

It was a five-minute drive. When they got there, Cooper was waiting.

"Cooper, good to see you," Jack said, extending his hand. He was glad to see him. "You remember Jojo."

Cooper gave a brief smile as he shook Jojo's hand. "Good to see you both," he said. "May I have your phones? I need to update them. You'll get them back when you leave."

Jack and Jojo handed their phones over.

"Thanks. Before dinner, we'll be meeting in the Situation Room to brief you," Cooper said as he led them inside. "It's located in the West Wing basement, not too far from here. The president will meet us there."

When they reached the room, Cooper told them to take a seat and the president would be there shortly. A large conference table took up most of the room; there were no windows but there were several large flat screens mounted on the walls. Two people were sitting at the far end of the room, intently focused on several computer monitors, their backs to them. They did not look up or turn around when Jack and Jojo sat down; Jack guessed they were intelligence analysts tracking communications.

They did not have to wait long for President Sutton. He strode into the room, his wife Cam right behind him, and Jack and Jojo both stood up. Sutton had a big smile on his face.

"Jack! Look at you," he said. "You look great. And Jojo! Congratulations. I'm so happy for both of you."

"It's so good to see you again," Cam said, giving Jojo a big hug. "And a baby is on the way! How exciting."

"We're thrilled to see you both," President Sutton said. "Now, let's sit down so I can brief you on a few important things and then we'll get to dinner."

They took their seats, this time Cam sitting where Jack had been, next to Jojo, and Jack sat to the left of President Sutton.

"First, Jojo," President Sutton said, "your dad knows that we're talking today, and he knows what we're talking about. He knows everything. And President Wang wants three things for China: One, a thriving economy with happy citizens; two, a happy and independent Taiwan; and three, a stable political situation with elections." Sutton paused. "The United States knows how to make this happen. And, unless certain things are done soon, there will be a coup in China. Wang reorganized people when he took office. Then, he further reorganized senior party officials as an outcome of Jack's most recent provincial project."

Jojo shot a worried look at Jack. "It sounds like there are many people who are not happy with my father."

"That's one way of putting it," Sutton said. "Then, there are others who do not like the move away from strict communism. They don't want to move toward greater openness. All these people have now gotten together and are plotting against Wang's administration. If these factions continue to have an impact, nearly all major countries will boycott the winter Olympics in China, due to a variety of concerns. This will be a big blow to China's prestige and to Wang Yang's leadership." Sutton looked at Jojo, then Jack. "That alone would likely end Wang's leadership."

Both Jojo and Jack were quiet. Everything Sutton was telling them was serious—if the factions organizing against Wang's administration were successful, Jack did not want to even think of what the outcome for Wang, for Jojo, for himself, would be.

"What I'm going to tell you next is highly confidential," Sutton said. "Jojo, your dad has promised me that he'll keep it confidential. May I have your agreement too?"

"Yes," Jojo said immediately, though Jack could hear the uncertainty in her voice. He wishes he was sitting closer to her so he could reach over and take her hand.

"I appreciate it, Jojo, thank you." Sutton took a deep breath. "The United States has developed Artificial Intelligence. I'm not an expert, but I know enough. We were able to input desired outcomes and then the computer has enough information and insights to tell us what exactly we need to do in order to generate those outcomes. We were also given a probability of success. I've been told that we can do this partly because we have greater data access than any organization in the world, and vastly better computational power and memory. A few things will happen soon. Riots will become more common in China. This will be seen as a sign of weakness by those wanting to instigate a coup. It will make President Wang look weak, and that he does not have control of the country."

"So what do you think should be done?" Jack asked. "Rather, what does AI say should happen?"

"To deal with the situation and achieve Wang's objectives, we need to do four things. First, Jack, you'll go with our Secretary of State, Ron Timmons, to Taiwan. This will infuriate traditional communists since they view Taiwan not as independent but as a part of China. Following that, Taiwan's main government building will be destroyed by China. People will be led to believe and think that it is actually the pro-communist faction that did it. Ultimately, the people of China will see this as a horrible harm to their brethren in Taiwan. Then, in retaliation, the

United States will bomb China's main administration building in Zhong-nanhai. People will think those in the building will have been killed, but there won't be anyone in the building at the time of the bombing. This, combined with the Taiwan event, will move the emotions of the public dramatically. They'll focus their attention on the entire situation."

Jack tried to digest everything Sutton was saying but he found it increasingly difficult. Is this what AI were telling them to do? Was it really the right thing?

"How will blowing up these buildings change anything?" Jojo asked.

"It will bring out the hardliners to disparage China's leadership. President Wang will have stationed his forces around China to arrest them. He has information from us on who these people are and where they are. America will freeze their assets in Western countries and revoke their visas, to support China. And finally, Jack, you'll need to say a few words to the nation to help calm things."

"Me?"

"Yes, Jack, you. You have a high trust factor amongst the Chinese. Now, I realize what I have just said is a lot to take in, but there is a massive amount of related information that I haven't shared with you. Most of it is how people's emotions will fluctuate while all of this is going on, which plays a significant role."

"What does Taiwan think of all this?" Jack asked.

"They are committed to the plan one hundred percent," Sutton said. "The benefits of this plan are great. And, given our experience thus far, we are very confident in its success. I'm just giving you the overview here. I don't want to overwhelm you. Plenty more details will be forth-coming."

Jack wasn't sure what to think, but it sounded like he was expected to play a central role again. Which he didn't want. "How can we know how accurate your AI is in predicting outcomes?"

"I thought you might ask that, Jack, and as I am decidedly *not* the expert in the field, I thought we might have someone who is, explain things a little better." Sutton looked toward the far end of the room. "Jeff? Would you join our discussion?"

One of the people stood, then turned. Jack's eyes widened when he saw it was his friend, Jeff. "Hi, Jack," Jeff said. "Good to be able to connect with you in person."

"Jeff!" Jack exclaimed. "No way! This is a surprise. But I guess if an expert in AI is needed, it's you."

"Well, your question is a good one, Jack. I've seen all the AI in the United States and what is being used. What makes the AI here unique is the amount of data collected and analyzed. AI is only as good as the information it receives. It goes beyond that in terms of its ability to facilitate connectivity. So, for example, there are about 200,000 protests a year in China, for any number of reasons—the seizing of property, tainted grain or livestock, or protests by Falun Gong. But there is no interconnected tissue linking the people of these different events together. Understanding this potential connective tissue adds a whole new dimension."

Jack was used to being able to assess and understand almost any situation quickly. It frustrated him that he felt he still wasn't entirely following what Jeff was saying. "Elaborate, please," he said.

"What it means is that the computer can also suggest interventions to accentuate or diminish emotions, and thereby, influence action. It's a given that it catalogues and understands things by individual, by friends, family, etcetera. In other words, in China, every person's phone calls, WeChat messages, Alipay purchases, WePay purchases, Weibo pages, and browser pages viewed—all of that is tracked. Psychometric profiles are then developed and updated real-time for individuals and groups. This is not just fancy regression analysis—it's the real deal. The computer is intelligent and learn in and by itself. The massive data and other information enable insights never before possible. So, Jack, we know the probabilities through tests, much like pharmaceutical companies test new drugs for efficacy before approval."

Jack looked at President Sutton, a question he wasn't sure he wanted to know the answer to forming in his mind. "Was my address at the Control Center part of this overall AI plan?"

Sutton held his gaze for a moment before looking away, first down at the table and then to Jeff. The silence in the room was heavy. Jojo sat straight up in her chair, looking at Jack from across the table.

"Jack," Jeff said. "We had no choice. But the original plan had never been for you to address the nation. There are, after all, some things that AI simply cannot predict."

"And President Wang knew all this, too?" It didn't matter what the answer was; Jack felt like shit. He'd been played this whole time.

"I'd be upset too, Jack, if I were in your shoes," Sutton said. "And I'm sorry. The way this thing works is that we have to do—and not do—certain things at specific times to generate desired outcomes. There were too many lives that would benefit to take a risk that we were explicitly instructed not to take. We couldn't risk telling you and were instructed not to. But that is the *only* reason that information was not shared with you."

Jack kept his eyes on Jojo as Sutton spoke, and he watched the subtle changes in her face, the way her brow furrowed slightly, the narrowing of her eyes. She was upset, on his behalf.

The door opened just then and Cooper walked in. Was this all part of their plan? Jack wondered. His mind was spinning, trying to think back to everything that he'd done, that he'd done believing he was doing of his own free will. But what it was sounding more and more like was that it had been predetermined, with probabilities of success and everything.

"Jack," Cooper said. "I know you've learned a lot in this short time you've been here. I'll be guiding you through this plan, step by step. Like last time, except it will be much easier. And safer."

"Safer?" Jack said. "I'm curious—what did the AI say about us almost being killed while driving in California? What did the computer say about me being killed by the guy with two swords in the Roosevelt Building?"

"We didn't know exactly what would happen," Jeff said, "but we knew your chances of survival."

"Which were?"

"Eighty-five percent."

"And what are our chances this time?"

"Ninety-five percent."

Jack glanced at Sutton, who nodded. "Jeff's number is accurate."

Jack took a deep breath and exhaled loudly. "I think this is a good time for a martini." Never had it crossed his mind that they would have actual percentages on his chances of survival.

"I think that's a good idea," Sutton said. "Cam will bring you two upstairs to the residence. I need to make a quick call and then I'll be right up."

Jeff gave Jack an apologetic look before he left the room. "Sorry, Jack," he said. "I know this wasn't what you were expecting to hear."

"Did AI predict that also?" Jack followed Jojo out of the room before Jeff answered. A few steps ahead of him, Jojo and Cam walked arm-in-arm.

188 The Probability of Success

"Jack," Cam called over her shoulder, "tonight is margarita night since we're having Mexican food. Would you prefer a martini or a margarita?"

"A margarita, I guess," Jack said. "If we're going to be having Mexican food."

"A margarita!" Jojo said. "Just what the baby wants."

They arrived in the personal dining area of the First Family, a place they had been before, and took a seat on one of the sofas while Cam went to get the margaritas.

"That wasn't what you were expecting to hear, was it?" Jojo asked. She took Jack's hand. "It certainly wasn't what I was expecting. And how could my father be okay with that? Putting us at risk? I can't believe it."

Jack squeezed her hand lightly. "I know," he said. "I'm still trying to process it all." AI had put a percentage on success and on whether Jack would live—information they had purposefully withheld from him. Elon Musk was right, Jack thought. AI was an existential threat to humanity and should be regulated. The computer had convinced both the American and Chinese government that they should put Jack's life in danger.

Cam returned with a pitcher of margaritas and poured a generous glass for both Jack and Jojo. For a moment, Jack thought about drinking half of hers, as he'd done previously, but decided not to. Jojo deserved at least a full drink tonight, if that's what she wanted.

Jack nursed his drink while Jojo and Cam talked. He was almost finished with the drink when President Sutton walked in. He poured himself a margarita and then sat down in a chair opposite Jack.

"I'm sorry about all that," he said. "Every commander in chief makes decisions he or she thinks are best. There are always percentages involved. Always. You were working for the CIA. You knew there were risks. I understand that learning now that there were percentages attached to things makes you feel bad. That's a normal reaction. Like I said, I'd feel the same way. But that's the ways things are done. It's been done this way since the days of George Washington through to Truman dropping bombs on Japan. They had to consider the percentages related to achieving outcomes. Nowadays, we have assistance from computers in making such judgments. This should be reassuring. And, things look very positive this time. It should run like clockwork. Since you'll know what you need to do ahead of time, everything should be easier. Safer."

"Dropping bombs on two government buildings," Jack said. "That makes me nervous."

"This plan could impact hundreds of millions of people for generations to come," Sutton said. "You and Jojo might be mad at Wang and myself, but I hope you understand the burden we have. The risk is manageable on this, and there will be security with you all the way."

The initial shock of what he learned was starting to abate. What Sutton just said *did* make sense. There was risk involved in anything.

"Jack, Wang Yang didn't really know what was going to happen when he brought you on board to do that strategy project for the provinces," Sutton said. "It was the outcome you produced that convinced him to move to the next steps we're talking about now. It was the computer that instructed everyone that you should do that assignment. Now he sees what you did as being unexpectedly transformative. Once again, you've had an extraordinary impact on Eastern civilization. He feels so indebted to you he doesn't even know how to show his appreciation. His words, not mine. And, it's not just him. He told me the entire Standing Committee was grateful."

"It wasn't an easy assignment," Jack said. "I was away from Jojo for two months. I had to travel all around China and deal with people who were skeptical, doubtful, or outright disrespectful in some cases. Fortunately, Wang came through in adopting the good plans and dealing with the bad apples. So, that was a good outcome."

"You can't imagine how much I wish I could send you around America to each state and major city to assist them in developing a re-organization plan. But they don't report to me, and their plans are their own. I don't think it's America's job to meddle in China. But, given the stakes and wishes of support from Wang, I cannot see us standing down. We have this one chance to really help facilitate change. It could change China and the lives of its people. The reverse could be devastating."

"I agree," Jack said. He understood why Sutton was president, why he had such remarkable support from American citizens. He was convincing, logical, and passionate. Yet at the same time, Jack now knew he'd been played this whole time, including tonight. Jojo and Cam's presence here was not necessary; nor was Jeff's, really. Neither was the dinner. Same with all the accolades Sutton was giving him now. All of this had been carefully orchestrated to ultimately impact how Jack felt about the assignment.

And it had worked.

"I have just one firm requirement," Jack said. "Previously, I spoke to you about security. Things were not properly taken care of, and because of that, Jojo and I almost died. I want your promise that Jojo will be protected like you and the First Lady until this thing is over."

"Absolutely," Sutton said, without hesitation. "You have my word."

"Okay," Jack said, feeling relieved. "I'm in."

Sutton clapped his hands together once, loudly. "Excellent," he said.

"I do have one other question, Mr. President," Jack said. "What should I do about that one billion dollars in the Luxembourg account?"

Sutton's brow creased momentarily and he looked up at the ceiling, then back to Jack. He shrugged. "Jack, that was a China and Iranian matter. You'll have to ask them." He grinned and then looked at Cam and Jojo, who had switched from English and were speaking in French. "How about we eat?"

The food was set up buffet-style, with both corn and flour tortillas. There was beef, chicken, and pork, as well as black beans and refried, lettuce, tomatoes, salsa, cilantro, sour cream, and guacamole. Jack moved out the way as Jojo made a beeline for a plate.

This part of the evening went smoothly. The food was delicious and Jack had another margarita. By the time everyone's plates were cleared, it almost felt like just another dinner party.

Cooper was there to meet them on their way out. He returned Jojo's phone to her and then asked Jack if he could have a word. "It'll just be a minute," he added to Jojo.

"Why don't you wait for me in the car," Jack said. "This will be quick."

Cooper and Jack walked a few paces from the SUV. "It's hard for me to know what is really going on and what might happen," he said. "Even with all this AI. So, I had our guys modify your black phone. It's a little bit thicker, if you look carefully. If, instead of entering your passcode when the phone is locked, you enter your birthdate twice, the phone will become a bomb and blow up."

Jack blinked and looked at the device in his hand. "Excuse me?"

"You heard me. If you enter your birthdate twice, your phone will blow up in ten seconds. It can blow out a wall or a metal door. It's more powerful than C4 and you'll have no problem getting it through an airport if you need to."

"Wow." The phone did feel slightly heavier than Jack remembered. "How come you never gave me any cool shit like this before?"

Cooper gave him a wry look. "Because you never needed it. And hopefully you won't now. Just think of this phone as your old one. Everything is the same. But—it's an insurance policy in case the unexpected happens. Computers might be smart, but they can't predict everything."

Jack slipped the phone into his pocket. "Thanks, Cooper," he said. He hoped Cooper was right and that he would not need it. But just knowing that he had it, and what it could do, reassured him.

* * *

At eight o'clock the next morning, there was a knock on the door. Jack went to answer it and was surprised to see Cooper standing there, uncharacteristically wearing a jacket and a tie.

"Cooper, hi," Jack said.

"Good morning," Cooper said. "Sorry to drop by unannounced, but I was hoping to speak with Mrs. Gold, if she's available?"

"Oh. Of course," Jack said. He stepped back so Cooper could come in. "Babe?" he called. "Cooper's here to see you."

Jojo started to get up from the sofa but Cooper held up his hands. "No need to get up," he said. "I just wanted to speak to you briefly. Jack stipulated to the president last night that his involvement was contingent upon you being protected like the president and First Lady are. The Secret Service knows this cannot happen if you are a Chinese national. We need to surround you with only those from America, since we are not sure who might be compromised on the Chinese side." Cooper glanced at Jack. "Jack was right in requesting this. But you'll have to temporarily give us your Chinese passport."

Jojo raised her eyebrows. "I will?"

"Yes. It will be temporary, though, and it's for your own protection. This way, we'll legally be able to protect you in China—" Cooper paused and pulled something out of his jacket pocket—"in case you didn't bring your diplomatic passport with you, here's another." She took the passport from him, glancing at Jack.

"Can I call my dad?"

"Of course," Cooper said. "The president did speak to him earlier and mentioned this."

Jojo reached for her iPad and called her dad over WeChat. They had, what sounded to Jack, like a rapid-fire conversation in Suzhou dialect, none of which Jack understood. She put the iPad down and then got her Chinese passport out of her purse.

"Here you go," she said.

"I assure you that I will keep this safe and return it to you as soon as possible," Cooper said. "And, just to forewarn you, we will be flying in another doctor to supervise your care. She's originally from Qingdao. You'll be in good hands." Cooper shifted his weight from one foot to the other. He looked uncomfortable, Jack realized, not a condition he was used to seeing him in.

"Thanks for letting us know," Jack said. "We'd rather hear the news from you than someone else."

Jojo nodded slowly. Jack knew she was disappointed to hear this, because she and Dr. Song had grown close, but Jack also knew whoever the new doctor was, she'd be just as good.

"I understand," Jojo said.

Now that he had her passport, Cooper seemed eager to leave. He said goodbye and Jack walked him to the door.

"Safe travels," he said to Jack before he stepped out.

Jack nodded. "I hope so."

He closed the door and walked over to the sofa, sat down next to Jojo. "That was a surprise," he said. "All of that."

"Yes, it was. Did you really say protecting me like the president and First Lady was a requirement if you were going to participate?"

"Absolutely." He put his arm around her and she leaned into him. His other hand went to her stomach. "I want you *both* to be protected."

"How does all of this work, though?"

"Cooper will communicate anything and everything that we need to know. I don't want you to stress or worry about this. We'll get all the specific instructions when we need to know."

"Okay," Jojo said. "I'll stop thinking about it. I do need to get some more iron pills. I'm getting hungry, too, I wouldn't mind going out instead of ordering room service."

"Whatever you'd like," Jack said. "If you want to get ready to go, I'll look online and see where the closest pharmacy is."

When he went online, he quickly found a nearby CVS, which was close to a bakery where they could get something to eat. Jack decided to check the Deutsche Bank account, and was again surprised to see that there was still a balance of over one billion dollars. The money hadn't been touched. Since Sutton had told him to take the matter up with China or Iran, Jack changed the password to "Dumplings4All!"

He closed the laptop. "I found a nearby CVS," he said. "And there's a bakery right across the street."

Before leaving the hotel, Davis came up and introduced them to two of their new agents, Victor and Sophia, both young, very fit individuals. They shook hands and Jack told them what their plans were for the morning.

They were shadowed by a number of Secret Service agents as they exited the hotel and headed toward the wharf. At the bakery, they ordered lattes, croissants, and a baguette, which they enjoyed as they strolled along the wharf, watching as the boats docked. Eventually, they made their way into CVS.

"Wait," Jojo said, only a few steps into the store. "I thought we were going to a pharmacy?"

"This is it," Jack said.

"Wow." Jojo's eyes widened as she looked around and started checking out one of the aisles.

"The pharmacy section is in the back," Jack added.

Pharmacies in China were small, dreary, and owned by the government. Most drugs were Chinese-made. The more serious drugs could be procured from the doctor's small pharmacy in their own office. This was the first time Jojo had stepped foot into an American pharmacy.

At the vitamin section, she stood, surveying all of the choices. "There are so many different types of iron pills," she said. "How do I know which one to pick?"

Jack looked at the options, of which there was an abundance. "Hmm," he said. "Well, I'm not expert, but we can ask someone who is." He walked a little further to the back of the store where the pharmacy was. The pharmacist was an older woman with glasses on a beaded chain around her neck.

"I was wondering if you could help us," he said. "My wife is pregnant. Her doctor in China was prescribing iron, but we don't know how much to get now."

"I'd be happy to help you," the woman said. She came out from behind the counter and walked with Jack back to aisle of supplements.

"Hello," she said, smiling at Jojo. "I hear you're looking for some iron. Pregnant women usually take at least twenty-seven milligrams." She reached out and took one of the bottles off the shelf. "This is a good brand."

"Thank you," Jojo said, taking the bottle from her.

"Congratulations," the woman said. "I can ring you up over at the pharmacy counter, if you'd like."

Jack was relieved when Jojo followed the woman back to the register at the pharmacy counter. He could tell from her wide-eyed expression and the way she kept looking everywhere that Jojo would probably be content to spend the rest of the morning exploring CVS. And, if she wanted to—he'd do it, but the truth was, he disliked pharmacies for the very reason Jojo was so enthralled: they stocked so much stuff, it was hard to not feel overwhelmed.

As they walked out of CVS, Jack's black phone beeped. He pulled it out of his pocket and looked at it: *Let's leave hotel at 4PM.*

Jack replied that they'd be ready. "Who was that?" Jojo asked as he slipped the phone back in his pocket.

"That was Cooper. We're going to plan to leave today around four."

"Well, at least that means we can walk around a little more," Jojo said. Ahead of them were five Secret Service agents, spread out and at a distance, but keeping watch. Davis, Sophia, and Victor were in closer proximity. Jack still found it hard to believe that he required Secret Service protection; in fact, he and Jojo were probably two of the best protected individuals in the United States right now, something that Jack took comfort in. He hoped it stayed that way.

CHAPTER 24

Back on the plane, this time headed home, an hour added to the length of the journey, thanks to head winds. A few hours into the flight, Jojo was napping so Jack took out his iPad and got caught up on the latest news from China. The areas of Guangzi and Chongqing were both hit by massive floods, which destroyed homes, infrastructure, crops, with an estimated thirty-five billion US dollars in damage. Lives were lost and mass protests were held at the lack of government infrastructure to prevent such occurrences.

Jack realized there were now four places in China that were facing serious protests. Mongolia was forcibly requiring students to learn Mandarin, and there was the cadmium-tainted rice in Hunan. Now the floods. The events did not seem interconnected, yet Jack couldn't help but wonder what might happen if more events like this occurred, followed by more mass protests. Given China's historic mass detention of Uyghurs and the destruction of their cultural heritage, he was surprised that there weren't more protests. Then again, he knew one of the key jobs of local officials was to squash such protests, as delicately as possible. It seemed like a ticking time bomb.

A message came through, jolting Jack from his thoughts. It was from his friend Ari. *Hello Jack. Mary and I would like to take you up on your offer—how about dinner this Friday at your place? We'll be in town visiting a friend of Mary's.*

Jack waited until Jojo woke up to ask if she'd be fine with that, though he knew she would be. Ari had been there the first night he had met Jojo, after all.

* * *

They got back home around lunchtime and spent a few hours sitting out by the pool. It was nice to be back on solid ground and outside, breathing fresh air, after their thirty-hour flight.

Jack was in the kitchen getting tea for Jojo when the doorbell rang. A young woman stood at the door; a few feet from her was a Secret Service agent, who gave Jack a discreet nod that she had been checked out and was no threat.

"Hi," Jack said.

The woman smiled. "Hi, Mr. Gold. My name is Ginger Sun; I'm Mrs. Gold's new ob-gyn." She spoke perfect English. She carried nothing and did not have a backpack or any other type of bag.

"Hi, Dr. Sun," Jack said. "Please, call me Jack. Come on in; Jojo's out by the pool." He led the way and then left Dr. Sun and Jojo to talk while he finished getting the tea, adding a cup for the doctor.

When he came back out carrying a tray with the tea, he heard Dr. Sun say, "I went to John Hopkins Medical School, then did my residency at USC. I was Chief Resident there, and I practiced for a few years and was then approached to teach obstetrics and gynecology at UCLA." Jack couldn't help but be impressed—he knew both of those institutions, and they were excellent.

Jack poured tea and then sat and listened while Dr. Sun asked Jojo some general questions. If he had to guess, Dr. Sun was probably in her late twenties and it was easy to see how she and Jojo had already hit it off.

"Is this the first time you've been to Dali?" Jojo asked.

"It is," Dr. Sun said. "I'm originally from a small town in Shandong called Jining, the hometown of Confucius. It's really beautiful here, and the food is delicious."

Jojo told Dr. Sun about the local market, the bakery, and the trail near the university. It seemed to Jack they were more like two good friends who hadn't seen each other in a while.

Finally, Dr. Sun stood up, though she did seem reluctant to go. "It was a pleasure to meet both of you," she said. "Truly. I look forward to taking care of all the medical needs for both of you. So if you need anything outside of obstetrics, let me know."

They walked Ginger back through the house and to the front door and said goodbye. Jojo had a big smile on her face. "I'd forgotten how nice people are from Shandong," she said as Jack closed the door. "Ginger is so sweet and she seems incredibly smart."

Jack nodded. "You don't become the Chief Resident at USC unless you are exceedingly smart."

"Yeah, what is a chief resident, anyway?"

"Hospitals ask the smartest doctor in training to stay an extra year to manage and educate the incoming students. It's a big deal."

Jojo's smile widened. "Well, I thought it would be difficult to replace Dr. Song, but I am glad to say I was wrong."

"In this case, I'm glad you were wrong, too," Jack said. "Now. We've got Ari and Mary coming for dinner tomorrow. What should we prepare?"

"I was thinking maybe we'd just order something. That way you don't have to spend the whole afternoon preparing something and we can just relax until they get here. What if we ordered something from The Backyard?"

"That sounds great," Jack said. The Backyard was a pizza and steakhouse in Old Dali, and Jack knew that his old pal Ari would certainly appreciate a meal that wasn't Chinese cuisine.

CHAPTER 25

There was a knock at the door the next day right at five-thirty. Ari and Mary came in, hugs were given, and then Jojo and Mary hurried upstairs while Ari stood with Jack and admired the garage.

"You have some nice toys in here," Ari said. "Are they yours?"

"They came with the place." Jack pointed at the Ducati. "I've taken that out a few times. It's a sweet ride."

"I bet," Ari said. "I can see you riding it. Me, though, I don't know if that's quite my style. I'm more of a Porsche-kind of guy. It's easier to ride around in that with a sandwich or beer in my hand." He grinned as Jack shook his head, laughing.

"Come on upstairs then," Jack said. "We can get you that drink."

Upstairs, Ari walked around and took in the view. "This is incredible, Jack," he said. "What a view."

"It's not bad," Jack said. "What can I get everyone to drink? Beer? Wine? Maotai?"

Ari perked up at the mention of Maotai. "Maotai sounds great. What type do you have?"

Jack pulled one of the bottles out of the cabinet and showed it to Ari and Mary. "This is what we usually drink."

Mary took the bottle and looked at it carefully. "Wow," she said, handing it back to Jack. "A senior business executive from Nike visited recently and wanted a good bottle of Maotai. This bottle no longer exists. So, it must be a fake. Or, it cost someone a fortune."

"Fake or not, let's have some!" Ari said.

Jack poured four glasses, filling Jojo's only halfway. They toasted, then took a sip. Ari grinned. "Tastes authentic to me," he said. "Jack, give me the rest of the tour."

Jojo and Mary took their drinks over to the sofa, so Jack went out the backdoor to show Ari the pool.

"This is a nice setup you've got here, Jack," Ari said. "Can we sit? Enjoy the view for a few moments?"

"Absolutely."

"How'd you find this place?"

"Jojo's dad hooked us up. My guess is that it's meant for senior party officials. Same as our current home. Everything is the best. No expense spared. Did I tell you that Wang gave us the boutique hotel in Beijing as a wedding present? The lease is for seventy years."

Ari held his glass up for another toast. "All my father-in-law does is offer me cigarettes, and I don't even smoke. Good for you, Jack."

"How are things with Israel?"

"Israel is doing er well. Its high-tech sector is growing strong. From a security standpoint, everything looks positive."

"That's great to hear." Jack cast a sidelong look at Ari. "Do you mind if I ask what you think about AI?"

Ari raised an eyebrow. "An interesting question, Jack. Is there something specific you want to know? We're brothers for life, remember? You can just ask."

"Okay." Jack paused. "Does Israel have AI?"

"No. Not yet. But the United States does."

"How do you know that?"

Ari took a sip of his Maotai and set the glass on the side table next to him. "Jack, the United States put more money into AI research than all other countries combined. How do you think that—seemingly out of nowhere—the Middle East deal was done? How did they discover an approach that no other administration could find? Trust me—Sutton's son-in-law is not that smart to come up with the plan on his own." Ari chuckled.

Jack was not surprised to hear that; he, too, had felt such a peace agreement had come out of thin air. "Maybe you can share your understanding of AI. I'm trying to learn more. It's rather overwhelming, to be honest."

Ari finished off his Maotai, rubbed his hands together, and settled back in his chair. "To start, let's take a little trip back in time. YouTube was started in 2005; Facebook in 2004. The purpose was to sell ads and get people to stay on their platforms as long as possible, in order to see as many ads as possible. How did they do it? They wrote and tested, then used, algorithms to predict how best to keep you on the site. To recommend things."

"Okay," Jack said. "Can you give me an example?"

"Here's a simple one from early on. If someone on Facebook searched using the words *new mother*, the algorithm would recommend inoculation groups. Or, let's say you've got a thirteen-year-old viewing diet videos. YouTube would suggest anorexia videos, because those are better at keeping a teen's attention. The scary part of this is that these algorithms have only gotten better and better. Those technology systems have taken control of human choice, because they're controlling the information we're getting. It's just we don't realize it. And when you control the information a population is getting, you are controlling their choices."

"Like censorship's role here in China."

"Right. But imagine it on a much grander scale. A machine learning everything, about everyone, in a country via *all* modes of communication. And using not just one, but a huge number of algorithms to not just *predict* but also *influence* behavior. What can be achieved is unimaginable. The intelligence and self-learning are like a never-ending turbo charge."

Jack realized he'd been clenching his jaw. He tried to relax it, took his final sip of Maotai, looked at Ari. "I think I need a beer," he said. "And maybe a shot of whiskey. What about you?"

"You know I never turn down an offer of food or drink. And Jack, I have some friends in tech companies, who know a lot about AI. If you'd like to learn more, I can make an intro."

Jack stood, collecting his empty glass. Ari did the same. "I appreciate the offer," he said. "I might take you up on it. I've been in touch with a few people who know quite a bit about it too, but honestly, sometimes it feels like the explanations go right over my head."

Ari looked amused. "Probably not a situation you're used to finding yourself in."

Inside, they were greeted by a delicious, savory aroma and found that Jojo and Mary had set everything out on the table.

"Oh my god," Ari yelped, upon seeing the table. "This looks amazing."

"I ordered some things from The Backyard," Jojo said. "We've got some lamb and steak with mash, salmon, salads, and two pizzas."

"I'm salivating," Ari said. "Seriously. This looks amazing. I'm so tired of Chinese food. If you took a Chinese person and said they had to eat white people food for one week, they would rebel."

Jojo and Mary looked at each other, seemed to be communicating something without using words, and burst out laughing. "Let's eat," Jojo said.

Ari sat down and began serving himself with gusto. Jack took some of the lamb ribs and mash and a portion of the salad. It was nice to have a plate of such delectable food in front of him that he hadn't cooked himself.

"Mary was just telling me how she doesn't work at Nike anymore," Jojo said to Jack.

"Oh?" Jack said. "How come?"

Mary had been about to cut into her steak, but she put her silverware down. "I left them a while ago," she said. "When China announced the new security law in Hong Kong, and there were protests, Nike did and said nothing. Nothing! They had signed a deal with the China's Ministry of Sports and would have been disowned if they did. More importantly, a very well-known NBA star told other players not to say anything. He was worried that NBA players would lose contracts in China if they spoke out. This person being a very outspoken proponent of other social justice issues, but apparently Chinese lives aren't that important. Same with the NFL. These people have a platform, a voice, and they didn't use it because they didn't want to lose a contract." Mary picked up her fork and knife and resumed cutting her food. "So," she said mildly, "I joined Adidas and got a pay raise. Ha."

"This woman isn't afraid to tell it like it is," Ari said. He let out a little groan. "Oh my god, this food is *so good*."

"Well, it's refreshing to hear candid views and see someone not backing away from what they believe," Jack said. "And hey, I like Adidas."

"This steak *is* quite good," Mary said. "Did you hear the news today? An alliance of eight countries are likely to boycott the Olympics next year. They referenced civil unrest. It's not official yet, but expect a final decision soon. And that would be a real shame. Adidas will lose out on a bunch of promotional opportunities."

Jack and Jojo exchanged a glance. What President Sutton said seemed to be coming true.

"That'll be a big blow to China's international prestige," Jack said. "I hope it doesn't happen."

"As you know," Ari said, "there are some things we just can't control."

Jack didn't mind when the conversation switched to Jojo's pregnancy. He didn't want the entire meal to be dominated by talk of politics and the state of affairs in China; he wanted a regular evening, with friends, like any other normal couple might do.

There was no need to worry about leftovers with Ari's appetite and enthusiasm. After dinner, Jojo made tea and they all sat in the living area, watching the last of the sunset through the big picture windows.

After they left, Jack and Jojo sat on the couch together. "Ari sure can eat," Jojo said. "Although, with my appetite being pregnant, I think I might be able to match him."

Jack laughed. "I don't think so. That man likes to eat. But it was good to see them. It's nice to get together with friends."

"Hopefully we can do more of that," Jojo said. "Just like a regular old married couple."

CHAPTER 26

The next morning, Jack was up early, drinking coffee and browsing the news sites. The Shanghai Stock Exchange had opened a little while ago and had immediately fallen five percent. The circuit breakers halted trading for fifteen minutes; once trading resumed, it immediately fell another five percent.

This was happening because people were cashing out of the stock market. But why? He typed RMB *exchanger rate* into the search bar and read the first article that came up: "RMB Status Won't Stick." People were trying to trade their RMB, also known as Yuan, into US dollars.

There was a protest with an estimated ten thousand people protesting the low labor wages in Shenyang factory. What exacerbated the seriousness of the strike was that there was a similar one in Guangzhou, also by migrant workers. They were communicating via WeChat and Weibo, too fast for the authorities to monitor.

So many protests. Someone was influencing them. Jack took a sip of his coffee and heard his black phone beep. The message from Cooper said that it was time to fly to Taipei and meet Ron Timmons, the Secretary of State. Tomorrow he'd meet with President Tsai Wending.

Plan to leave in an hour, Cooper's message concluded.

Jack finished his coffee and went into the bedroom, where Jojo was just waking up. "Good morning," she said with a yawn. "I can't believe this, after all the good food we had last night, but I have such a craving for a breakfast sandwich from McDonald's."

Jack lay down next to her. "I will definitely order you one," he said.

"I was thinking maybe we could go out, take a walk after."

"That sounds great, babe, but . . . I just got a message from Cooper. I have to go to Taipei today, and leave in an hour. I'll only be gone for a day or two. Will you miss me?"

The expression on Jojo's face darkened. "Jack, we just got back. Do you really have to take off *now*?"

"I have to," he said. "We discussed this with the president. And this is for your dad, too. It's important."

"I'm just . . . I'm afraid that you won't come back. This whole thing seems really dangerous. Is that what you want? For me to be raising our child on my own?"

"Of course I don't want that. That's the last thing I want. But . . . you know me, Jojo. You know I have to finish what I've started. And I thought we talked about this. It's not going to be forever. But I can't stop now. I gave them my word."

"You also gave me your word when we got married," Jojo said.

Jack sighed. He didn't want to leave on this note, but he knew the only thing that would assuage Jojo now would be if he said he wouldn't go. He wished he could explain it to her in a way she would understand, *truly* understand—he had always been like this, he had always finished what he started. It was who he was. Something that his father had instilled in him at a young age, and not a trait that he could simply discard because it was making someone upset. Even if that someone was his beloved wife.

"I love you," Jack said. "And I will be back soon." He moved to kiss her on the forehead but she pulled back and rolled over, so her back was to him.

* * *

Midway through his flight, which, at just over three hours felt like nothing, Jack got another message on his black phone. *Meet Ron Timmons for a drink tonight, at 6PM, in the lobby of the Mandarin Oriental. Yes, Taipei has one too. The Taiwan's Presidential Office Building will be bombed by China and demolished at 10:30AM, shortly after your meeting. No casualties.*

It was a drastic measure, though Jack knew such a measure was needed to get people to wake up. Not that it was a guarantee—some people would never think anything was more important than looking at WeChat and shopping online.

A thought suddenly occurred to Jack—how did he know the messages he was receiving were actually coming from Cooper? There wasn't any reason to think they weren't, but who was to say that they weren't coming from a machine that knew how Cooper texts?

No, he thought. *That's a ridiculous thought.*

But was it? *Unimaginable things*, was how Ari had phrased it. Jack picked the phone back up. He typed: *How do I know I am actually texting with Cooper?*

The reply was almost instantaneous. *Because I gave you an upgraded phone recently at the White House. Good thinking to ask that question, though.*

Okay, he wasn't communicating with a machine. That was good. But it now did not seem that farfetched to think that eventually, computers would be smart enough to use ubiquitous cameras that could pick up conversations. Then things would be much different. He didn't want to be around then, maybe he and Jojo could stay in Dali forever. But then Jack realized he had not one, but two phones, as well as a MacBook and an iPad. Five devices. He was wrong—they had already arrived. He, and everyone else who used digital technology were being monitored, all the time, everywhere. He'd been living with it, utilizing it, and enjoying it, the entire time being blissfully ignorant about the existential reality of it all.

*   *   *

Jack met with Secretary of State, Ron Timmons, in the lobby lounge of the Mandarin Oriental after he had checked in. Ron was tall, with dark hair and blue eyes, and he had a friendly demeanor which did little to calm Jack's nerves. Jack couldn't explain it, but after his last text conversation with Cooper, he felt more and more unsettled about this plan he was partaking in. Yet he couldn't pinpoint exactly *what* was making him so uneasy.

"Have you been to Taiwan before?" Jack asked Ron. Obviously Ron was on board with this plan, but what would happen if Jack backed out?

Ron shook his head. "No, actually, I haven't. Though not because I haven't wanted to; the politics have prevented me. It really would have pissed China off. So, that's a great segue for me to ask you for your insider take on Taiwan."

Jack tried to keep his face neutral, despite finding it unbelievable that the United States Secretary of State was asking *him* for insights into

Taiwan. He took note that Ron had used the word "Taiwan" instead of the word "country."

But he decided to humor him. "Chiang Kai-shek fled Mao and the communists in 1949 and formalized the island country of Taiwan. The capitalist economy steadily grew, unlike China, and the people maintained their cultural values and the small country evolved. China constantly perceived Taiwan as a renegade province and wanted unification. China cringed when other countries or companies referred to Taiwan as a country, but it was and is. Now, President Wang is much more receptive to a formally independent Taiwan and just wants peace and prosperity for all." Jack shrugged "That's the abridged version. Does that make sense?"

"It does, Jack, and I appreciate it."

"So, where do you focus most of your time, if not in Asia?"

"Mostly in Europe. We still haven't finalized a comprehensive trade deal. Germany is buying oil from Russia. NATO. Well, NATO is NATO: No Action Talk Only. Each country has a different agenda and culture. Wheels spinning in the mud."

Jack thought that was a good point. He had been only dealing with Chinese, and although there were many differences, there was still a band within which they operated. The French were so different from Germans, and Germans were so different from the English. "The word *Europeans* is almost useless," Jack said.

Ron smiled. "You're right. It's a geographic term—as is Asians."

Jack felt a little more relaxed as his conversation with Ron continued. "What do you expect tomorrow?"

"Well, it'll be quick. We enter at 10AM for a photo-op. We reassure President Tsai that America stands with her, in front of the cameras. Then, we are out of there by ten-thirty. At the latest." He gave Jack an apologetic look. "Seems like a long flight for such a short visit, if you ask me."

"If things go according to plan, I think we'll be communicating a message globally that will help both President Tsai and President Wang." Jack paused. "My guess is that it could be the most consequential meeting of your life."

Ron's brow creased. "I'll have to give that some more thought. But, interestingly, Jack, I believe you."

"I'm glad we had this chance to talk before tomorrow," Jack said. And he was; his prior doubts were dwindling. If things did work out as planned, it could help usher in the real change that Jack hoped to see in China. "So I guess we'll meet tomorrow and go there together?"

"No," Ron said. "I heard that, for security reasons, we'll be traveling separately."

"Oh," Jack said. "Okay, then. Well, I'll see you there."

He and Ron stood and shook hands; then Jack made is way back to his room. Davis walked with him.

"Let's plan on leaving at nine-forty tomorrow," he said. "As Ron mentioned, you'll be traveling there separately. Make sure you bring your luggage; we'll go directly to the airport afterward."

"Sure thing," Jack said. "Have a good night, Davis. See you tomorrow."

Jack went into his room. Neither he nor Ron had mentioned that Taiwan's Presidential Office Building would be bombed, minutes after they left. It occurred to Jack that perhaps Ron did not know that part of the plan. Or, if Ron *did* know, did he also know that it was actually the Chinese government who was responsible?

Jack got undressed and hopped in the shower. He wouldn't say something about it unless Ron asked. Had a computer somehow known beforehand, maybe by using their psychometric profiles, to determine how their conversation would transpire?

When he got out of the shower, he looked at his phone to see if there were any messages from Jojo. He hadn't heard from her, though he also hadn't been in touch. He opened WeChat and typed a quick message: *Thinking of you. Hope you had a good day. I'll be back tomorrow.*

CHAPTER 27

Given the friendly relationship between Taiwan and America, four of Jack's security detail were permitted to join him as he was escorted into the president's office. President Tsai immediately stood up and walked over, grasping Jack's hand with both of hers. "Jack," she said, speaking in Mandarin, "I've heard and read so much about you. It's truly an honor to meet you."

"President Tsai, it is I who am honored to meet you." Jack smiled. "These seem like positive times. I want to share that there are many influential people who support you and Taiwan."

"I understand we need to leave this building no later than ten-thirty."

"Yes," Jack said. He felt she not only wanted to confirm what was about to transpire, but also to receive acknowledgement that her passion for an independent Taiwan was receiving the support she had always hoped and dreamed it would. "That is my understanding, Madam President."

"Well, we better keep this news conference brief, then." She looked over Jack's shoulder. "The Secretary of State is here. Hello, Mr. Timmons. I think it best we get started." She politely guided Jack and Ron to the next room, where they were greeted with about thirty members from the press, holding cameras and video recorders. Flashes began going off immediately.

President Tsai began to speak in Mandarin. "Ladies and gentlemen," she started, "I was just meeting with US Secretary of State, Ron Timmons, and Mr. Jack Gold, who I believe you all know. We had a productive discussion about the global recognition of Taiwan. I am grateful for their support."

It was smart of her to speak Chinese, not English, Jack thought. That way, everyone in China could clearly understand her message.

President Tsai turned to Ron and shook his hand. In English, she said, "Thank you, Secretary Timmons, for coming to Taiwan." And now, any

Americans and other English-speaking nations would also understand clearly what was being said. She then pivoted to Jack, and switched back to Mandarin. "I know you have been to Taiwan many times before, for business. But this is my first time meeting you, Mr. Gold, and I am honored."

"It's my pleasure, Madam President," Jack said, in Mandarin. "I hope on my next visit I can see more of Taiwan's modern infrastructure and, once again, visit your amazing hot springs."

President Tsai smiled at him and then turned back to face the cameras. Dozens of hands went up for questions. "Ultimately," President Tsai said, "what Taiwan wants is peace and prosperity for all. Now, I know that the secretary has a busy schedule in Asia. Thank you all for coming today."

Jack stood there, watching the waving hands, feeling like a prop. It was a strange feeling, that he was simply going along with some larger plan, all because of AI. But he continued to play his role, mostly because he knew the president was being sincere, and because he hoped the plan would indeed be successful. And he *did* have credibility in China from his previous broadcast from the Control Center and the recent province project; his presence added credibility to President Tsai achieving her objective of international acknowledgement for an independent country. The Chinese had received mixed signals about Taiwan over the years, but Jack being there would assure them that what President Tsai said was true. Previous administrations in China had been adamantly against Taiwan being its own country; only Wang's administration wanted a independent Taiwan.

Ron took a step closer to Jack. "You said the exact same words to me last night," he whispered. "*Peace and prosperity.*"

Jack was surprised he recalled that. He felt someone touch his elbow and he turned his head slightly, saw Davis.

"Sir, we have to leave, please," Davis said in a low but firm voice.

Jack nodded briskly. He shook President Tsai's hand, then Ron's, and then followed Davis out of the back of the Taiwan Presidential Office Building.

What happened next was broadcast on every Chinese CCTV channel, and Jack watched on his laptop on the plane back to Dali. China fired two supersonic cruise missiles that penetrated the US missile defense system, delivering a conventional but effective payload. The Taiwan

Presidential Office Building was instantly obliterated. The prior broadcast, showing Jack, Ron, and President Tsai, had been aired around the world by every news station. According to the broadcasts, it was unclear if all three had been killed in the blast or made it out safely.

Online, Jack saw that the 50-cent party had been unleashed. They had gained that name because they were paid fifty cents for every social media post they made; there were over 200,000 such individuals and total yearly posts by the government and government-sponsored internet commenters generated about 500 million posts in a year in China. They swayed the online conversations and opinions that the bombing of Taipei was the responsibility of an anti-Wang administration group that commandeered a bombing center.

Jack's black phone beeped. The message from Cooper read: *Good job. The two missiles have hit their target and the explosion was contained. Everyone is safe. Please spend the night in Beijing. Wang would like to meet with you tomorrow at 4:30PM. You must leave by 5:30PM.*

OK, Jack wrote back.

This will all be over soon.

Jack put the phone down and glanced at Davis, who was seated across from him. "I understand we are going to Beijing?"

"It's a shame we're not earning frequent flier miles," Davis said dryly. "Do you want to know what the worst part of a mission is, besides getting and reviewing all the intel?"

"I don't."

"It's having to wait. The waiting sucks. Everything needs to be done not just correctly, but at the proper time, otherwise things can go wrong and kill you and others. When I was in special forces, I had to rely on my team members for everything. The challenge in your case is that you cannot see all your teammates, they're too far away. But we're here with you, Jack."

"I appreciate that." Jack leaned his head back and closed his eyes. His thoughts went to Jojo, and he opened his eyes and took his iPhone out to call her.

"Hi, babe," he said when she answered.

"*Hi babe?!*" she said. "Jack, once again you're all over the news! They're saying they don't know if you're dead or alive! Are you safe? What is going on?"

"I'm okay," Jack said, relieved that she had answered the phone in the first place. "We're all okay."

"I called my father but he didn't pick up, I've been freaking out . . . I thought the morning you left might have been the last time I saw you!"

"I'm sorry," Jack said.

"But you're on your way home, to Dali, now?"

He paused. "Um, well, actually . . . I'm on my way to Beijing. We're almost there. Your dad wants to meet with me tomorrow."

There was an even longer pause on Jojo's end. "Babe?" Jack said.

"Have you ever considered at all how your actions might affect me? How I felt when I saw the footage of the building exploding? Followed by the not knowing if you were in there or not? How could you do that to me, Jack?"

He closed his eyes and pressed his thumb onto one eyeball, his index finger on the other, little explosions of colorful fireworks going off behind his eyelids. "Jojo, I'm sorry. Nothing I have done has ever been to stress you out or make you feel bad, I swear. I had no control over what was going to be broadcast."

"Yes you did," she snapped. "No one *forced* you to go. You could have said no. You had control over making the choice to go or not, and you chose to do it."

"Can we talk about this when I get home? Please?"

"Home? Jack, you're in Beijing. I'm in Dali. Where is your home?"

"My home is with you, Jojo. I'm in Beijing because your father wants to meet with me tomorrow. After that, I'll be on my way right back to you. We agreed that I would do this, remember? You were there, you heard the president explain things."

"He didn't say this would happen!" she shrieked.

The line went dead.

Jack kept the phone pressed against his ear for a moment longer, knowing that Davis had at least heard his side of the conversation, and maybe he'd even heard Jojo's final retort because she hung up on him. He put the phone down.

"It's not easy," Davis said. "I'm not trying to eavesdrop, but . . . it can be hard for the spouses." He gave Jack a chagrined look. "I learned that the hard way."

In all his travels with Davis this past year, Jack realized that he knew very little about the man's personal life, though he had always felt that Davis had wanted it that way.

"You were married?" Jack asked.

"It was a while ago, and it didn't work out because I wasn't around as much as she wanted me to be. She was unhappy; I was unhappy that I was making her feel that way, but at the same time . . . we had discussed such things prior to getting married. Sometimes, people agree to something they think they understand but then it plays out and they realize they're not pleased at all with the outcome. And . . ." Davis paused. "You might want to factor the pregnancy hormones into the equation, too."

"I know." Jack sighed. He felt he was being pulled in opposite directions and he was beginning to wonder if this was really all worth it. But he had to see it through. He looked at Davis. "I'll be glad when this is all over."

CHAPTER 28

It felt strange to return to their home in Beijing after being away for a while, and without Jojo. He took a shower and then tried to reach Jojo for a video call on WeChat. She didn't answer.

He browsed some news sites and found it interesting how the Chinese websites were focused on whether he, Ron, and President Tsai were still alive. Every article he looked at replayed the destruction of the building. Did people care? Jack knew that one event seldom was able to convince people or impact them enough emotionally to initiate real change. Multiple events were required; personal feelings needed to be triggered. And, there needed to be an interconnectivity amongst people to sufficiently amplify and unify emotions.

Over the years, Communist Party members had been indoctrinated about China's history, that the South China Sea and Taiwan were part of China. They believed what they were originally taught: that Taiwan was a province of China, where Chinese lived. They had never visited, nor ever seen the country that shared a common historical lineage, yet had evolved much differently. Jack had a feeling that the bombing of Taiwan was only the first of things to come.

The BBC's website had the Taiwan bombing as front page news, with a picture of the demolished Presidential Office Building. The article began: China launched two supersonic missiles, destroying Taiwan's Presidential Office Building. It is believed that this was in retaliation for Taiwan's recent actions seeking international recognition as an independent country. No casualties were reported. It is unclear how the United States might respond, since historically, it has strongly supported Taiwan defending itself, though has not guaranteed military protection or retribution."

The other articles he read on the Western websites were nearly identical. Someone had sent out press releases; the information was too similar for that not to be the case. Jack wasn't sure if it was the US or China; nothing had yet been released outside of China that indicated those responsible were a fringe group of disgruntled Chinese officials. The stories simply said the missiles came from China; there was no mention of Chinese troops landing in Taiwan. While this might be the case to the external world, Jack suspected that a completely different plan within China's social media was being played out. Unfortunately, his reading ability in Chinese was not good enough to comprehend the various news boards.

China's key English newspaper, the *Global Times*, only repeated the BBC taking points and mentioned there was a fringe group within the Chinese military that was responsible. "An investigation was being conducted to determine exactly who was responsible for the missile launch," the article stated. Jack knew what was likely happening in the US: Chinese students living there were bombarding their friends and relatives in China about the news. This influential external group massively heightened the attention of Chinese in China on the story, augmented by the sharing of stories from Chinese students living throughout Europe. Concern and suspicion as to the true situation and motivations dominated a good portion of the global Chinese population's perception.

But, Jack knew, that since Wang took over, there had been many positive changes in China—Hong Kong was a good example of this. It was still ruled by China, yet freedoms had been restored. Other positive examples: Re-education camps had mostly been emptied in Xinjiang. Tibet was given great autonomy, but open transportation meant too much commerce was being brought into the previously closed region. Citizens of China had open Internet access but the propaganda bureau continued almost as before. Regulations opening free and fair trade had been adopted in earnest and foreign companies were entering and treated as domestic ones. These were all good changes that Jack was pleased to see.

Just before going to bed, his phone beeped; a text from Jojo. *You know those days that can change your life for good or bad?* It read. *You not being here with me was one of those days.*

He read the message over again, then waited, hoping another might come, but it did not. He wasn't sure if any response from him would help things at this point; he didn't want to upset her more, but he also could not do what she wanted, which was to return to her right this very moment. He turned the phone off and put it on the bedside table. If only there was a way to make her understand that his need to see this to completion had nothing to do with how much he loved her or valued their relationship.

*   *   *

Jack wore his new Armani suit, with the nontraditional collar that came slightly up his neck, for his meeting with Wang. Davis drove him the short distance to Zhongnanhai, but before turning into the main entrance, he caught Jack's eye in the rearview mirror. "We decided this morning that it would be best to meet you at the Eastern Gate Entrance when we leave. We must be out of here by 5:30PM. There should be very few people in there, hence no reason for any delay."

"Got it," Jack said. He got out when Davis stopped at the Eastern Gate, where a woman stood, waiting to receive him.

"Hello, Mr. Gold," she said. "Follow me. The president is waiting for you by the lake."

He followed her inside, through several long corridors, then back outside, where Jack saw Wang Yang sitting at the exact table where Jack had first formally met him. This time, though, there was no stack of paperwork in front of him; instead, he sat comfortably, drinking tea, the smoke from his cigarette curling up in tendrils toward the sky. He stood when he saw Jack.

"Jack," he said with a warm smile. "Great to see you. Please, sit down."

Jack did as Wang suggested, though he thought it might be better to get the pictures taken for news media circulation first, and then get out. Wang pushed the pack of cigarettes toward him. "We found out who is behind the small fraction of communist party members causing the rebellion," he said as Jack helped himself to a cigarette. "They are also causing and enflaming the protests with the aim to dimmish the government's standing and compel other nationals to boycott the Olympics."

"Who?" Jack asked after he lit the cigarette and exhaled a plume of smoke.

"It's Li Keqiang. He used to be the Premier of the State Council under my predecessor." Wang smiled. "Sutton calls him a 'hunting dog,' which is a pretty big insult in Chinese."

"I know of him," Jack said. "He's quite adept at finding problems but not solving them."

Wang raised his eyebrows. "Exactly. That's why I removed him. But he didn't take kindly to it. This evening, after . . . after the bombing occurs, all of them will be arrested. They will be charged with subversion, undermining the power and authority of the central government. It'll be over. But the people will still need help to understand what has happened and make sense of it, both logically and emotionally." Wang looked over Jack's shoulder. "The photographer's here," he said, standing. Jack did the same.

The photographer took several photos of them; Jack smiled but he knew it probably looked forced. The photos were necessary, though, to show them together at Zhongnanhai, to arouse the concern in people that they might have perished, to create that emotional reaction and distract the public from other matters. It would be a shock, since both of them were well-known. He couldn't help but wonder how often people were manipulated, both subtly and more blatantly. Far more than he knew, he was realizing.

When the photographer finished, Wang turned to Jack. "Before we leave, I must get something from the bunker. You were down there before; there are some important keys I must keep on myself, even though they are likely to be destroyed in the blast." These keys, Jack knew could manually override the entire system. Taking those keys would ensure an extra layer of security.

Jack recalled the bunker, which was full of offices, as well as the government's situation room. It was fortified enough that it could withstand a nuclear blast.

Wang started to walk and Jack kept pace next to him. They traversed a different set of corridors that led to the elevator that would take them many floors underground. Wang pressed the button.

Just as he did so, Jack heard soft footsteps, like the footsteps of someone trying to move undetected. The footsteps sped up and a person appeared suddenly, maneuvering in front of them just as the elevator doors opened. Before Jack could register what was actually happening, the man thrust a gun first into Jack's face, then pointed it at Wang. It was only then that Jack realized who it was: Liang, the head of the security regiment at Zhongnanhai.

"Liang," Jack said, shocked. "What are you doing?"

"Enough is enough," Liang said, a hard look on his face. There was a part of Jack that expected the look to change, flip to a smile, this was just some sort of practical joke, wasn't it? "Wang is demolishing China," Liang continued. "Dismantling communism. We cannot take it any longer." That look on Liang's face was a mix of anger, frustration, and determination. Jack could see in his eyes that he believed in what he was doing, and that made him both predictable and dangerous. If they did not do what he demanded, they would face consequences, Jack had no doubt.

Jack glanced at Wang without moving his head. Wang's shocked expression matched how Jack felt. Did AI predict this? Jack wondered. From the look on Wang's face, he'd have to guess no.

"Cào nǐ mā!" Wang hissed. *Fuck your mother.* Appropriate for the situation, but Jack had never heard Wang swear before, not even jokingly. Wang's feelings of being betrayed were evident and valid: he had entrusted the safety of Zhongnanhai, its occupants, and the boutique hotel where Jack and Jojo lived, to Liang. Only to be betrayed like this.

Jack suppressed the fear and panic that were trying to bubble up. He raised his hands, let Liang see they were shaking a little, though Liang did not need to know this was intentional. Jack wanted him to think that he, Liang, was in complete control and that Jack was terrified. Liang looked at him as he raised his hands, and then Jack rotated his left shoulder, knowing Liang's gaze would go there. Jack kept his hands in the same place.

"Get behind me," he said to Wang.

Liang pointed the gun at Jack's chest. "You want to be the hero?" he sneered.

"I'd rather not get shot," Jack said. He had zero doubt Liang would shoot him; the man had some of the best training of anyone in China. "Liang, what do you want?"

"I want keys and all of the codes to the systems below. And, I want your black phone. Unlock it so I can see your discussions with your CIA. We have been unable to crack it."

"Okay," Jack said slowly. "I'll give you the phone first." Liang stood at the threshold of the elevator, preventing the doors from closing. Once he had the phone, Liang would force them into the elevator. Or, he'd kill Jack and force Wang into the elevator. Jack lowered his arms. "I'm going to get the phone out of my pocket, okay?"

Liang nodded. Jack took the phone out. "I have to enter the passcode," he said.

"Do it quickly."

Jack did it quickly. He entered his birthdate twice. The phone started to flash red; the bomb was activated. Ten seconds until it detonated. Jack took a step toward Liang, his arm outstretched. As Liang reached out to take it, Jack raised his left hand. Liang's eyes followed the movement of his arm. As he looked up, Jack brought both his hands down together, colliding at an angle with Liang's wrist and knocking the gun out of his hand. Jack kicked out, hard and fast, knocking Liang back into the elevator, the black phone with him. With nothing blocking the threshold anymore, the doors closed and the elevator began its descent.

Jack turned to Wang, grabbed his arm. "Run," he said. "East Gate. Let's go!"

They had only take a few steps when the floor under their feet shook, the muffled sound of an explosion radiating out from underneath them.

"What was that?" Wang asked, his eyes wide.

"Keep going," Jack said. "That was my phone."

They exited the building and walked along a path and over a quaint bridge that stretched over a tranquil stream. Jack felt like he was in a dream as he made his way through all this natural beauty, which would soon be destroyed. Davis was there at the East Gate, as anxious a look on his face as Jack had ever seen.

"Come on, come on," Davis said, waving them on. They both got into the back of the SUV and Davis jumped in the front, punched the gas, and they took off.

"Jesus Christ, Jack," Davis said. "What the hell happened?"

Jack's heart was racing. "Liang tried to stop us," he said. "He pulled a gun on us and demanded the codes to all Chinese intelligence and military assets. He also wanted my black phone."

"What?" Davis said, incredulous. "Liang? Holy shit."

"Somehow, Jack disarmed him and blew him up with . . ." Wang paused and looked at him. "Your phone?"

Davis looked at Jack in the rearview mirror. "You blew him up with your phone?"

"We've got Cooper to thank for that."

Davis shook his head. "I would say so. Damn."

At that moment, it felt as though there was a seismic shift under-neath them and the SUV shuddered. Jack looked over his shoulder but did not see anything. "Tomahawk Missiles?" he asked.

"America's finest," Davis said. "I'm going to take you to your place right now. It's one of the most secure in China."

"Sounds good." Jack settled back in his seat and looked at Wang, who still had a look of genuine shock on his face. "We're good," Jack said to him. "We made it out."

"I can't believe it was Liang," Wang said. "I trusted him." He shook his head. "I hope you don't mind if I spend the night. General Wang Shaojun augmented the security there with trusted lieutenants. I also made arrangements for Mini to be walked and fed."

"Of course it's fine if you stay here," Jack said. "As long as you don't mind the rules of the house."

"And what would those be?"

"You have to drink some Maotai, and we have to call my wife."

"Can we smoke in the house?"

"Smoking when you drink Maotai is mandatory."

Wang smiled, a genuine one this time. "Well, then, I will strictly adhere to the house rules."

When they arrived, they said goodbye to Davis and went inside. Jack showed Wang to the guest room, though when Wang said he was going to lie down, Jack suggested they first have that drink and a smoke.

"You've just been through a very intense situation," Jack said. "You're now just starting to experience the effects of adrenaline. Let's have a drink, take some deep breaths, and talk about what happened first."

Wang hesitated but then followed Jack back downstairs. "You seem to know what you're doing," Wang said. "Not just now, but in every situation."

Jack opened a bottle Maotai and poured them each a generous glass. He appreciated the compliment but he certainly didn't feel like he knew what he was doing when it came to Jojo, who might not even be on speaking terms with him currently. He handed a glass to Wang, who took a long sip.

"Liang was one of our best," Wang said, sounding almost wistful. "And you handled him expeditiously. I can't believe Liang was working with Li Keqiang. I just can't believe it."

"I guess it was that five percent," Jack said, referring to the odds of a positive outcome.

"And your phone? It was a bomb?"

"Yes. It wasn't always like that, but . . . the last time I was visiting the White House, my black phone was modified. I guess Cooper knew more than we did."

Jack finished his glass and poured a little more for himself. While he did that, Wang drained the rest of his and Jack filled his cup back up. "I should really call Jojo," Jack said.

Wang nodded. "Yes, by all means."

Jack got his iPhone and tried to reach her through WeChat. Three rings, four rings, five . . . she didn't answer. She wasn't going to. Jack set the iPhone down on the counter. "Your daughter is very pissed off at me for being involved with all of this and being away for so long. Understandably so; she's eight months pregnant."

Wang took his phone out of his pocket. "Let me try to reach her." She did not pick up. He slid the phone back into his pocket. "She's upset, yes."

"Time for some more Maotai, I think."

But before he poured them more, he sent her a text: *Your dad and I are both safe now at our home.*

Jack's black phone beeped as he was taking a sip; he put the glass down before that sip was fully taken, wishing it were a reply from Jojo on his other phone. But it was from Cooper: *Nice work. We need to get you a new phone. Please broadcast tomorrow night at CCTV Control Center at 6PM. Details to come.*

Jack put the phone down and looked at Wang. "That was Cooper," he said. "Something about broadcasting tomorrow night at the Control Center?"

Wang kept his eyes on him as he took a sip. "Yes," he said. "Tomorrow night, at the Control Center, we'd like you to speak. I know you probably thought you'd never be doing something like that again, but the nation trusts you. They will be elated that you are safe, after the bombing of Taiwan and Zhongnanhai. You can share what has happened. It will unite the nation. This is the last step in liberating Taiwan and China adopting a new constitution. You will be ushering in a new era for China and the Chinese people. I know it's a lot to ask of you, but I don't request it for myself. I do so for your child, and for future generations."

Jack swallowed. It was, indeed, a lot to ask, even though it would not be his first time doing such a thing. But if he did, he would lose Jojo. That would be it. He knew this as surely as he knew anything. She would be watching. There would be nothing he could do to repair the mistrust and pain he had created.

But Wang's last sentence lingered: *Your child and for future generations.* As much as Jack wanted to decline, and as much as he loved Jojo, for he truly did, he knew that this transcended all of that. It went beyond his own personal desires, and it even went beyond his wife's desires. To not do as Wang asked would mean there was a real chance that everything up until now had been in vain, that he might have just as well stayed with Jojo right here, the whole time. The past several months played back to him like a film reel—traversing the entire country, meeting with the various leaders, finding out how, in some ways, he was being used as a prop. But again—this was about more than just himself, and more than just his own child.

CHAPTER 29

The next morning, Jack woke up and showered. Wang was still asleep. There was no contact from Jojo.

He was making coffee when Wang came down and said good morning.

"I'm not so sure," Jack said.

Wang smiled. "Jack, it will be a great day."

"How can you say that? Did your AI give you the likely outcome of that?"

"No. But today is the last piece of the puzzle. The Chinese people have seen what has happened in both Taiwan and Beijing. They are now in a better position to stop rioting, and I just got off an important call. It seems last night was very successful in beginning the round up of those who were causing serious revolts against the government and country. More will continue today, and in particular, after you make your broadcast."

Jack put the water on for tea for Wang. He was in no mood to make breakfast for either of them, but he could make the tea. He turned and faced Wang. "America bombed Zhongnanhai. China bombed Taiwan. It was *not* revolutionaries who were responsible for that."

"You're correct," Wang said mildly. "But we are blaming them to drive support for the true Chinese government. Taiwan agreed. This was part of an overall plan that we all bought into. Including you."

Jack frowned. "It's the lying that is bothering me. I don't like lying to people. The situation is being misrepresented in order to achieve what you want."

"Not just what I want," Wang said. "What is best for the country. You know this, Jack. It is essential to achieving the desired outcome of unifying the nation and its citizens, and, in the process, avoiding chaos. It is unfortunate that each step cannot be pure, but that's just how it is.

How humans are. If the outcome is otherwise unobtainable good, then I think it's justified."

"The ends justify the means," Jack said softly. A good outcome did not excuse the bad things done to obtain it. He looked at Wang. "You sound like an ad for artificial intelligence."

"Tell me what you would have done differently," Wang said. "Tell me how it could have been done."

But Wang knew the answer to the question—there was no other way. Not doing what they did would only mean more of the same. Drastic and sustained change did require extreme actions, and, sometimes, dishonesty. It didn't seem right. But he had played a part in it, and his role still wasn't over yet.

The water for the tea boiled. Jack turned the burner off. What Wang said was correct, but that didn't make Jack like it any more.

* * *

Later that afternoon, Davis drove Jack and Wang to the CCTV Building, which was just as unattractive and uninspiring as Jack remembered it. But unlike the first time he had entered this building this time, Jack did not want to go in. His attempts to reach Jojo continued to go ignored; though there was a part of him that wanted to keep calling until she picked up.

Jack was flanked by two of his security detail, along with two Chinese military officers. A tall woman approached them as they entered; Jack recognized her right away.

"Hi, Tingting," he said.

She was unable to hide the look of surprise on her face as her eyes darted from Jack to Wang. "President Wang," she said. "This . . . this is such an expected pleasure to see you."

"They are expecting us in the Control Center and adjacent broadcasting room," Wang said. "Will you please escort us up there?"

Everything was happening so quickly, yet somehow Jack felt like things were in slow motion, as Tingting led the way, just as she had the first time Jack had gone into this building. The six of them crowded into the elevator, and as they did, Tingting looked right at Jack. He gave her a small smile, but she did not return the gesture; instead, her sculpted eyebrows came together and a muscle twitched near the corner of her mouth. She was angry at him about what had previously happened, which, Jack supposed, was valid.

The elevator moved at ultra-fast speed and delivered them to the thirty-ninth floor. Never did he think he would be back here again, expected to address the nation. Jack realized, as they walked down the hallway, that he had not even considered what he might say.

Inside the Control Center, there were about sixty people sitting at work stations in front of monitors. They all stood when they saw Wang. A man walked hurried over. "Let me take you to the broadcast center next-door, Mr. President," he said.

It was hard not to feel déjà vu, though this situation was nothing like the first time he had been here. Ari was not here, as he had been. There was no anxiety, no adrenaline, just that uncomfortable feeling that he had to do something which needed to be done but would have negative consequences on his own life. All he wanted now was to be with Jojo. Hadn't he done enough? Sacrificed enough of his time, his energy, his knowledge? Now he was being expected to sacrifice his marriage and his chance at having a family, a happy life.

In the broadcast room, Jack was seated at the large desk, facing the main screen. "Jack," the man said, "we're going to run this introduction, and then you may begin. Okay?"

He nodded, even though he hadn't at all considered what he was going to say. What if he just sat there and said nothing? What if he told people how much he had given up in order for them to live in a free and open society? Might that play to their emotions enough to instigate lasting change?

A video began to play, narrated by a man speaking formal Mandarin. Jack tried to push his thoughts out of his mind and focus on what the narrator was saying. "Mr. Jack Gold visited every province and munic-ipality in China to work with secretaries and governors to develop a plan for their region." As the narrator continued, the screen flashed to different places, showing different images of Jack and various officials. There were also short video clips, material that Jason had collected.

Jack was startled to hear his own voice, dismissing Secretary Hu for his non-participation. He was surprised they showed such blatant crit-icism by him, a foreigner, of an official. It was typical in Chinese society that everyone respected and feared officials. Clearly, Jack did not.

The next clip was of Jack, with another official, pleading with him: "*You have to understand why I am here. China must evolve. This is the reason the Standing Committee sent me here. To help change attitudes. All you have to do is present recommendations, how you'll do it, and what will be the impact on revenue over a few years.*"

Another image showed Governor Bo at Jack's place, relaxing by the window, looking out onto Erhai Lake. The final clip was of Jack and Bo, discussing Dali University, and Jack's assertion that every citizen who could have, but did not, receive an education was a loss for the nation.

It was a good clip to end with, as that one quote would resonate particularly with Chinese parents. They would support and follow what he said. The preamble finished a moment later—they had turned Jack into a hero, and had paved the way for whatever it was he was supposed to say now.

"You can start now, Jack," Wang said.

Jack sat up straight in his chair, looked directly at the camera. "Good evening, ladies and gentlemen," he said. He had been paying attention to the introduction and hadn't thought of what he might say now, but was that necessary? He had lived it, after all. He simply had to speak from his heart. "Three days ago, China launched two supersonic missiles from the Spratly Islands, aimed at Taiwan's Presidential Office Building. The building, as you know, was completely destroyed. Even though Taiwan has never been controlled by China's ruling Communist Party, some in China insist the democratic, self-governing island is an integral part of their China." He paused. "Two days ago, to fulfill its commitment to protect Taiwan, the United States reciprocated by firing two Tomahawk missiles, which struck and destroyed the heart of Zhongnanhai, the home of China's Communist Party and leadership. I was at each site just minutes before the missiles hit." He looked right into the camera, knowing he was looking out into the eyes of millions of Chinese citizens, even though he couldn't see any of them.

"Here's the thing: the United States was mistaken about China sending the missiles to Taiwan. A few former Chinese government officials took action on their own. As you just saw in the introduction, President Wang and the Standing Committee asked me to assist province secretaries and governors in detailing plans to improve their cities. I visited every province and discussed with them what they were going to do, how it would be done, and what the impact would be. This is an important change from how things were done in the past. Usually plans are top-down from the central government. However, in this new way, the province officials would present their plan, and then *they* would be responsible for achieving them. The intent being they would earnestly own their plan.

"But something happened during this process. When the province leaders presented to the Standing Committee, the committee discovered that many leaders did not develop a good plan, or were incapable of implementing one. Unlike before, the Standing Committee took bold action and relocated or dismissed roughly thirty percent of all provincial secretaries and governors. They did this because you need the very best to grow your city, to make them efficient and attractive; to grow wages and increase the quality of life." Jack paused, letting what he just said sink in.

"Unfortunately, those officials who were let go got mad. They unified with others who wanted *more* restrictions and hoped for a more traditional form of communism. They fueled protests, they seeded doubt amongst people, and they illegitimately took military action aimed at making Taiwan part of China."

There was plenty more he could say now, about all sorts of things. He had seen all of China and had insightful observations he wanted to share—he wanted to tell everyone what an incredible country this was, the people, the cultures, what a privilege it had been. He thought about emphasizing that Taiwan should be free and independent. He could talk about China adopting a new constitution. Or maybe mention the right to vote and that it was the most important tool in democracy. After all, without access to the ballot box, people were not in a position to protect their rights.

He was aware of the others in the broadcast room with him, including his father-in-law, the president of China. He realized that he did not feel used by them; rather, he had gone along doing what others wanted, because he made that choice, but that was because he was trying to prove himself. Prove to himself, to others, that he could do things, get the job done. Just like his father had ingrained in him. Just like his father had always done.

It felt as though a veil had been pulled back, a fog in his brain cleared. He raised his eyes back to the camera, letting out a deep breath. "I've been very stupid," he said. "My wife is eight months pregnant. I am going home to her, where I should be, where I should have been this whole time. So I beg you, all of you, for peace. That your country will grow, and be a wonderful place for my child, and all children in China. There is nothing else to say. Thank you, and goodnight."

The silence was heavy. Jack stood and walked away from the desk. Wang came over to him, the look on his face hard to read. But there was kindness in his eyes, Jack saw, and understanding. "Jack," he said. "You are right. We will get you home immediately. That was not entirely what I expected you to say, but you couldn't have said anything better, or more authentic. And that is what will speak to people. Your broadcast will be part of *Xinwen Lianbo*, and it'll be played continuously over the next few days. Articles will be written and disbursed throughout online news media. It's all done, Jack. Thank you."

He thought he would have felt something–some sort of relief, or satisfaction, upon hearing those words. But he felt nothing, only the growing need to get back to his wife, to his home, as soon as he could.

CHAPTER 30

It was close to eleven that night when Jack arrived back in Dali. He had gone back to the boutique hotel only briefly to get his bag; while he was there he passed his desk and saw the package from Cartier he hadn't given Jojo yet. He grabbed it and slipped it into the bag.

He quietly let himself in and walked up to the second floor, hearing the soft sounds from the television. Jojo was on the couch, her back to him. She turned as he approached. Her expression was neutral, and half hidden in the shadows.

"Hi," Jack said finally. "I'm home."

She got up from the couch slowly, clearly pregnant. Jack wanted nothing more than to go over and take her in his arms, whisper in her ear that she had been right this whole time, he should have listened. He was a fool not to. But he didn't know how she'd react; it felt like it had been so long since they'd last spoken. Too long.

"I saw you on TV," she said. "You really know how to address an audience. Maybe you should consider a career in television."

"I don't want a career in television."

"That last part about your wife was pretty good. People like that sort of thing."

There was only one person whose opinion he cared about. "I meant it," he said. "I meant everything I said. But especially the part about my wife. Who was right this whole time. I didn't say that part. But I could have added that I thought I was doing the right thing and was so blinded by that that I was willing to go against what my wife wanted. And I'm so sorry."

The reality of his situation cascaded down on him. They were at a crossroads now, and it was not up to Jack to decide which direction was going to be taken. Jojo had been very clear. Had it been he just hadn't believed her? Or that he truly thought it was worth it, to sacrifice his own family, his own life? Because even if he still woke up each morning and drew breath into his lungs, how could he really call it living if Jojo and their child were elsewhere, never wanting anything to do with him?

Jack swallowed. His shoulders slumped. He was tired, but if Jojo told him to leave, that they were done, he would go. He would respect her wishes this time. It was the least he could do.

But then—a smile slowly came to her face. A genuine smile, and, if he wasn't mistaken, she was looking at him as though she were truly glad to see him. She came over to him and he put his hand on her stomach, feeling their baby kick right as he did so.

"I'm sorry too," she said. She looked up at him, smile widening, and shrugged her shoulders. "What can I say? Maybe it was the pregnancy hormones. Maybe it was just me being selfish and wanting you all to myself. But you did great. Not just on TV, but everything you've done. For us, and for the nation. You did things no one else could, or would, and instead of punishing you for it, I should be grateful. I couldn't ask for a better husband."

He wrapped his arms around her, buried his face in her hair, as he felt her arms go around him. "I want you to be selfish and want me all to yourself," he said. "I'm not going anywhere. I'll always be here for you, and for our baby. I love you, Jojo." Relief flooded him. This was all he wanted. None of his efforts would have been worth anything if he'd lost Jojo in the process, and that he had another chance to show her that he truly felt this felt like the greatest gift in the world.

* * *

They slept in the next morning and had just come down to get coffee— for Jack—and tea—for Jojo—when Jack's iPad began to ring. It was his father, on FaceTime.

"Hi, Dad," Jack said after he pressed accept.

"Jack!" his father exclaimed, a clear blue sky in his background. "I've just figured out how to call you using FaceTime!"

Jack smiled. "Yes you did," he said. "Good job. How are you?"

His father's eyebrows shot up. "How am I? Everything's fine in Cabo as always, but how are *you*? What on earth have you been up to? I just heard from one of my buddies that you almost died? I don't watch much news Jack, it's too stressful, but apparently there was talk of your demise both in Taiwan and Beijing?"

Jojo came over and sat down on the couch next to Jack. "Hi, Dr. Gold," she said. "It's nice to see you."

"Hello, Jojo," Jack's father said. "You're looking radiant. How are you feeling?"

"I feel good! I'm ready to not be pregnant anymore. So, it seems you heard about everything Jack's been up to. I swear, I tried to keep him out of trouble."

"Apparently a very tall order," his father said. "But I'm glad to see you're safe, Jack. Did you get paid this time, for your efforts?"

"Well . . . it was offered but it would have been a conflict of interest, since I'm the president's son-in-law. So I asked them to give the money to charity."

His father snorted. "Jack, those Chinese will probably keep the money for themselves."

"Dad," Jack said, glancing at Jojo, who was suppressing a smile, "surely you are aware that my wife and my father-in-law are Chinese. You've just insulted them."

"I'm not insulted," Jojo said. "And my dad wouldn't be either. Dr. Gold, you should be so proud of your son. He did indeed put his life on the line for the entire nation, in the hopes that people here would have a better opportunity at a happy and prosperous life."

"He always finds a way to get himself into these things. So, what's next?"

"What's next?" Jack said. "We're going to have a baby here soon. I expect there's a lot of sleepless nights and diaper changes in my future. Honestly, I'm looking forward to slowing down and spending as much time with Jojo and our baby as possible."

"I'm very happy to hear that, Jack," his father said. "And—I'm proud of you. You have become the man I always hoped you would. I'll let you two get back to your morning; I'm just glad to see that everyone is well and healthy."

Jack couldn't recall his father ever being so open emotionally with him before. It might not sound like much to someone else, but just hearing those words meant the world to him.

"Thanks, Dad. We'll talk soon. I love you."

"Love you too, Jack. Jojo, take care of yourself. I can't wait to meet my new grandchild." His father gave them a wave and then the call disconnected.

"That was nice to hear from your dad," Jojo said. "He was worried about you."

His father was smart—maybe one of the smartest people Jack knew. He had, in fact, previously worked for the CIA, though he'd always downplayed it. And suddenly, Jack wondered: Had his dad been treating him a certain way all these years, perhaps knowing that Jack could do certain things but he needed the right guidance and motivation? Would AI be able to predict his dad's impact on him, and who he was? Did it matter? Jack knew his dad well enough to know that, even if he asked, his father wouldn't admit to anything.

CHAPTER 31

Jack sat at the table, the sunset beginning to descend beyond the lake behind them, watching as Jojo artfully wrapped Chinese dumplings. She was so close to the end of her pregnancy but she had insisted on making dinner tonight, since her father was coming over for a visit.

"What type of dumplings are you making?" Jack asked. She was barefoot, her hair twisted up into a top knot, as she spooned filling onto the center of each homemade dumpling wrapper.

"My dad's favorites are leek and egg. So we've got those here—" she gestured, "and I made cabbage and pork for you."

Jack smiled and stood. She was barefoot and pregnant, sure, but nothing was going to slow her down. "I'll set the table."

He'd just put out the bowls and napkins, along with some garlic and chili oil, when the doorbell rang.

"Would you mind getting that?" Jojo asked. "I'm almost done here."

Jack went down and answered the door. "Hello, yùe fù, please come in," he said to his father-in-law. Wang had Mini with him. "Hi, boy," Jack said, patting the dog. "You look like you're even smarter than the last time I saw you."

"Good evening, Jack," Wang said. "You look relaxed and well-rested. Good to see you." He followed Jack upstairs. "Something smells delicious."

"Hi, Dad. Ah, you brought the dog with you!" Jojo had just finished with the last of the dumplings, and she came over and gave her father a long hug.

"It's been years since I've come to Dali," Wang said. "Now I can see why you both like it so much." The last rays of sun were just disappearing. "Wow, that is some view."

"Isn't it? It's so beautiful, with the lake and the mountains. The architecture is incredible, too, and I can get amazing vegetables at the local market for about a third of the price of those in Beijing or Shanghai."

"Do you know what Former president Zhao Lihong said of Dali?" Wang asked. "He said, *Lucid waters and lush mountains are invaluable assets.*"

"I would have to agree," Jack said. It had been about two weeks since he'd returned to Jojo, and they'd spent that time together, going on walks, exploring the city, and enjoying this slower pace of life.

"Are those leek and egg dumplings I smell?" Wang asked.

"Why yes they are. I know they're your favorite."

"How about I get some Maotai while Jojo cooks up the dumplings?" Jack offered.

Wang grinned and shot Jojo a look. "I think Jack is starting to enjoy life's simple pleasures. Yes, let's have some Maotai."

They drank Maotai while Jojo cooked the dumplings, each dumpling perfectly crafted from the hands of a gifted sculpturer. Jack was filled with love and pride for his wife, who was so talented in so many ways.

"So," Jack asked, when they were seated at the table and a platter of freshly cooked dumplings in front of them, "how did everything turn out? I've read almost nothing since the broadcast."

"Your part was done, Jack, so we didn't want to distract you with getting back to your life," Wang said. He took his first bite and let his eye close as he chewed. "Jojo, this is delicious." He looked back to Jack. "We rounded up all of the conspirators, as you may have suspected. What we did *not* expect was the level of contrition. People genuinely felt bad for what they had done. The important thing, though, is that the riots immediately stopped. We consulted several psychiatrists about what happened, and they all said that people liked what you said, Jack, and how you said it. You didn't tap into what people were feeling, necessarily, but what they were thinking. When you said you were stupid and were going to go home to your wife, we think that reminded everyone of their own life and family. They knew what you were saying was truthful. You showed great humility by admitting that, right there in front of everyone. You did the exact things that were needed to de-escalate the situation and calm the people of this nation. Also, I've received calls from a number of countries, reiterating their attendance to the Olympics next year."

"What about Liang?"

Jojo looked quizzically from Jack to her father. "Liang?" she asked. "What did he have to do with this?"

"Liang pulled a gun on us. He betrayed me. And the nation. But, the elevator helped protect the bunker entrance after Jack gave him his phone with the bomb in it. The contained blast decimated him; there was only his liquid remains and a few bone fragments."

Jojo's jaw dropped. "What?! Are you serious?"

"I was having a hard time believing it myself," Wang said. "I *still* cannot believe it. Liang." He shook his head. "But thank goodness Jack was there, because if he hadn't, and if he hadn't had his phone, who knows how things would have turned out."

"How did your *phone* blow up?"

"Cooper gave me a new phone," Jack said. "As a contingency."

"Good thing he did," Wang said.

"Would you like one too?" Jack asked Jojo with a smile.

She rolled her eyes. "Oh my goodness, *no*."

"Liang's betrayal hurt, yes," Wang said. "But other than that, everything worked out better than we could have imagined." He smiled at Jack. "Thanks to Jack."

Jack shook his head, raising his glass. "You mean thanks to AI."

"Jack, don't do that," Wang said, as he raised his glass. "*You* did it. AI just helped us figure out *what* to do. All the AI prediction in the world wouldn't matter if there weren't people willing to step up and do what needed to be done."

"My dad is right," Jojo said. "You should be proud of what you did, Jack. Don't downplay it. I'm proud of you, too."

Jack's face flushed; he could blame it on the Maotai but it was really the earnestness of their gazes that was making him uncomfortable. Or was it the fact that they were speaking so openly about what he had done. He smiled. "Does this mean I can have another glass of Maotai?"

"Jack, this means you can have as much Maotai as you want for the rest of your life."

"Really?"

Wang nodded emphatically. "Really. It's the least we could do."

"Well, that's a great thing to hear. It'd be horrible to ever run out. Also . . ." He paused. "By the way, there's still that money in that Luxembourg account. What should be done with it?"

Wang tipped his Maotai glass back, draining it. He set it down and looked at Jack. "I don't know what money you're referring to."

"The one billion that got transferred over after I said I'd leave the project."

Wang poured Jack some more Maotai, then some for himself. "Jack," he said, "I know nothing about this."

Jack took a bite of his dumpling, part of him wanting to push the issue, insisting that of course Wang knew about it, and what on earth should he do with it, all that money sitting there in an account with his name on it. Sutton had not seemed concerned with what happened to the money at all, and now Wang, too, was feigning ignorance. They wanted him to keep it, was Jack's gut feeling. A billion dollars was an unthinkable amount for the average person, but for world leaders like Wang and Sutton, it was nothing. And perhaps Wang knew that there was no other way that Jack would accept payment for what he'd done, though surely he deserved to be compensated. How many times had his life been in danger? How much had he put Jojo through?

"Okay," Jack said after he'd swallowed his food. He nodded, glancing at Jojo, who had as surprised a look on her face as Jack did. "Okay, then."

Wang helped himself to some more of the dumplings from the platter in the middle of the table. He ate a small bit of raw garlic with each bite. "These are delicious," he said. He put his chopsticks down. "There's something else I was thinking. This place is lovely, but it's a little awkward, isn't it, entering on the first floor in the garage and having to come up the stairs just to get to your living space? Especially when you're going to have a baby so soon, you don't want to have to lug all the baby stuff up and down those stairs every day. Also—there's really no good area here to plant watermelon . . ." He let the thought trail off.

"What are you thinking?" Jojo asked. "I can tell by that look on your face that you've got something in mind."

"Well . . . it's just a thought, really. A suggestion. There's a good-sized vacant lot just up the street. You could design and build something, exactly how you wanted. So it fits all your needs. Plenty of outdoor space for grass and gardening. A child will want a nice yard to play in. It's worth at least looking at."

"I'd be open to that," Jack said. He enjoyed this place very much, especially the incredible view, but it had always felt temporary. He looked at Jojo. "What do you think?"

"I do love this area," she said. "And of course I'd love the chance to design our own place. That would be great. Although maybe I wouldn't have the time for such a thing with a newborn."

"We have a great architect who can provide some suggestions," Wang said. "He can also supervise the construction. Why don't you two take some time to think about it, and then let me know."

They would certainly do that. And Jack had enjoyed living here in Old Town; it was charming, safe, the air was clearer here than any other part of China that Jack had visited. Dali was what Jack had thought China should be, and he could envision them splitting their time between here and Beijing, although honestly, with a child, they'd likely spend more time here than the capital city. It was a wonderful place to raise a child, with the mountains and the lake, the cobblestone streets and the small shops, the friendly locals and all the tourists. There were very few white people here, but Jack didn't mind that. Dali might be his favorite place in China. It would be wonderful to be able to really put down roots here, even if they did split their time between here and Beijing.

When the evening came to a close, Jack and Jojo walked Wang downstairs. Wang shook Jack's hand and gave Jojo a long hug. "Thank you for a wonderful evening," he said. "I am so excited to meet my grandchild. And let me know once you've had a chance to take a look at that lot; I'll send over the architect over after."

"We will, Dad, thanks."

Jack opened the door for his father-in-law and he stepped outside, waving goodbye. Jack waved and saw a familiar figure walking toward him.

"Hey, Davis," he said.

"Hi Jack. I figured this could wait until your dinner was over. Here you go." He handed Jack a thick manilla envelope, the words on the outside read: *Jack Gold, Eyes Only.*

"Thanks, Davis," Jack said.

"Oh, hi Davis," Jojo said, sticking her head out the door.

"Hi, Jojo. I'll let you two get back to your evening. Have a good night."

Back upstairs, Jack opened the envelope. It was Jojo's Chinese passport and his black phone. Well, a new black phone.

"I didn't really miss this," Jojo said when Jack gave her the passport. "I've come to realize that I'll be Chinese no matter what passport I have; it's just some paper that allows you into one country or another."

"That's very true," Jack said.

She looked at his phone. "Is that a bomb, too?"

He inspected it. "No," he said. "This one hasn't been modified."

"That's good. I mean, the whole idea of a phone that's also a bomb is I'm sure every guy's dream toy, but . . . I'd rather not have something like that around with a baby about to be here and everything."

"There's one more thing," Jack said. "Hold on." He brought his phone with him when we went into their room to his bag, where the Cartier package was still nestled. Before he went back out to Jojo, he sent a text to Cooper.

Thanks for the new phone. Also, I changed the password on the bank account.

Cooper's reply came in a few seconds. *I haven't the slightest idea what you are referring to.*

Jack left the phone on his bedside table. It seemed that he had a lot of money and no one to return it to. Certainly not the Iranians. He could live with that. He would have returned it if Sutton, Wang, or Cooper had wanted him to, but they were all acting as if they had no clue what he was talking about. It was a lot of money. As he walked back out to Jojo, his mind began to wander, thinking about what he might do with all that money. But there really wasn't much—he had everything he already wanted.

"This is for you," he said to Jojo. "I wanted to wait for the right time to give it to you. For a little while there, I was wondering if I might not get the chance at all."

Jojo unwrapped the package and slowly opened the box. Jewelry was not something she was particularly fond of, but he knew she had a few pieces she loved, and he hoped this would be one of them.

"Jack," she said, breathing in, when she saw the diamond Love bracelet. "It's beautiful. Which wrist should I put it on?"

"I was thinking your left. It will go nicely with your ring. Here, I'll help you screw it on."

He reached over and plucked the little screwdriver that came with it out of the red velvet it rested in. He caressed her wrist before securing the bracelet on and tightening it. When he was done, he put the screwdriver in his pocket.

"Isn't that part of the present?" Jojo asked with a smile.

"It is, but we're going to throw it into the lake together. The bracelet stays on forever. Is that okay?"

"It's okay as long as we're always together," Jojo said, holding her wrist up so she could admire the bracelet. "I don't swoon over jewelry, but this is lovely. And it fits perfectly." She went over to Jack and put her arms around him and tilted her head up. He leaned down and gave her a long, slow kiss.

"Let's go to bed," he said.

"You can read my mind." She smiled. "Shàng chuáng ma. You lead the way."

CHAPTER 32

A few weeks later, in a hospital room down the street in Dr. Ginger's home, Josephine Gold was born. She weighed six pounds, six ounces, and scored perfect tens on her Apgar tests. The first weeks of her life went by in a blur; they settled into a comfortable routine that saw Jack getting up most nights when the baby awoke so Jojo could sleep. Josephine would cry but was easily soothed, and Jack would hold her and walk back and forth in front of the big windows overlooking the lake, sometimes the moon shining down on the water, as he rocked his daughter back to sleep.

Even though she had only been with them a short time, Jack could barely recall what his life had been like before Josephine. He felt complete now, in a way he hadn't realized could be possible, in a way he hadn't realized he had so badly wanted. He often felt sleep deprived and had never been so happy in his entire life.

One warm, sunny day he got a notification on WeChat and saw that it was from Bo, who had been promoted to Provincial Secretary. *Jack*, the message read, *it's a beautiful day. Can you come out and visit with me briefly at the tip of Erhai. I need your help.*

Jojo had just put Josephine down for a nap. "Now's the perfect time," she said. "I wonder what Bo needs your help with. I'm going to look over some of the plans the architect sent over. Tell Bo I said hi."

Jack typed back a response, saying he'd meet him.

Bring your swimming suit, please, Bo replied.

"He says I should bring a swimming suit," Jack said. "What does he have planned?"

Jojo grinned. "I don't know, but you better take a picture to show me!" She gave him a kiss. "Have fun."

Jack went and dug his swimsuit out of his drawer and changed. Then he went down to the first floor, opened the garage, and started the Ducati. Jack loved the motorcycle; he was able to swiftly navigate the bike onto the main highway, which right now was largely free of cars.

When he arrived where Bo had requested, he was amazed to see an all-new beach, as well as a small marina and a few docked ski boats. People milled around everywhere. Jack parked the Ducati and walked out to the dock, where Bo was waiting, in a suit but no tie.

"Hello, Jack!" Bo said with a big smile. "I'm so glad you could make it out." He gestured with an arm. "What do you think?"

"Bo, this looks amazing. It really does. But . . . why am I the only one in my swimsuit?"

Bo's smile turned a little mischievous. "Well, Jack, as I mentioned—I need your help."

"With . . . what?" But as he asked, Bo shifted and Jack noticed a brand-new ski boat behind him, in the water. A white guy sat at the wheel, and there was a Chinese man also on board, holding a camera. Jack raised his eyebrows.

"I need you to go wakeboarding," Bo said. "There are lots of people here, as you can see, but . . . they don't seem quite to know what to do. Or don't want to be the first to do it. You know how it can be. So, you told me when we first met that you'd help me however I needed—you're going to be part of my marketing campaign that was approved by the Standing Committee."

Jack laughed. "Wakeboarding . . ." he said. "Well, Bo, that's certainly not at all what I was expecting to hear from you, but . . . you are right. I did offer you my assistance in any way that I could, and I'm certainly not going to go back on that offer now, especially if your campaign has already been approved by the Standing Committee."

"I think that's partially why the approved it so willingly," Bo said. "When they heard that you were going to be a part of it."

"We've got a college student, Eric, here to captain the boat," Bo said. "And that is Huan, who is going to document all of this."

Jack said hello to both of them and went to the edge of the dock and leaned down, shook both their hands.

"Great to meet you, man," Eric said, the sun shining brightly off the top of his blond head.

"Where are you from?"

"Florida State. I was asked to come out and teach some of the drivers and skiers out here."

"Eric has a wakeboarding scholarship," Bo said.

"Wow." Jack nodded. "I didn't realize you could get a scholarship for that. You must be excellent. So I'm in good hands, then."

"You are," Eric said. He handed Jack a blue life jacket. "Come on aboard."

Jack put the life jacket on and started to step down into the boat. Before he did though, Bo put his hand on his shoulder. "If you could, Jack, do something . . . impressive looking. Like, a jump or something? I hope that's not asking too much, but . . . the press will be thrilled and it will go a long way in promoting Dali."

"I'll see what I can do," Jack said, laughing. He hadn't come out here today expecting to be used as a marketing and promotional tool, but this looked like fun, and, more importantly, Bo had taken the initiative to ask. That was a rare thing in China. But perhaps it would now be less so. Jack climbed into the boat. Huan began taking photos.

Once Jack was in, Eric pulled the boat away from the dock. Bo waved, like a proud parent seeing a child off on the first day of school. About fifty yards out, Eric stopped the boat.

"This is good," he said. He helped Jack get his feet strapped onto the wakeboard and then Jack fell backward off the edge of the boat, into the refreshing mountain water.

"You want some gloves?" Eric asked.

"No, I'm good," Jack said. Eric tossed the handle, connected to the line, to Jack, who caught it and took a good grip. It had been a long time since he'd last wakeboarded. Like riding a bike. At least, he hoped it would be. Jojo would not be pleased if he ended up injuring himself.

"All right, let's do this," Eric said with a grin. Huan snapped more pictures. The boat slowly pulled away, pulling him. "Hit it!" Jack yelled.

Eric expertly accelerated the boat, popping Jack out of the water immediately. Getting up on the wakeboard was the easy part, though it required the use of muscles that Jack did not regularly use. But it was just as exhilarating as he remembered it and he began to jump the wake, catching some decent air. Huan gave him a thumbs up and began filming.

All right. He felt comfortable enough now to go for the money shot. He'd try a helicopter, which was the flashiest move he knew how to do on a wakeboard. He went wide to the right of the boat, then turned toward the wake. He had to time this just right. He jumped as high as he could, then turned his body in the air. He didn't get high enough though, and had only rotated about halfway around when he crashed back into the water.

Eric turned sharply and brought the boat back. "All good?"

"I'm good," Jack said. "Trying to give Bo what he wants, but I might not have it in me."

"Aw, sure you do. Pull the bar really close to you before you jump, throw your arms around you, and transfer the handle to your other hand behind you when your back is facing the boat. You've got this."

Jack wasn't so sure, especially when the steps were laid out like that. But, he'd give it another try. Eric straightened the boat and Jack easily got back to his feet, did a few practice moves before going wide to the right again. He took a deep breath as he approached the wake. Even if he didn't succeed doing the helicopter, this was more fun than he had expected. He was almost at the wake. He timed it just right this time and, as Eric had said, used his arms as he turned in the air. The board landed back on the water's surface and he was still upright. Eric let out a whoop and pumped his fist in the air. Huan had a huge grin on his face.

They stayed out there a little while longer, but then Jack's arms were starting to get tired. He swam back to the boat and got in. On the ride back to the dock, Jack really took in the scenery, the placid surface of the water reflecting the surrounding mountains like a mirror. He'd never seen Dali from the lake before, and it was exquisite.

"It's really beautiful out here," he said.

Eric nodded emphatically. "Hell yeah," he said. "All my friends are jealous I get to be out here."

Back at the dock, Bo looked overjoyed. He handed Jack a towel. "Jack, that was incredible! It's going to be such a help with the marketing. I know you have a new baby at home, so I won't keep you, but thanks so much for coming down. And feel free to come back any time you want, and I promise, there won't be any more marketing events."

Huan gave them a wave as he left. Jack saw him get into a van with CCTV written on the side. He knew what that meant.

Jack bid Eric and Bo farewell and got back on the Ducati. He was perfectly dry by the time he got home, excited to get inside and tell Jojo about what he'd just gotten to do. But as he walked up the stairs, he heard her scream.

"What the *hell*?!"

He rushed up the remaining stairs, his heartbeat accelerating. But all he found was Jojo, on the couch, looking at her iPad.

"What's wrong?" he asked.

She looked up at him, her eyes wide. "Um . . . was that a video of you on a *wakeboard* that I just saw? It's all over social media. How could this be? You just left. That couldn't have been you, they must've found a body double. Right, Jack? I didn't know you could do something like that on a wakeboard, you could have really hurt yourself!"

Jack shook his head, smiling. "Well, that was fast. Bo wanted me to see the lake, and, uh, also help promote it. That's why he wanted me down there."

"So . . . this just happened?"

"It did. The lake looks great; Bo should be proud of himself. He wanted my help, though, to make some promotional videos. There were some people down there but no one was in the water and everyone seemed a little unsure of what they should be doing."

"That's probably because they don't know how to swim."

"Well, maybe some group swimming lessons could be some of the lake's first offerings."

Jojo looked back at the screen and then stood up. "You've certainly given people plenty to strive toward," she said. She shook her head "I really didn't know you had moves like that."

"It was a little questionable at first. I doubt they posted the first attempt, which was a total fail."

"You're grinning like a little kid! I wish I had been there to see it."

"Maybe you can try it some time."

He held his arms out and Jojo stepped into him, wrapping her arms around his waist. He leaned down and kissed the top of her head. In the other room, he could hear Josephine start to coo and murmur. Sometimes, he still had a hard time believing that everything that had happened had actually transpired, and it wasn't just a riveting movie or page-turning novel he'd stayed up late indulging in. But everything he'd been through had led him here, to this moment. Jack had always felt that life was about striving toward something, something un-nameable and always seemingly out of reach. He realized now that feeling was gone; he no longer wanted to strive or chase after something, he wanted to enjoy each day, really *be* with his family, here in China, a country that was on the precipice of lasting, positive change.

Please leave a review
and if you have any inquiries visit
www.bradleygood.com

THE CHINA DECLARATION

THE CHINA AFFAIRS

BOOK 4

CHAPTER 1

Jack Gold got out of the shower and looked at himself with dismay in the mirror. He'd never been one to care much about his physical appearance, though he was beginning to suspect it was because he'd always managed to stay in shape, whether through his long-time practice of karate or the fast pace his life had taken these previous years.

So much had happened since he'd met Jojo that it was sometimes hard for Jack to reconcile the slow, more mundane nature his life had now taken.

It wasn't that long ago I was in the Control Center, he thought, instantly recalling exactly how it felt when he'd been there, how improbable it had all seemed the way his life was suddenly more akin to something out of a high-octane action flick. Sometimes Jack wondered if it had all been a dream.

Yet if it had, he would not be here now, living in a boutique hotel, married to the daughter of the sitting president of China. If it had been all a dream, he likely would not be standing in the bathroom, looking at the twenty pounds he had gained in the mirror he'd just wiped the steam from.

He'd gained exactly as much as Jojo had gained during her second pregnancy. Since having children, sleep and exercise had been much harder to come by, despite their live-in nanny, Sherry, and visiting relatives. Jojo's aunt and uncle had been visiting from Suzhou to help out and her dad, President Wang, was always coming and going along with a constant train of Jojo's friends. Unlike in America, a new child in China was not just a new family member but a cherished heir and member of the social strata. Two kids—first their daughter, now a son—meant something for everyone. It was also a great excuse for everyone to bring food.

Jack's dad and brother had not visited. Beijing was too far away from the west coast of America. He didn't mind; they often visited via FaceTime. But the contrast to Jojo's family and friends—and their constant presence—could not be more distinct.

Jack helped whenever he could, getting meals for Jojo, taking care of Kai, their daughter. Jack Jr. always slept in their bed, as Jojo insisted, since it was Chinese custom. It was exhausting waking up in middle of the night and always being attentive. And to Jack, it seemed a little bit ridiculous. The baby was so young he did not recognize much except when he was cold, hot, hungry, or needed a diaper change. Occasionally on these sleep-deprived nights Jack entertained the thought that kids should be delivered to their parents when they were over two years old—that would be great.

Jack threw on a pair of jeans and a black cotton t-shirt and then descended the stairs. He could see Jojo holding Kai; next to her was her father and her friend, Jennifer, cooing over the child. Jack felt like an outsider entering an event that he was not invited to.

"Jack," Jennifer said, turning to him. "I saw a picture of your mother. Kai looks just like her—with some Chinese mixed in."

He smiled. He'd heard so many such comparisons to every member of both his and Jojo's family. "She's my daughter, unique and beautiful in her own right."

Jennifer looked at Jojo. "He knows all the right things to say."

Jack sat down in a chair across from them. Since he last spoke at the CCTV Building, everyone had left him alone. The population felt a renewed sense of well-being as the economy motored along and property prices had, until only very recently, continued to increase, which had been one of the most promising signs of all, as property accounted for seventy percent of all wealth in China.

President Wang looked at Jack. "How are you doing?"

It felt strange to have the question directed at him; it had been a long time since someone had asked. His father and brother had not. And the family and friends who visited were (understandably) most concerned with Jojo and the children and how they were faring. And, truthfully, Jack didn't know how to answer. What he did know was he was not meant to be a stay-at-home dad. This was simply not something that made him happy. He needed to do something but did not have the slightest idea what.

Before Jack could answer Wang, Jojo chimed in. "Honey, you shouldn't be afraid of doing other things. You have taken great care of us. Think about yourself."

Think about himself. This wasn't something Jojo would have said in the past; she'd felt the opposite, in fact, that their relationship was always taking the backseat to the needs and concerns of the country, made up of over a billion citizens Jack would never personally meet. Yet she had stuck with him, through it all. He looked down at his soft midsection, then up to Wang. "I need to get in shape."

Wang chuckled, patting his own midsection, which was much bigger than Jack's. "Welcome to the club. Good luck making that go away."

The front door opened suddenly, no knock, or at least not one Jack heard. His good friend Ari walked in and negotiated his big, heavyset frame down the few stairs as everyone turned his way. Jack jumped up and gave his friend, who was now more like a brother, a big hug.

"Ari!" he exclaimed. "Come sit down. I think you've met Jennifer. And of course you know President Wang."

Wang leaned forward to shake Ari's hand. Wang did not speak English well and warmly smiled and said, "Hello."

Ari sat down after shaking hands with Wang and took in the entire scene. "You don't look busy enough, Jack. When is your third child coming?"

Jack suppressed a smile. Ari had four children; it seemed to Jack that all Jews had big families. "We were just talking about how out of shape I am. Imagine what a third child might do to me?"

Ari let out a loud laugh and looked down at his own bulging stomach. Jack did not want to join that club, though he wouldn't proclaim such a sentiment out loud. Jojo bounced Kai in front of her and in Chinese, for the benefit of her father, said to Jack, "Why don't you convert one or two of the rooms upstairs into a gym?"

That wasn't a bad idea. The boutique hotel they were living in was not being fully utilized, as there were five extra rooms, only two of which were ever used by guests. "How about we convert three rooms into a nice gym?"

Jojo frowned. "I was thinking two. That will leave us three rooms for guests."

"Three rooms would make a really nice place to work out."

"Okay, you win. Three rooms it is. But I get to convert them and design everything for you. That'll be a fun little project."

"You have great taste and know what I like. It's a deal."

Jojo looked at her dad. "I'll send over some guys tomorrow," Wang said.

"If you are serious about getting back into shape," Ari said to Jack, "why don't you visit Israel and join the IDF training? We could assign one of the lead instructors to you."

"Israel!" Jojo said. "How long would he be there for?"

"It's a month-long program. It'd be fun and you can't get better training anywhere else in the world. You and the kids can come too, of course."

Jojo translated what he said into Chinese for her father, then turned back to Ari. "No. Jack is not leaving for an entire month."

"Fair enough," Ari said. "How about we send someone out here to train him, then he can visit Israel for a week or so for in-person tactical combat shooting training? It'd be a shame to miss out on that."

Jojo smiled. "That sounds better."

Though Jack was doing little in the way of formulating this plan about himself, he liked what he was hearing. "I wish President Sutton were still in office; he could help with someone from America and maybe Japan."

Wang leaned forward. "Yes, President Sutton could have. I miss my interactions with him. I actually spoke with him the other day; he and Cam are enjoying their time in Florida. They said to send their regards to the both of you."

President Sutton had lost his bid for a second term. His successor, President Glendon Smith, was a progressive hands-off operator who thought America should collaborate with all other countries and not impose its will globally. His liberal ideas appealed to a number of America's different factions and Smith promised a "level playing field" and "equality of opportunity" which was a message people were ready to embrace.

"Anyway, I'd offer something similar with China's special forces," Wang said, "but honestly they do not compare to what Israel has to offer."

Jojo was beaming as she sat on the sofa holding and bouncing Kai in front of her. "Jack is a just big boy. Now he gets to play." She gave Jack a stern look.

Jack knew what that meant. "Okay, I'll only go visit places for one week at a time." He was thrilled with this unexpected development. He'd get to train with some of the best people in the world. It wasn't just about getting in shape; Jack was a third-degree blackbelt, but his skills needed to be honed and improved. Perhaps, more importantly, his brain was out of shape. Martial arts at a high level required practice, thinking, and creativity. It required using your brain instinctively. That's what excited him. That's what he missed—what he felt he had lost.

"You'll need a partner for all the training," Ari said. "And I'm sorry to say I'll have to decline your offer, but it'll be best if you have someone to practice with while being instructed."

"Where is Davis?" Jack asked. "He has been on vacation for weeks now." Jack knew his longtime bodyguard would cherish the opportunity and suspected he too needed to get back into shape after so much relaxation.

Jack looked at Ari. "You really think you can get someone to come here to train me?" He was a little skeptical. These people had their own lives, they were important, and why was Jack so special?

"Jack, the Israeli prime minister would be delighted with the idea. Plus, they'd be thrilled to have you visit Israel again."

Jack's mind was already at work forming a plan. One month of training here followed by a visit to Israel—he'd be a changed man.

"Well, now that that's settled, what have you been up to?" Jack asked Ari.

"Some interesting stuff, actually. I was approached by a laser communication company. They've developed some new technology that will enable communication with astronauts in outer space, using lasers. I'm focused on using the system to bounce lasers back to Earth to provide ultra-fast internet to major cities."

"How fast is the connection?"

"20Gbps, with 99 percent up time."

"Wow. That's fast. Elon's Starlink is only 500Mbps and that's their premium service."

"It's a game changer; that's why I decided to get involved. There are all sorts of applications for such fast internet. Israel is really good at this sort of technology."

"What's the business model? How will you make money?"

"Close to seven trillion dollars of foreign exchange transactions occur every day globally. They need a fast and reliable connection—and they'll pay for it. Starlink requires too many satellites. And it's slower. We'll have receivers placed in all major cities by the end of this year. We'll put institutional customers on a subscription fee plan, except the price will be much higher than normal plans. There are also military related customers we're talking to. They like the security features."

"What about other customers who might need fast internet but who are in more remote locations?"

"We'll get to them eventually, maybe three to five years down the line. Providing the service to our military is a priority. Simultaneously, we'll be placing receivers in secondary cities eventually." Ari glanced at Wang. "No plans for China yet."

Jack was fascinated. "What would it take to place receivers in China's more isolated cities in the mountains for use by schools and hospitals?"

"At the right time that won't be a problem. Regulations will be the biggest hurdle. Later this year we'll have all the satellites in place. But, positioning receivers in all the towns is not enough. Once a beam reaches a city it can be diverted to other areas within the city and two-way communication is possible. But still, infrastructure needs to be built out connecting customers to a nearby receiver or cell site. In most cases, China does not have such cable laid out."

Jack looked at Jojo, who had also been listening intently as she held Kai on her lap. Jack nodded for her to translate what had just been said to Wang.

He turned his focus back to Ari. "What do you think it would cost to connect remote Chinese cities, to get it done earlier, for educational institutions and medical facilities, along with the cables connecting them to a laser node?"

"Oh, Jack, I really don't know. Someone would have to do a study to figure it out. My best guess is a few hundred million."

"A few hundred million." Jack had been wondering how he might be able to use the one billion dollars sitting in his Luxembourg bank account, money that had been deposited in the account in exchange for Jack no longer participating in a transformative project for China. Neither the US or Chinese government acknowledged the money existed and so, by default, it belonged to the account holder—Jack.

He hadn't given any real thought of what to do with such an enormous sum of money. but now he had a few ideas. "If I can arrange the investment," he said now to Wang, "will you agree to the concept of helping isolated hospitals and educational institutions in China? Mostly those in isolated mountainous areas. They can ramp up remote medicine and teaching. China can leapfrog the rest of the world technologically."

Wang sat back in his chair, clearly not anticipating having to address such issues while visiting his grandchildren. "I'll have someone from our Ministry of Health and Ministry of Education contact you for a discussion."

Jack could tell Wang liked the idea, but as a prudent leader he could never commit too quickly to something. "Maybe you join that meeting," Jack said to Ari. "And we can see if we can work something out."

"Sure. Sounds great. Let me know." Ari stood up. "Anyway, I should be going, I was just in the neighborhood and wanted to drop by to see my buddy." He shook Jack's hand and then turned to Wang. "President, it's a pleasure as usual. And Jojo, you look amazing. Good job with your kids." He looked at Jack and grinned. "All *three* of your kids." There was good-natured laughter as everyone bid Ari goodbye. Though his visit was quick and unexpected, Jack felt buoyed and eager and engaged in a way he hadn't in a while.